BERMUDA

KARIM SOLIMAN

BERMUDA

Edited by Yasmin Amin
Cover art and design by Stefanie Saw

ISBN-13: 978-1-07421-782-2

This is a work of fiction. Names, characters, places, and incidents are either the product of the author's imagination or are used fictitiously, and any resemblance to locales, events, business establishments, or actual persons—living or dead—is entirely coincidental.

For the Nosseir brothers who lent me a book about Bermuda. Please forgive me. I lost your book when we moved eighteen years ago.

Prologue

"Perfect weather for a vacation." Owen gazed at the clear sky above the Atlantic Ocean, stretching out on his seat at the right side of the cockpit. The long non-stop flight that had started from Lisbon was going to end in seventy minutes at Miami International Airport.

"Lucky you." Cruz shook his head, grinning. "You might have the chance to enjoy the Fourth of July fireworks live. I'll be watching from Rio de Janeiro at that time."

"Not bad at all, Cruz," said Owen. "I spent a week at Ilha Grande with my ex. It's so close to Rio, but it's something else. It's relaxing, quiet and—"

"It's the perfect place for a dreamy, boring guy like you," Cruz interrupted, teasing his second-in-command. "I'm not surprised she left you though."

Come on. Give me a break. Owen wanted to strike back. Should he remind the *not-so-boring* pilot of the Australian chick, who had dumped him after a *long*-standing love story that lasted for the entirety of two minutes and thirty-two seconds? Officially, Cruz now held the world-record of...

"What the hell is this?" Cruz's voice alarmed him. Did they both doze off or what? From nowhere, a flying object appeared on the radar screen. The bad news was: it was headed directly to their plane.

"Too small for a plane," Owen pointed out.

"And too big for a missile," Cruz muttered when he tried the radio. "Mayday! Mayday! This is flight AAL 256. We will have impact with an unidentified flying object in fifty seconds."

"*Flight AAL 256, identify your position,"* came the answer from the radio.

Hurriedly, Owen replied, "Latitude twenty-nine degrees—" *Dammit!* The buzzing sound declared the death of the device that connected them to the world. Could this get any worse? Sure thing. In forty-four seconds, he was going to witness his first, and surely also his last plane crash. Live.

The remaining seconds to collision were the slowest and heaviest he could remember. Heavier than waiting for his turn to enter the surgery room for an appendectomy. Adrenaline rush hit a top score. Maybe they weren't exaggerating after all when they said that waiting for death was worse than death itself. But how the hell would anybody know if they didn't taste death before? Anyway, it was a matter of seconds to *live* that unique experience.

BERMUDA

The experience of death.

1. Unthinkable

Virginia, three months later,

Two years in the Pentagon and still those men with their harsh voices and stars on their shoulders intimidated her. Heather understood that being firm was part of their military nature, but she wasn't a soldier; she was a scientist.

"They're ready for you now, Heather." Holly came out of the room, which Heather wasn't sure whether to call a meeting hall or an investigation room. It depended on those guys *ready* for her inside.

"So, am I," Heather lied as she stepped into the hall, the butterflies in her stomach killing her. It was too late to go to the ladies' room now. *Pull yourself together, Heath.* She had presented to hundreds of people in several international conferences, in bigger halls than the one she was stepping into right now. But still, the Pentagon had its own ambiance. Today her audience was not a group of researchers who had come for the love of science. Today her audience was a bunch of big shot officials whom she was seeing for the first time, save for the man at the head of the table; her boss, the Secretary of Navy, also known as the SecNav—they were rather fond of abbreviations here.

The big shots stared at Heather, their faces grim. Were they pissed off, or were they born like this? This was not an audience; this was the jury.

Holly—the only friendly face in this cursed hall—handed Heather a presenter. "You sure you put the right file, huh?" Heather asked. "I don't need any surprises in this meeting."

"Just a click, and it's your show," Holly whispered. "Good luck. Your boss is not in the mood today."

The scowling gray-haired man had never been in the mood any day before that either. Maybe *that* was the mood.

Holly stood at the nearest corner to the door, while Heather was walking toward the spotlight. "Good afternoon, gentlemen." She managed her best smile for the time being.

"Do you know why you are here, Heather?" Her boss narrowed his deep-set eyes.

"I'm supposed to present the progress of the Bermuda Unit so far," replied Heather.

"*Progress?*" The SecNav clenched his square jaw, his voice thick with disapproval. "Let me make this clear. After the jet crash, Mr. Secretary of Defense is expecting *conclusions*. That accident has drawn too much attention, and the pressure on the White House is growing to allow the Germans and the French to *help* our investigation teams. I guess you understand that the last thing we want is those Europeans sticking their noses in our business."

So, he knew how it felt when someone stuck his nose in another's business. Should Heather tell him that she was sick of military noses in her work? But hey, screw them all. This could be the right moment to get a positive answer to her request—at last. Now was the right moment to say, "We need the HG-3 to give you a conclusion, sir."

"You know I can't do that without convincing reasons," he said gruffly. A typical answer she was expecting from her boss.

"I do have convincing reasons. That's why I'm here."

"We're listening." The anticipation in his eyes as well as in the eyes of all those big shots' boosted her confidence. Heather was the one with the magic wand now.

One click on the presenter, and a map of the Atlantic Ocean appeared on the screen behind her. "My team inspected the water in a ring of two hundred square miles around the point of collision," she clicked again, a circle surrounding a specific part of the ocean, "looking for parts and even splinters from the mysterious object that hit the jet. Using a virtual builder that Kenji and Jay from our team had developed, we did succeed in building an image of the outer skeleton of the flying object."

Heather had succeeded in capturing their attention; she could see it in their eyes. The butterflies in her stomach were gone, and now she was starting to enjoy the show—

her show. She couldn't wait to watch their faces when they saw the next slide.

"*This* is the object that hit the plane?" Pointing at the shown image, SecNav was doing his best to keep his cold poker face, but there was no doubt, he was astounded. "A TBM Avenger?"

"We're sure of it, sir." Heather smiled confidently. "We used radioactive analysis to detect the bomber age. And guess what?" Maybe, it wasn't the most proper way to address these big shots, but *screw them all again.* "The bomber is seventy-four years old."

"This doesn't make any sense." SecNav frowned, his arms folded over his chest. "Where would a World War II bomber lead you in this investigation?"

"An excellent question." She nodded. "It leads us into possibilities that may sound crazy to you, gentlemen. But we're scientists; we should think of the unthinkable. You all know, there are several theories about the Bermuda Triangle that—"

"Please, proceed with your findings, Heather," SecNav put in. "We're not here to listen to academic theories."

Nobody interrupts me. Heather hated it when someone disrupted her train of thought. Taking a deep breath to calm herself, she feigned a smile. "We went beyond theories, Mr. Secretary," she slowly said. "The picture you're gazing at is not an archived one."

Her boss shot her an inquiring look.

"Even with ninety percent of the damaged parts of the mysterious bomber, the physical rebuilding of the real plane was much harder than creating a virtual image of it," Heather continued. "But we did it."

The top brass were not able to keep their stony faces any longer, their eyes betraying their obvious astonishment. "You have restored an original TBM Avenger?" One of them adjusted his glasses, as if he was making sure his eyes weren't playing tricks on him.

"We didn't just rebuild the external skeleton," she bragged, "we reconstructed most of the inner parts as well." She flipped to the next slide which showed the bomber engine.

"Is it working now?" SecNav asked.

"Not yet." Heather shook her head. "Some parts of the engine are still missing, but that wasn't our issue. We restored most of the engine for this." She zoomed into the engine to magnify the digits on it.

"The engine serial number." Her boss had grasped her idea. *He's not bad after all.*

"Exactly." Heather nodded with a smile. "As we didn't find any DNA traces that might lead us to the pilots of that bomber, we thought that the engine serial number would help us verify the origin of the plane itself, and it did. Actually, the plane's identity shocked us all."

Their widened eyes were on her, their ears ready for her next announcement.

"This plane belongs to Flight 19 that vanished in 1945."

2. Mr. Colgate

Well, that had gone better than she had thought; Heather could tell from Holly's wink at her when she walked out of the room. Still, it wasn't a crushing victory. The HG-3 would be under Heather's disposal in five days, *but* she had less than nine days to complete her damned mission. Once and for all. She wondered how the crew of the Bermuda Unit would react to the deal she brought to them. Daniel would probably rub his rugged beard for five minutes before finally saying, *'Ok, Heather. We'll do it.'* She knew he would never protest, but he couldn't make any decision without meditation. Anyway, it wasn't up to him or her or anyone else in the team to decide. *SecNav* had spoken.

Santino would be a headache, as he had always been. He was an ill-tempered guy, and Heather easily got ill-tempered with ill-tempered men—that was why she had broken up with her last two exes. But she had no other choice than being nice to him. He was the one who had designed the immune skeleton of the HG-3; a good enough reason for Heather to even fall in love with him.

The others wouldn't be a problem. Linda, Kenneth, Walter, and Joshua would nod their approval. Susan would do the same, but not before she found something about the matter to criticize. Kenji and Jay, the two IT whizzes would shrug carelessly, smiling. '*As you wish, Heather,*' Jay would say.

"Dr. Heather?" a deep voice called out to her. As Heather turned, she recognized the bald head of one of the *big shots* who had attended the meeting. But this hazel-eyed guy in particular had remained silent during the whole session. She didn't remember he had even cleared his throat or nodded with an *um.*

"Yes?"

"That was a good show you gave." The slightest of smiles lifted the corner of his mouth. "I'm really looking forward to seeing you reach the finish line."

"Thanks," she cautiously replied. "We didn't get acquainted, sir."

"I know you already, and that's enough for me." He leaned forward, the same slight smile on his face.

"But not for me." She tilted her head.

He seemed to be enjoying this. "I work for a classified special unit that is concerned about our national security; you need to know nothing more about me."

A classified special unit? Could the IMF team be real after all?

"You didn't stop me just to wish me good luck, did you?" she asked.

"You're *alone*, and you need some help." His Colgate-grin together with his deep voice and hazel eyes made her swallow this time. *Alone?* The way he stressed the word made her believe he was hitting on her. Not that she would mind...

"I'm not alone, sir." She cleared her throat, dismissing her wild thoughts. "As you've heard in my presentation, *we* are a team. More than a team; a family." What if he was really hitting on her, the *lonely* her, not *Dr.* Heather? That would be awesome.

"You and *your team* are alone, Heather." His smile vanished while he insisted, and she couldn't deny she was a bit frustrated. "The Navy, National Security, the CIA; *no one* will help you reach the only man who knows the truth."

Well played. Now she knew how her audience had felt during her show. "What truth?" she impatiently asked. "And who knows it?"

He grinned again.

"Do you mind if I walk with you?" he asked.

"Do you know where I'm going?" she teased him.

He killed her again with his Colgate-smile. "After you."

Walking side by side with her along the corridor, he said, "Jeff Burke, a former assistant professor of Geology at the University of Oklahoma."

"*Former?*"

"He was fired for perversion. But that was the *official* reason."

"What's the real reason then?"

As they stepped into the elevator, he didn't say a word, and neither did she. Not with twelve ears around them. Even when they were alone after everybody else had exited, his mouth remained shut. Surely, every word was taped inside this big can.

The door slid open, revealing the quiet corridor behind it. "He claims he has a relative among the victims of USS Proteus—the ship that was lost in the Triangle in 1941," he resumed the story. "But that's not the best part. He also claims he made a journey nine years ago on his own to find the wreck, and that was when things turned ugly for him. When he tried to publish a paper about his journey, a crusade was declared against him."

"For what? For his academic work?" Heather didn't get it. Even if his work was based on delusions, that shouldn't be a reason to fire him.

"Well," he tilted his head, "let's say there were some *big shots* who didn't want him to spread his *reflections*."

She couldn't conceal her grin. *Does he have issues with big shots as I do? We have something in common, then.* "I wonder who those guys were," she said.

"You met a few of them today already."

Today? Heather stopped and faced him. "My boss is not one of them, is he?"

Her shoulder numbed when he gently patted it, motioning her to resume their little walk. "We can't blame him, though. Our fellow, Burke, wasn't playing nice. And you know how sensitive we are in this country about anything that might compromise our national security."

"National security?" She couldn't believe what she was listening to. "Come on."

"The termination of his academic career didn't stop him. He went to the online community to spread his nonsense about Bermuda. Of course, it's not hard to imagine how headlines like *Bermuda: Still Alive*, *What They Didn't Tell You About the Devil's Triangle*, *The Five Lies of Pentagon About Bermuda* can pique the curiosity of sci-fi nerds and mystery fans."

"It seems his *nonsense* about Bermuda wasn't nonsense at all." She glanced at him to catch his reaction. His smile confirmed her point.

"He passed the lie detector, so we know he is not pushed by the Russians to make up the stuff about Bermuda and USS Proteus."

The lie detector? Such a treat for the poor guy. "A schizophrenic would do better than any of us with the lie detector," she pointed out.

"His behavior might be a bit odd, but we can't say he is a schizophrenic." He opened a door, and suddenly she realized they had reached the roof, a helicopter waiting already at the helipad. How and when had she got there with him? Was she so smitten by his charm that she wasn't aware of where she was heading?

"What do you want from me?" Heather asked him directly, knowing that there was no free lunch here in the Pentagon. For all this information, there would be a price, a heavy one, most probably. *Unless he's telling me all of this because he's fallen for me. I know I was stunning today during the presentation.*

He looked at the waiting helicopter, his Colgate-smile back. "I want what you want, Heather." *Seriously, do you have any idea what I want now?* "I want you to succeed in your mission. That guy has gone to the Triangle *and* returned. I'm quite sure that all he has told us in two years of interrogations is just the tip of the iceberg."

"But he will reveal the whole iceberg to me. Is that what you want to say?"

"Burke could be eccentric, but he's no fool. You'll earn his trust because you're a scientist like him. And if he trusts you, he'll feel more comfortable to talk and spill all."

The idea made Heather a bit sick. Her sitting in a windowless room with a criminal wearing that orange prison uniform, guys from the CIA or wherever they were from listening in and watching through the one-way mirror of the adjacent room. She wasn't sure if she could really handle that pressure, but she couldn't resist her curiosity, either. *That guy has gone to the Triangle and returned.*

"I've never been to prison before." She harrumphed. "I suppose he is...jailed or something?"

"His jail?" He chuckled. "You could never imagine having your honeymoon at a better destination."

Here he hit on her again. *I know it.* "I have to be prepared for that meeting, then. I must return to—"

"This helicopter is leaving in one minute," he put in. "The pilot knows the way."

So, everything was already set up. That was more worrying than astonishing. "But..." she stammered. "Shouldn't I inform my boss at least?"

"Let me worry about your boss." His confident grin settled it.

Still, she was a bit confused. *What are you doing, Heath?* After listening to a nameless guy she had just met, she was about to take a helicopter to a destination she didn't know, to meet another bizarre guy with weird behavior.

"About the *official* reason for firing him," she said. "He is not a pervert for real, is he?"

He stared at her for a moment. "You'd better hurry."

3. Tiger Woods and the Chick

Playing golf with a tennis ball turned out not to be that bad at all. Yet it could be much better if that garden had holes like a real golf course. And if he had a golf club, not a broomstick.

"No, please, don't go." Panic overwhelmed Burke as he looked for his only *golf ball* in the bushes. No ball meant going back to his indoor activities that had caused him cabin fever and had been driving him insane for eight years. What were they thinking when those guys with black suits brought him a laptop with a web browser that couldn't upload a single byte?

"Ouch!" He should be more careful. Those thorns were nasty, just like the two guards of this *prison*. Which brought a question to his mind: what if he asked for their help?

"Hey." Burke waved to the two guards standing at the entrance of the villa. "Yes, you." *Who else could it be, you idiots?* There was nothing alive or even dead around this remote house. "Would you give me a hand?"

The two brawny men exchanged a look, a mocking smile on their faces. Usually they ignored him when he tried to start a conversation with any of them, but today one guard seemed to be in a good mood and so decided to respond to his call for help. Those two rhinos must be as bored as he was.

"Drop the weapon, Burke," the guard demanded as he approached Burke. *A weapon?* He must be kidding, right? Because the poor wooden thing wouldn't harm that mountain of muscles. Burke could only wish though...

"I said: drop it," the guard insisted, his voice a bit more menacing this time.

"This is my golf club."

"I'm not sure about that, Tiger Woods." The guard snatched the broomstick from Burke's hand.

"What are you doing?" Burke protested. "I need that."

"You'd better stay inside." The rhino walked away with his golf club. "Or enjoy the view here."

Burke balled his hands into fists. For a second, he thought of taking his chances in punching that rhino in the face. But thank God, he came back to his senses before making such a foolish move. He would crush his knuckles if his fist hit that granite chin.

Maybe he should try talking *nicely* to him. Quietly, he walked toward the gate, where the two rhinos usually stood. As it was theoretically impossible to climb the electrified wire surrounding the whole perimeter of the villa, the steel gate was the only way out of this lake-view prison.

"Where do you think you are going?" The other brawny guy looked like a real rhino as he peered at Burke. "Step back."

"I come in peace." Burke raised his empty hands. "Just give me my club, please."

"Playtime is over, *Mr.* Burke. You should do the right thing and go inside now before we report you for lack of cooperation." The rhino pointed the stick at the house. Not the first time they used that card against Burke. Lack of cooperation could lead to depriving him of a few of his *perks*, like the laptop they gave him to kill his boredom.

"No need for that." Burke forced a smile and returned to the house. *I must find a way to kill those assholes and run away. Seriously, this time.* Because the same idea had crossed his mind one hundred times before. He was sick of them. Sick of that garden. Sick of that house. Sick of that quiet world that was slowly driving him insane. That was the declared reason for bringing him here; being insane and spreading false news that concerned the national security of the United States of America. Now he was becoming insane for real. The good news was he was still *aware* that he was becoming insane. Because if he became insane, he wouldn't know he had become insane. Got it?

Not knowing what he was going to do, Burke turned the laptop on. For years, he had resisted the temptation to write his diary because he knew it was a trap. At some other end, there were those tech guys who would analyze every word written on that device. Every word might be used against him. Shame the National Security guys hadn't installed any games on that laptop.

A new game; that was what he needed to break the routine. What about identifying his location as à start?

The guys in black suits who had brought him here eight years ago never told him where he was. All he remembered was that the plane took three hours to reach this place from Miami. Well, an interesting clue to start solving the riddle.

As a hacker, he wouldn't consider himself the best, but he wasn't bad at all. Hacking was just a hobby, and he used it only to *borrow* some useful information, especially the hidden pieces. They were always the most interesting, or else, why would they be hidden in the first place?

First, he had to fool the firewall and override all security settings. In fact, that was what the whole game was about. If he succeeded in that part, the game was over. All he could bank on were his old tricks.

The mission seemed tough, but it wasn't an impossible one. His old tricks still worked with the operating system of that laptop. A feeling he had thought was long dead, but now it was back; it was excitement.

A car door was slammed shut outside. Burke had been so immersed in his new game he was unaware that the time for the next watch shift had come so quickly. But wait, that wasn't true. That wasn't the arrival of the guards of the next shift—more than three hours still remained. That could be the arrival of some unexpected *guests*. And usually, those guests came from the National Security Agency for some *friendly*, warm chatting. And he had thought they had forgotten him here. The last time they paid him a visit had been three years back. It had been a while indeed.

Or maybe they had detected his attempt to hack the system.

The second probability forced him to halt the ongoing process before someone might notice what he was up to—if they hadn't already. His fingers ran over the keyboard quickly, all windows and tabs closed. In three seconds, he was lying on the nearest sofa as if he had been napping for a while.

"Dr. Burke?" a soft voice called out his name. Surely, this one wasn't here to arrest him.

Stretching and yawning, Burke rose from the sofa and faced his *guests* with a sleepy face. Actually, it was one guest, a cute black-haired chick. The man standing behind her was just one of his two friendly rhinos, his firm eyes fixed on his, as if he was telling him '*I'm watching you.*'

But screw that dumbass. Back to the chick. She was nervous; Burke could tell from the cautious look in her brown eyes and the way she balled her small hands into fists. "In the flesh."

"I'm Dr. Heather. May I have a few minutes of your time?"

"I have plenty of minutes, Dr." He ushered her to the couch opposite to his. "Please."

She looked uneasy as she slowly approached, the rhino following her. "I'm afraid I have no minutes for you today, big fella." Burke dismissively waved him away.

The rhino glowered at Burke.

“I’ll be fine,” Heather told the brawny guy, not looking so sure, though. The rhino, in return, didn’t leave them completely alone, but stood near the doorstep of the house.

“You won’t regret it,” said Burke when he seated himself opposite to her. He liked her face, her nose delicate and straight, her chin short and narrow. “Unlike what they told you, I don’t bite.” Well, he would do his best to keep his word.

Her nervous smile made him doubt if his pathetic attempt to reassure her was working. *She doesn't think I bite for real, does she?* He could never know what sort of crap about him the NSA guys had filled her head with. The chick looked like a little girl whose parents were urging her to feed a caged beast in some zoo.

"Ah! Where are my manners?" Burke broke that moment of awkward silence. "Want to drink something? The coffee they bring me here is not that bad. But you may have some ice water if you don't like to take risks."

"Please, no need for this, Dr. Burke."

"You may call me Burke. Do you mind if I call you Heather?"

She shrugged. "Of course not."

"Good. Now tell me, Heather: you work with them, right?"

"Who are they?"

"The US government."

"I work for the Pentagon."

"So, you are here for the Triangle."

A deep breath escaped Heather's lips. "Listen, Burke. I'm not here for yet another interrogation. I'm here because I need your help," now more encouraged, she leaned forward, "as a colleague."

Burke allowed himself a self-mocking smile. "When I told my *colleagues* what I knew about Bermuda, they called me a lunatic." He lowered his voice. "Those men in black made me disappear for good because I tried to tell the world the truth."

"What truth, Burke?" Despite her attempt to sound impassive, Burke could sense her curiosity.

"For decades, they have been promoting the notion that the Bermuda accidents that occurred—especially in the middle of the twentieth century—were due to the Triangle's high gravity forces which affected the poorly designed planes and ships at that time. And they didn't stop at that level. They hid from the world the fact that the accidents of disappearing ships and planes *never* stopped."

"How do you know that those accidents never stopped?"

"Heather, I'm not short of charges. I guess you're not here to extract confessions of more crimes." He leaned forward. "If you were here for the Triangle as you said, then you wouldn't be interested in the *how*."

Heather nodded. Now she was taking him more seriously.

"I knew that you made a journey to the Triangle," she said.

"I was looking for Paul, my grandfather's brother, who was lost in the Proteus journey."

"You were looking for the ship wreckage, you mean..."

"I know what I mean, Heather, and it's Paul. He is still there."

"I'm really sorry for your loss, Burke." The smile on Heather's face was a fake one, he could tell. "Sometimes our grief about those who we are attached to makes us—"

"Attached?" Burke put in, a mocking smile on his face. "The ship vanished in 1941, before you and I were born. How could I be attached to him?"

Heather paused for a moment, as if she was weighing what she heard. "Very well. You're not attached to him, but somehow you believe he is still alive. Can you tell me why you believe so?"

"Because he was a boy when the ship was gone. The poor man must have aged by now—"

"Burke, Burke." Heather snapped her fingers. "Age is not the issue now. It's the place. Where is he right now if he has not drowned with the ship?"

"He did not drown. He's on that island."

She furrowed her brow. "What island?"

Her query seemed genuine to him, though. She wasn't like the agents he had met before. "I can't believe your bosses didn't tell you about it. What are you doing here, then?"

"I told you I needed your help, remember? Now tell me what island you're talking about."

Maybe she could help him, he reflected. What might he lose if he told her anyway?

"That island is the main reason for keeping me here." He sighed. "It's in the heart of the Triangle, but it doesn't exist on any known map. I told your bosses about that island, but they never managed to validate its existence."

"That shouldn't be an issue in the age of satellites." She looked Burke in the eye. "If that island really exists."

Her reaction wasn't much different from the agents who took him for a lunatic. "Would you believe a satellite more than your eyes?"

Heather was silent for a moment. "What do you think you saw, Burke?"

Think? The underestimation in her question irked him. "I did see the damn mountains, Heather. It wasn't there on the map, and the satellites couldn't spot it, but I *know* what I saw."

She leaned back in her couch, a puzzled look on her face. Believing him wouldn't be easy, he should have known.

"Did you go ashore?" Her question made him feel flattered, he had to admit.

"I was one mile away when, suddenly, the ocean went crazy, as if the island was preventing any uninvited guests from getting any closer. My boat and I survived the colossal waves by a miracle until I returned to the calmer part of the ocean."

"If that island had no existence on any map; how did you find it in the first place?"

"Patience and persistence." He grinned. "And some luck in the end."

Heather shot him an inquisitive look. She needed more elaboration.

"When something becomes your obsession for a lifetime, you never stop going the extra mile," he said, recalling his grandfather's tale about the brother and the father he had lost in the Proteus Accident. *Paul could still be saved*, had always been his grandfather's words. "A long time ago, I knew I would have to inspect the whole Triangle with my own eyes to find our lost Paul. Away from my academic study and research, I dedicated a whole year for field inspection, in the ocean, in the heart of the Devil's Triangle."

"You're not the only one who scanned the whole Triangle."

"I doubt, even if you don't believe so. I didn't miss a square mile of the ocean."

"You don't have to inspect every square foot even. That's why they invented those satellites you hate."

He liked her spirit. "Satellites, radars, and compasses can be fooled. But you can't fool your naked eye."

Heather didn't seem satisfied.

"Burke, I told you when we started our conversation that I needed your help." She rose from her seat. "I thought you would tell me something my bosses didn't know, but obviously I was wrong. I'm wasting my time here."

She was walking away. Heather could be his golden ticket out of this place, and here she was, leaving him, probably for good. He couldn't wait eight more years for another rare chance like this one.

"I can take you there," he voiced the thought that suddenly crossed his mind.

She shook her head as she stopped at the doorstep. "This is not going to work, Burke." She seemed to be mulling over the idea, though. "I'm really sorry for your painful situation, but this is out of my hands."

"You said you're a scientist, right? What if I tell you that the island harbors more secrets than you can imagine?" He pushed to his feet, hurrying to the photo frame placed on the table in the middle of the hall. Time to use the card he had saved for a desperate move like this one.

"While I was headed to the island, I saw this with my binoculars, well-drawn on a wide sandy area of the coast." He approached her, handing her the paper photo. "Having my super-zoom camera, I was able to capture this in one shot."

"What's this?" She must have expected something else other than the gorgeous girl in the photo.

"That's why they ignored it." He grinned. "They took from me everything that looked even remotely relevant to Bermuda." He scratched the picture with his fingernail to reveal the hidden one. Heather arched an eyebrow, impressed by the simple trick that had fooled the National Security agents. After he was done revealing the picture of the symbols drawn on the sand, she looked confused. Before she posed her next question, he said, "I'm not an expert in ancient languages, but I thought I might find something if I researched them. With the help of a competent friend, we found out that these symbols formed one short sentence, written in three different languages; two of them were ancient Egyptian and Latin, but we never figured out what the third one was." He paused for a moment, enjoying that look on her cute face. "Impressive, huh? I bet you're dying to know what this short sentence says."

"You win." Heather was on her toes, her eyes betraying her anticipation. "What the hell does it say?"

Maybe he had teased her more than necessary.

"Only two words," he said. "Help us."

4. New Rider

All the way back to the Pentagon Headquarters, Heather couldn't help thinking of that island in the heart of the Triangle. It could be the key to solving the long-standing mystery, and it could be nothing. But the island itself was a mystery on its own. Could it be possible that the government was unaware of it as Burke thought? *Hell no*, she told herself. Most probably, they knew more than he did. But that would raise the following question: why would the government hide this valuable piece of information from the very team whose mission was nothing but that damned Triangle?

Heather was too impatient to meet her boss and ask him all the questions occupying her restless mind. *You should calm down, Heather,* she reminded herself. An argument with SecNav wouldn't take her anywhere. And she would never forget that, more than once, her bad temper had almost cost her her career, had it not been for the unparalleled dedication she demonstrated in her work.

Yes, the dedication that killed my son and ended my short marriage...

Gazing at the Pentagon building at the horizon, Heather dismissed the dark memory that haunted her every now and again. Until the helicopter landed on the helipad, she busied herself with the upcoming *conversation* with her boss. Should she start by telling him about the mysterious guy with the charming smile? Or should she cut it short and ask him directly about the professor he had ended his career?

Still unsure how she should manage that confrontation, she headed to SecNav's office. Holly rose from her desk when Heather entered. "Where have you been? He has been looking for you after the meeting to have a word with you."

Hadn't they talked enough in that damned meeting? And where was that mysterious guy who hadn't handled her boss as he promised her? "Here I am. Is he available?"

"He's all yours," Holly scoffed.

Heather knocked before she pushed the door open, her boss beckoning her to come in. "Your phone was unavailable. I was afraid you might have decided to quit the mission after the meeting."

You can only wish, she thought. "I was in a classified facility to gather some info."

"A classified facility?" He furrowed his brow, a hint of disapproval in his tone.

"Jeff Burke." Heather didn't wait for SecNav's permission to seat herself opposite his desk. "Does this name ring any bells, sir?"

Her boss was renowned for his stony face, but he lost his reputation for one second when a hint of a smile barely lifted the right corner of his mouth. "You found any of his articles?"

"I'm afraid the situation is worse than that." She looked him in the eye, waiting for his reaction when he knew. "I met him in person."

Her boss's eyes widened. "Jeff Burke does not exist right now. Who took you to him?"

Heather ignored his question. "I wonder why you never told me about him. What he knows could be really valuable to our mission."

"He knows nothing but crap," he firmly said. "You just wasted a few hours of your limited time."

"The island in the Triangle. You know where it is, don't you?"

"The island?" he echoed nervously. "You listened to his fairy tale, then."

"You are not telling me that the US Navy is not able to locate that island."

"That island exists only in his sick mind, Heather."

"We both know that his mind is not sick, sir."

Her boss let out a deep breath of air. "Demoralizing you a few days before your expedition is not my intention, Heather. But I have to ask you: do you know how many boats the Navy has lost in the Triangle?"

The timing of his question wasn't helping indeed. "I didn't count."

"Neither did I. You know why? Because they're too many." He leaned forward toward her. "Now tell me why you believe he managed to do what everybody else failed in."

Heather produced the photo she had taken from Burke.

"What is this supposed to mean?" he asked.

"This photo is captured from the coast of the island that exists only in his *sick* mind." She brought it closer to his face. "Do you see the text on the ground?"

SecNav wasn't impressed at all. "Nonsense. This photo could be captured from any beach in Miami. If it is real in the first place."

"You have a whole army of experts who can tell us if it's real or not."

"My *army* of experts has more urgent matters to handle."

"I thought Bermuda had a priority."

"Speaking of priorities, why didn't he reveal this alleged photo to us eight years ago to spare himself a lot of trouble?"

"Maybe he didn't want to lose his photo in vain because he knew you wouldn't believe him."

"You're absolutely right, Heather." He peered at her. "Because he knew he couldn't fool us with his crap."

Her boss's resistance was so frustrating. "Fine, sir. I'm not going to ask you to believe his crap anymore. But if you don't mind, I need an ancient languages expert from your *army* to join the expedition."

"That's one seat on the HG-3 you've just wasted." He curled his lips. "But if you insist."

She hadn't wasted any seats, she believed. She had Daniel and Linda for electromagnetism, Susan and Kenneth for oceanography, the designer of the HG-3 and his assistants Walter and Joshua, in addition to two IT experts. Knowing that the passengers' cabin in Santino's masterpiece could accommodate ten people, she was quite certain she still had another available seat. One last seat for one particular person. "I need Burke as well." She looked him in the eye. "If there's a 1% chance he's telling the truth, I will take it."

Unlike what she expected, her boss didn't get infuriated. "Even if I want to, the guy is in the custody of the National Security Agency."

"That's why I need your help, sir. I'm quite sure you can persuade them at the NSA to let us make use of the services of their captive."

"Nonsense. I'm not going to wage a war for him."

"This is a matter that concerns the national security of this country. They can't say no."

"Heather." He glared at her. "You had better go to your team and make sure you are 100% ready for the upcoming expedition instead of wasting your time as well as mine in some futile argument. I'll give you your language expert, but a National Security prisoner? No."

Trying to convince him was a waste of time and effort indeed. Her boss with his military head would always be on a different wavelength from hers. The likes of him, who were raised on following cold orders without questioning them, would expect nothing from their subordinates but obedience.

Frustrated, she left his office and strode through the corridor, heading to her team's partition. Thanks to her boss's stubbornness, she had to rely on her currently available resources to find that island on her own.

"Heather."

And she was wondering when she would hear that deep voice again. The sound of her name made her heart flutter as she turned to face Mr. Mysterio. "How do you manage to always find me?"

"Is that supposed to be difficult?" He flashed Heather a smile. "How was your meeting?"

"Frustrating."

His eyebrows rose in astonishment. "Wasn't he cooperative?"

Now she realized which meeting he was asking about. "Oh, you mean Burke? It went well. No accidents."

"Good to hear." The way he stared at her made her nervous. "Did he feel comfortable enough to reveal anything that might be useful for your expedition?"

The existence of Bermuda Unit was classified in the first place. And here she was, about to share details about her mission with a man whose name she didn't even know. "You promised me you would handle my boss, but you didn't. Why should I trust you?"

"You just returned earlier than I expected." He shrugged, his hands in his pockets. "Has your sudden visit upset your boss that much?"

"You could have spared me some trouble if you had kept your word," she teased him.

"Trouble? Why?" He furrowed his brow. "Wasn't the visit outcome satisfying?"

"For me? It was. But my boss doesn't share my belief."

"Burke told you about the island, didn't he?"

Heather didn't feel he was asking. He knew. "Which conversation were you spying on? The one I had with Burke? Or my little prattle with my boss? Or both?"

"You think anyone would admit that?" The bastard didn't bother denying.

"What are you doing exactly? Enjoy messing with me?" Heather started to feel irked after she got over his charm.

His smile faded. "I thought you were smarter than that."

"Don't turn the table on me." She wagged a finger. "You tell me now: what the hell are you up to?" She should mind her language, shouldn't she? After all, she had no idea what post this handsome guy could be occupying in this accursed building. A man who had the power to watch anybody in the Pentagon was someone she had better play nice with.

"Isn't it obvious that I'm helping you?" He didn't seem offended by her tone, but the smile was gone now. Was he disappointed for real?

"I'm really confused right now. If there's the slightest probability that Burke is not demented and he has really managed to return from the Triangle, why would my boss be so determined not to even consider making use of his experience, which might prove beneficial to the mission?"

He looked right and left, as if he was making sure that no one in the corridor was following their conversation. "Burke caused an embarrassment to your boss." He lowered his voice as he leaned forward, his proximity electrifying her. "With all the Navy resources under his disposal, your boss failed in what an ordinary man managed to do with a simple boat."

Heather found herself taking one step back to rouse her hypnotized mind. "So, you all know he is telling the truth," she mused. "While I may understand my boss's reasons for silencing Burke, I cannot understand yours for helping me."

"Because that's my job." He peered at her, his voice firm. "Your mission is a national security matter, remember?"

His job? So far she had no idea what the hell his job was.

"You will never find that island without Burke's help," he said. "Would you mind if he joined your crew?"

Heather squinted at him. "So, you admit you spy on SecNav's office."

"You didn't answer my question."

"You know my answer already."

"I don't know what you're talking about."

Heather sucked in a deep breath of air and slowly let it out. "You know what irks me the most? Men thinking they can fool me."

"You insist on dragging me into side issues while I'm asking you a simple question. If you don't want Burke on board with your team, then fine. Your call." He turned and started walking away from her.

Had she gone a bit far with him? "Wait." She didn't think twice when she caught up with him before reaching the elevator. "He is held by the NSA. Is it possible they might release him for the mission?"

"They might." He stopped as they reached the elevator. "If your boss talks to them of course."

You must be kidding me. Heather did her best not to lose her composure. "I don't think my boss is in *the mood* to talk to them."

"Let me worry about your boss's mood, then." A faint smile played at the corner of his mouth. "You had better stay focused on what you do best."

Not the first time he asked her not to worry about her boss. But anyway what was she going to lose? After she tried her luck with SecNav, her options were not that many.

He stepped into the elevator when the door slid open. "When will we meet again?" she asked.

The door was sliding shut when he said, "We won't."

5. Inevitable Failure

Heather gathered her team in the meeting room of the Bermuda Unit Command Centre—or the BUCC as Daniel liked to call it—to brief them on her recent updates, starting from her meeting with the 'big shots' until her return from her unplanned journey to Burke's lake-view prison.

Daniel gave a *whew*, a smile on his round face. "Quite a full day you had, Heather."

"Did they tell you when we would take off?" Santino's thick eyebrows almost met together; an expression he made so frequently that one day it would be carved on his face. Anyway, he looked awkward in those rare moments he wore a smile. A frown suited him more. The bigger mystery than Bermuda itself was that sweet girl Linda, who had accepted his proposal to marry her. The electromagnetism expert must have been drunk when she said yes to spending the rest of her life with him until death did them part. Jay's theory postulated that it was Santino—not Linda—who got zonked. The IT geek swore he had seen Santino laughing once after a heavy dose of tequila.

"We have less than nine days to get the whole mission done," said Heather. "So, if we deduct the five days remaining before we put our hands on the HG-3, we will practically have less than four days of field inspection."

"Nine what?" Santino curled his lip. "Why?"

Heather shrugged. "Because that's the time limit we are given."

"And you said nothing about that?" Santino protested. "How did you leave that damned meeting without demanding more time for field inspection? We have been working our butts off for three months to prepare for that expedition. How didn't they put into consideration our huge efforts that would be wasted and in vain if we were not granted the adequate time to finish this mission?"

"All I know is that there is a global pressure on the White House to allow the European Union to interfere. We cannot hold them off forever."

"Screw them all," Santino spat. "This mission is none of their concern."

"Not after the AAL crash. The world is expecting an explanation."

"Dammit, Heather! I need a whole day to set up the vessel system and find out what the Navy engineers have done to my masterpiece." Santino turned to Kenneth. "You think we can cover all points in three days?"

"The red ones at least." Kenneth folded his broad arms. "Half of the yellow ones perhaps."

"I'm afraid you will have only six hours to finish the system setup," Heather addressed Santino, her hands on her waist. "Kenji, Jay, and Dani will help you."

"Nonsense," Santino mumbled. "This is not going to work."

Being accustomed to Santino's bitching about anything and everything, Heather ignored him and turned to Kenneth, her finger pointed at him. "Start working on a forty-eight-hour route."

Kenneth narrowed his eyes, a bit confused. "I thought we had three days for field inspection."

"I need one day for Burke's island," she said.

"Burke's island?" Daniel echoed, a nervous mockery in his tone. "You have given that non-existing island a name?"

Heather might be able to handle Santino's bad temper, but she wouldn't stand Daniel's reluctance. Besides his experience in electromagnetism, he was her unofficial second-in-command whose opinion mattered to her and, more importantly, to the rest of the team. Without his support, she would need anticoagulants to survive this mission.

"This could be our only chance to go into the Triangle," Heather reminded Daniel. "We might be on the verge of a shocking discovery. What happened to our scientific curiosity?"

"We are here to accomplish a mission, Heather." Daniel glanced at his colleagues, who were not showing any reaction so far. "And unfortunately, our time is too tight to satisfy our scientific curiosity."

"What if that island is the key to accomplishing our mission?"

"What if it is not? What if there is no island in the first place?"

Heather pulled Burke's photo out of her pocket and placed it on the table her team members were sitting at. "Have a look at this before I send it for lab investigations and think of the possibilities if this photo is real. An island in the Bermuda Triangle. Writings in ancient languages calling for help. Don't you wonder why they are not written in English or Spanish or any other modern language? Come on. I didn't imagine I would be the only one who would be excited about this."

"You're not alone in your curiosity, Heather." Walter harrumphed. "Finding that island could be a huge milestone, but as Daniel said: we have a mission to accomplish. That island needs another expedition fully dedicated to it."

"I agree with Heather," said Susan. "The island is the key."

"We are not even sure it exists in the first place." Joshua shook his head.

Heather sighed as she watched the debate between the two parties. While Susan and Jay agreed with her, Walter and Joshua adopted Daniel's point of view. After two minutes of back and forth, Heather presumed that Linda and Kenneth, who were silently watching the discussion, hadn't made up their minds yet. As for the grumpy Santino; his mind was somewhere else, probably preoccupied with the HG-3 system setup dilemma. *Wait, someone is missing.* Heather needed a few seconds to realize that Kenji had taken his seat away from the heated discussion, busying himself with one of the computers at the corner of the room.

"We must vote to decide," Daniel suggested, voices of approval from both parties rising, all eyes on Linda and Kenneth whose votes would decide this farce. Heather was losing control on this.

"Stop." Heather slammed her hand against the wall. "What the hell do you think you are doing? This is not the Congress."

Her reaction took them all off guard. Even Susan and Jay, who had seconded her opinion, gaped at her.

"We all know you're the boss here, Heather, but we never got things done this way," Daniel warily said. "Are you sure this is how you want to manage the team in the coming few days?"

Her dear second-in-command was rebuking her. Maybe she had gone a bit far, but she couldn't help it. Regardless of the lack of any solid evidence, she had that strong belief about the island. All answers were on Burke's island.

While she was seeking diplomatic words to handle the tension, the wide screen behind her was on. "Kenji?" Heather peered at the busy IT guy.

"I think you all need to watch this." Kenji left his spot at the corner and pointed his finger at the screen. "I found it while I was looking for that island you were talking about."

"You found the island?" Heather exclaimed.

"No." Kenji shook his head. "But I found something more interesting: an attempt to record an expedition to Bermuda three years ago."

On the screen was a top view of a lonely boat in the ocean. "That was captured by a satellite," Kenneth pointed out, or maybe he was asking, but no one paid him heed as they watched the video in anticipation. Kenji was showing that to them for a reason, right?

"Is this a video from *inside* the Triangle?" Heather asked Kenji.

"The boat is about to enter the Triangle." Kenji gestured to her to look ahead. "Keep your eyes on the screen."

Now Kenji was raising her expectations about the climax of this mute video. The entrance of the boat into the Triangle had better be dramatic. Otherwise, she would...

"What the...?" Kenneth exclaimed when the boat simply disappeared, as if it evaporated into thin air. As if it never existed in the first place.

"Are you sure there is nothing wrong with this video, Kenji?" Daniel asked, his eyes fixed on the vacant blue ocean on the screen.

"It's original, no edits." Kenji shook his head. "The boat vanished the moment it entered the Devil's zone."

"Well, thanks, dude." Jay rubbed his black beard, a nervous smile on his face. "That was really inspiring to watch before the mission."

"No electromagnetic waves." Heather gazed at the empty ocean.

"The satellite transmission was not interrupted." Daniel nodded, seconding Heather's finding.

"And not a minor disturbance at the surface of the ocean," Susan added, glancing at Kenneth, whose specialty was oceanography like her. The sudden formation of rogue tidal waves was one of the two main assumptions explaining the events of disappearances in the Triangle.

"So, Kenji, you're implying that the smart lead box Santino has designed will be obsolete inside the Triangle," Heather concluded.

"Oh no! We're back to square one this way." Susan was frustrated. Well, she wasn't alone.

"Very well, then." Santino pouted. "Does anyone here have an explanation for this video other than demons and paranormal powers?"

"Even if it's real, this video doesn't mean anything," said Kenneth.

"Guys, guys." Kenji gestured with both hands to calm everybody done. "I showed you this because you were debating about how we should get this mission done while we should ask ourselves *why* we should accept it in the first place. I mean: look at the givens we have in hand; that exiled Burke that nobody told us about, his 'invisible' island that doesn't seem to be abandoned at all, and this video that I only found while I was looking for any piece of information that might lead to that island. Can anybody here explain why Mr. Secretary of the Navy has been hiding all these clues from us? From the team that is supposed to be working on this mission?"

Silence descended over the meeting room, all voices hushed, the team members exchanging looks with each other. It was the same issue that had been bugging Heather since she met that bald man. That secrecy about all those *givens* didn't make sense at all.

"You know what," said Daniel, glancing at Kenji. "All we have been doing since we learned about those *givens* is the perfect answer to your question. The arguments we had about the existence of Burke's island are futile because there is no way to prove or deny its existence. That video we just watched; what's new in it? Are we suddenly surprised to know that boats do disappear in the Triangle?"

"If it's not so surprising, why do they keep such a video out of our reach?" Kenji leaned his hands on the table, addressing everyone.

"What do you want to prove?" Daniel asked.

"I'm raising an alarm. You're debating about some island while you have to worry about our return. Because I'm afraid we're nothing more than the White House's official answer to the question about the measures taken to solve the mystery of the jet crash." He pointed at the screen. "Were you watching carefully? They know we can never come back. They know this mission is an inevitable failure."

Seriously, that video was the last thing Heather's team needed to watch at such a critical time. "Kenji, what the hell are we doing right now?" She glared at the slender IT expert. "We were all aware of the risks of our mission the day we signed in. Are we going to back off now?"

"Why not?" Kenji shrugged casually. "I signed in for a *risky* expedition, not for a suicide mission."

Though humor was something Kenji lacked, Heather studied his face to be one hundred percent sure he wasn't joking. "You are not quitting, are you?"

"I'm not quitting alone. Either we all walk away or we all stay." Kenji faced the rest of the crew. "Shall we vote?"

Most of them were looking at Heather now, as if they were seeking her approval.

"I feel sorry to say this." Heather peered at Kenji, her arms folded. "You don't have to come with us if you don't want to."

An awkward silence took over the room.

"You know I have been working hard since the first Bermuda investigation, Heather." Kenji pressed his lips together. "But I have a son I want to come back to. That mission into the heart of the Triangle is not more important than my son."

He had a son to come back to...unlike her.

"I guess Daniel is the only one who knows this about me," she glanced at her unofficial deputy, "but I was offered to work for the Pentagon two years ago."

Kenji sighed. "We know you are the first one in this room to—"

"You have no idea how excited I was when I received that phone call. A one-to-one meeting with Mr. Secretary of the Navy himself! I was ecstatic and terrified at the same time."

"Okay, Heather. That's enough," Daniel urged her. "Let's vote and end this."

But Heather was determined to resume the story only a few knew about. "My husband Larry was a petroleum engineer. He was drilling outside the state, so I was alone on the day of that big meeting in the Pentagon.

"I was scared, but the meeting went better than I thought. After two hours with the Secretary of the Navy, he gave me the green light to establish the Bermuda Unit from day one. And you know what? I didn't leave the Pentagon until I was done with my plan of action. I explored the facility and assessed the available resources. I identified my requirements in terms of manpower and equipment. My new boss was impressed with my dedication." She allowed a self-mocking chuckle. "But my husband wasn't.

"After twelve hours in the Pentagon, I forgot where I parked my car." She heaved a deep sigh as she recalled the memory she had suffered to overcome. "It wasn't the only thing I forgot on that day; I realized that when I found my car with my four-month baby trapped in it, breathless, pulseless. I left my son to boil to death because I was totally preoccupied with my new job."

"Stop it, Heather," Daniel urged again. "Please."

"Larry and I got divorced two months later," Heather went on. "He told me he would never bear looking at my face again, not because of my carelessness, mind you. It was my heartlessness, he said; because I didn't quit the new job that killed our son. He wanted me to simply quit the job I *earned* after years of hard work."

Susan cleared her throat. "I say we take a five-minute break."

"Let's make it ten," Kenneth suggested as he turned to Joshua. "Don't you feel like smoking a cigarette right now?"

"We will take a break after we are done voting," Heather said firmly. "But I want you all to know that whatever the result is, I'm riding the HG-3 to the damned Triangle, even if it is only me on board." She turned to Kenji, looking him in the eye. "Because I don't have a son to come back to."

6. Obsession

Four Days Later,

Sitting opposite Heather was Nathaniel, the ancient languages expert who had recently joined her team. The short, slender fortyish fellow adjusted his thick glasses as he studied the magnified copy of Burke's photo. "Help us," he read. "It's written in Ancient Egyptian and repeated in Latin." When he reached the third row of words, he squinted, rubbing his black hair. "What do we have here?"

Heather waited for an answer from the *expert* to his own question. "Don't you have a translation for this?" she asked him.

"I'm sorry to disappoint you, Dr. Heather." He shook his head, his eyes fixed on the screen. "That language doesn't seem familiar at all. May I ask where these writings are?"

Now a member of the expedition, Nathaniel could learn the story behind that photo. He seemed astounded after Heather told him about Burke's journey to and back from Bermuda Triangle. "Mr. Secretary didn't tell you where we would be headed to, right?" she asked.

"He told me it would be an expedition in the Atlantic Ocean. That's all." Nathaniel shrugged. "I guessed you might be trying to discover the ruins of the lost continent of Atlantis. But anyway, I won't mind if you take me to that island. I'm really curious to discover what that call for help is for."

"I'm sorry to disappoint you, Nathaniel, but we are headed to the Atlantic Ocean as Mr. Secretary told you." Well, most probably. Without any updates in her boss's stance toward the idea of letting Burke join her crew, she had no clue how she could reach that island. That was why she had agreed to stick to the original plan of inspecting the locations of recent disappearance incidents. *I shouldn't have trusted that bald bastard in the first place. Men will always be men.*

"I bet you're not taking me to help you read the surface of the ocean."

His sense of humor was worse than Kenji's, but he was right. "I'm taking you just in case," said Heather. "Because I have no idea what the hell I'm going to find in that cursed Triangle." She leaned forward toward Nathaniel. "You understand that this journey could be a one-way ride."

Nathaniel seemed to be giving the matter a thought. "A journey with a team of scientists into the heart of the Bermuda Triangle," he mused. "How many times will I be offered that?"

"You're in the right place, then. Welcome to Bermuda." Heather allowed a faint smile as she rose to her feet, heading to the big meeting room.

"What could be in common between Ancient Egyptians and Latin and an island in the Atlantic Ocean?" Heather heard Nathaniel mutter behind her back.

"What do you think? You're the expert here." Heather looked over her shoulder.

Nathaniel let out a deep breath of air as he leaned back in his seat, his hands clasped behind his head. "The possibilities are insane. Such a shame if you don't go to that mysterious island and uncover its secrets. Because I'm sure it has a few."

Such a shame indeed. But Heather had an agreement with her crew. Too late to weep over that island now.

Heather left Nathaniel and joined Daniel, Santino, and Kenneth who were meeting with Major Powell, the other new member of the team. With his muscular build, he looked like a wrestler rather than the pilot of the HG-3.

"I can't believe you brought me for this." Pushing to his feet, Powell shook his bald head in disapproval.

"Is everything okay here?" Heather managed a smile as she approached them, glancing at the virtual map of the Atlantic ocean with red and yellow circles on it.

"No, it is not, Dr." Powell scowled when he addressed her. "I am supposed to be doing simulations for steering the vessel, but instead, I wasted two hours in coming here to learn the difference between red and yellow."

Another Santino in the team. "We have too little time to cover a large area, Major." She folded her arms, her voice impassive. "So, it matters a lot to me that you do know the difference."

"I get it: red for recent events, yellow for older ones." He curled his lip. "You could have sent an email."

Heather feigned a smile. This back and forth might take forever. "I need to have a word with Major Powell if you don't mind." With a nod, she motioned her team members to the door.

Daniel, Santino, and Kenneth didn't seem bothered as they left the meeting room. When Heather and Powell became alone, she seated herself. "Have a seat, Major." She gestured to him. Reluctantly, he sat opposite to her.

"I understand that it is hard for a military person like you to work with civilians like us, let alone work under their leadership." Heather looked him in the eye; that point in particular was her main concern. The last thing she wanted was some rebel who loathed the chain of command.

"No need to remind me who is boss, Dr," Powell said impassively. "I was briefed about everything regarding this mission. Yes, it might be hard for me to work with civilians, but I can live with it."

"Very well, Major. Because when we enter the Triangle, I will have more pressing issues to worry about than our pilot's temper. Are we on the same page?"

Looking down, Powell pressed his lips together before he turned to her. "Anything else you want to brief me about?"

"Yes." Heather gave him a genuine smile this time in an attempt to reduce the tension. "Actually, it's me who wants to hear from you about the simulations. I presume they include exposure to electromagnetic waves, right?"

"Of course, they do." He shrugged. "Anyway, the vessel skeleton is made of a smart experimental alloy that is immune to EMP without compromising the vessel's communication with satellites."

The muscular pilot had some basic knowledge, then. "What about hurricanes?" she asked. "Did you test—?"

"Up to level five," he put in. "Believe me, Dr, I was well briefed."

Heather leaned forward toward him. "Believe me, Major, we are not one hundred percent sure of what we are going to encounter in the Triangle."

"There is nothing to worry about. Our hovercraft can fly at a maximum speed of one hundred ninety miles per hour in the worst weather conditions ever known. Thanks to its fortified skeleton, we have the option to evade any probable storm by diving to a depth of two thousand feet. The vessel is even equipped with a defensive missile system, just in case we encounter any hostile actions in Bermuda Triangle." A hint of mockery was in his voice when he stated the last part. *One briefing session and he seems so sure.* Should she show him Burke's photo?

Her phone peep interrupted their conversation. Heather gestured to Powell to wait before she walked away to answer her boss. "You never told me you had powerful friends," her boss impassively said.

So, her powerful *bald* friend came through at last after she had lost all hope. "I didn't want to involve them, but sometimes you have no choice."

"Listen, Heather. I don't bother if you waste the remaining five days in looking for that island as long as you get the job done. Now tell me: is your team ready?"

Heather needed a couple of seconds to grasp the point of this question. "Yes?" They still had twenty-three hours at least before departing for the Triangle.

"You must be sure, Dr." He used the title every time he wanted to sound assertive. "To give your crew enough time to set up your customized vessel, we will release it for you seven hours earlier than designated zero hour."

"That's great news, sir." She meant every word.

"We have provided you with everything you requested, Dr, so we have high expectations."

"Not everything, sir," Heather countered gruffly. Did he think she would allow him to get away with that?

"Ah, about that. I talked with the Head of the National Security Agency, not because of your *powerful* friend or my belief in that stupid island. I did that to deprive you of any excuse to fail."

"Very well. When will Burke join us?"

"He won't. Three days ago he was arrested for his attempt to hack the system."

"Arrested? He was exiled already."

"Transferred, Heather. He was transferred to another facility. And trust me, the guys at the National Security are so pissed off with him. Forget him and give me a final answer now: is your team ready?"

* * *

Obeying her boss's simple order to forget Burke was not that simple.

With a restless mind, Heather attended her team's wrap up, their last meeting before heading to their new office in Miami to get ready for the departure. Daniel and the rest were rehearsing their plan of action for the coming four days of field inspection, yet she wasn't listening. She wasn't able to.

"Heather?" Daniel's voice interrupted her endless thoughts.

"What?" she snapped.

Putting his hands on his waist, Daniel exchanged a look with the team, a smile on his face. "We just want to make sure what this silence is for. May I safely presume that you agree with everything we said?"

"Without doubt, Dani." Why did she say that? Why didn't she voice the idea that had been haunting her since her last call with her boss? Oh, wait, she remembered now. She had given her team her word before. She would stick to the original plan. No Burke. No islands in the Triangle.

"Excellent." Daniel grinned. "Let's—"

"Burke was arrested." Heather couldn't help cutting him off. From the way her team members stared at her, she could tell how stupid she sounded.

"Damn!" After a moment of awkward silence in the meeting room, she nervously chuckled. "Listen. I know this topic is supposed to be settled, but I'm really sorry, guys. I can't help it. Maybe I've become obsessed with Burke's island, but forget about me. You look at the facts for yourselves, and you'll simply realize that there is something wrong."

"Heather," Daniel warily said. "We had our final say about that. Your boss had his final say about—"

"My boss approved my request to take Burke. But when he contacted the NSA bastards, they refused to let Burke join us."

"So what?" Daniel shrugged. "He is their prisoner, and they can do whatever they want to do with him."

"Listen, Daniel. For some reason, Burke has been hidden from us. And when we got closer to him, *someone* made sure he was out of our reach." She addressed the whole team, "I'm telling you that there are people who don't want us to succeed in our mission. Don't ask me who those people are or why they would do that, because I don't know and I don't care. All I care about is getting this job done. And I'm getting it done by taking Burke with us to find that island."

Daniel shook his head, a nervous smile on his face. "I can't believe we're starting this debate all over again."

"There is no debate, Dani." Heather looked him in the eye. "Burke is coming with us, and that's a final decision. We will all work on that in the next nineteen hours." She turned to Kenji and Jay. "Especially, you two."

Jay grinned, Kenji furrowing his brow.

"You accessed satellites classified files to show us that video, right?" she asked Kenji. "Now do it again to find out where Burke was moved to."

Kenji seemed hesitant, and she wasn't surprised at all. The only one who had voted against the mission was supposed to break a few laws for the sake of the very mission he wanted to quit.

"You can do that, can't you?" Heather peered at Kenji.

"Yes, Heather, but—"

"Do it now," she firmly demanded. "We have no second to waste."

"And then what, Heather?" Daniel asked. "Do you think you can just go there, knock on the door, and nicely ask the NSA guys to let you take Burke?"

Heather glanced at the eyes fixed on her. *They think I've lost my mind.* But she knew she could do whatever she wanted as long as her trustworthy right-hand man approved it. "Who said I would ask nicely?"

7. Some Little Hacking

Burke's bathroom in his villa had been bigger than the room he was locked up in right now. Except for the two metal chairs and the small table, the room lacked any sort of furniture. After desperate attempts to sleep on those chairs, he had spent the previous three nights on the floor.

Burke hated to admit that, but he missed the house with the lake view.

None of those who had taken him from Maine—yes, he knew where he had been kept thanks to some little hacking—had told him why they brought him here or what they were going to do with him. They were National Security guys, Burke presumed, and they were kind enough to provide him with three meals a day and allow him to visit the toilet whenever he wanted, but not without an escort, mind you.

Time for lunch had come. As he listened to the approaching footsteps, Burke wondered what kind of sautéed vegetable would be served today. A blond guy wearing a blue pullover and gray trousers entered the room, his hands empty, though. "Where is my lunch? I'm starving here," said Burke.

"I'm not your damn waiter, punk." The blond chap curled his lip in disdain as he seated himself. "Sit."

That sounded like the beginning of an interrogation. "You know what is worse than imprisonment for someone like me? That after those years of studying and teaching, I end up being called punk by some guy whose IQ doesn't qualify him to be one of my students."

"My IQ is high enough to know that you're just another nerd who doesn't deserve all those measures," the blond spat. "They should have let you rave about your nonsense. Only nerds like you would listen to you anyway."

"Oh! Someone here hates his job," Burke teased him.

"Of course, I do. Especially, when it requires wasting two years of my life in an office to keep an eye on a lunatic and report any attempt from his side to escape from his *fancy* villa."

"You're jealous of me because of my fancy villa?" Burke scoffed. "Is that why you keep me here in this rabbit hole? I hope you feel better now."

"I followed the procedures and no one bothered to pick you up to take you to your next destination. You got what I mean? You're nobody. The whole matter is just a live example of absurdism."

Burke arched an eyebrow. "You're well educated for an underestimated agent who is assigned to pick up and guard a *nobody* like me."

The agent chewed on his lip. "You think you are smart, don't you?"

"I'm a genius."

The agent narrowed his eyes. "And who's that genius who thinks he might get away with his attempt to hack our system?"

I'm so gonna enjoy this. "Is this your way to get a confession from me, *genius*?"

"We have more brilliant ways to extract confessions, you know." The agent leaned forward, his tone menacing. Perhaps it was time for Burke to play nice.

"Oh, come on!" Burke waved him away. "That's not the right way to break the ice." He ambled toward the table. "You may call me Burke without 'Dr.' if you want. What can I call you?"

"Jonathan." Jonathan smiled crookedly. "Without *Agent*."

Burke tilted his head. "That's not your real name, is it?"

"It's real for you," Jonathan curtly said. "Now *sit*."

"I assume it's not you who is supposed to interrogate me."

"You're not in a position to decide who does what."

"Will you get a promotion for that?"

"Maybe."

"Then, I'll be glad to help." Burke grinned as he sat down, his hands clasped on the table. "What do you want to know?"

Jonathan peered at him for a moment. "Your plan to escape will be a good start."

Burke shot him an inquiring look.

"Trust me, you need to cooperate this time. The cell you're headed to is nothing like your lovely villa."

Burke harrumphed. "Trust me as well, I want to cooperate too, but I wasn't trying to escape."

"Then, why did you hack the system?"

"I didn't hack anything, and again, I wasn't trying to escape. I was just trying to fix the bug that blocked the GPS signal from reaching the device."

"A bug?" Jonathan echoed in disbelief. "Is that the best story you can come up with?"

"I'm telling you the truth."

"And why do you want to unblock the GPS signal?"

"Just curious about where I am."

"Curious?" He arched an eyebrow. "After eight years?"

Burke shrugged. "You can never imagine what boredom might inspire you to do."

"Is it a coincidence that your inspiration came right after Dr. Heather's visit?"

Burke was at a loss for words for a couple of seconds. For some reason, he didn't like the notion of involving Heather in the matter. He had only met her once, and their meeting had been brief, but he liked her already. Although he didn't exclude the possibility that she could be just another agent whose job was to extract information from him, he still thought of her as a nice lady.

"She has nothing to do with it," Burke replied curtly.

Jonathan's eyes were still scanning Burke's face. "Why do I feel that you are protecting her?"

"Protecting her from what? Did you catch our conversation?"

"I'm watching you right now." Jonathan gave him a lopsided smile. "And I have seen enough. Now I know where the next interrogation should start from." He rose from his seat.

"You're not going to interrogate her for real, Agent Jonathan." Burke had no idea what that victorious look on Jonathan's face was for.

"You should rather worry about who is going to interrogate you, punk." Jonathan gave him a wry smile. "Trust me, it's going to be a very long week."

8. That Phone Call

Jonathan squinted into the screen when he saw her pacing in the corridor outside his office. That was Heather, the scientist from the Pentagon who had visited Burke in Maine. "What is she doing here?" Jonathan asked his assistant. Only a few in this country knew about this place.

"She says she's here for Burke," his assistant replied. "That's why I brought her to you."

"Bring her in," he urged his assistant. Heather's presence here was not a coincidence. He knew she was involved with that punk.

His assistant went to the door, and the moment she opened it, Heather rushed inside. "Are you the one in charge here?" Heather took him off guard with her firm tone.

"Any help, Dr. Heather?" Jonathan gave Heather a studying look, but she didn't seem impressed at all by the fact that he knew her name without any previous acquaintance.

"I presume you know who I work for, Agent. The man you hold in your custody belongs to us now."

"What are you talking about?" he snapped.

"Jeff Burke, Agent," she curtly said.

"Bullshit. I have nothing official about that."

That bitch dared to glare at him. "I would mind my words if I were in your place. The whole matter is highly classified and above your pay grade."

What the hell is going on here? "That Burke is not leaving anywhere until my bosses say something else."

"I have no time for your bosses." She picked up her cell phone from her pocket. Did she think she could scare him that way?

"Call Mr. President himself if you want, but you will never get—"

"I am so sorry, sir," Heather interrupted with a firm hand gesture as she talked over the phone. "I know, I know; this number is only for emergencies, and I believe I am having one now...Well, it seems that they haven't received their orders about our man yet...Hold a second, sir." Heather turned to Jonathan. "What's your name?"

"Jonathan," he replied impassively. He had to admit he was a bit curious about the identity of the person talking to her on the other end.

"Agent Jonathan, sir." Heather was back to her phone conversation. "He's the one in charge here."

He doubted if he should feel flattered by that description at this very moment.

"He wants to talk to you." Heather handed Jonathan her phone.

"Who?" Jonathan held the device in his hand.

"Mr. Secretary of Defense himself." Heather looked him in the eye. "Haven't I told you yet? He's my boss."

She couldn't be bluffing. She wouldn't dare to. Jonathan had made a quick investigation about her before and he knew she was just a scientist in one of the Pentagon research units.

"I wouldn't leave him hanging there if I were you." She arched an eyebrow. *Dammit! What if she is right?*

Clearing his throat, Jonathan lifted the phone to his ear. "This is Agent Jonathan."

"Good afternoon, Agent Jonathan."

The voice coming from the other side was his indeed; the voice of the Secretary of Defense of the United States of America.

"Sir?" he warily said.

"This is an unprecedented measure, Agent Jonathan," said Mr. Secretary. "But the time we have is too tight to follow any usual protocol. Soon you will receive your official orders from your direct boss, but *now*, you must release Jeff Burke. Starting from this moment, he is in Dr. Heather's custody. Is that clear?"

Releasing Burke? That didn't sound quite right. "But, Mr. Secretary..." Jonathan was at a loss for words.

"That's not a discussion, Agent Jonathan. That's an order." Mr. Secretary's voice was getting firmer. "Make sure you don't delay Dr. Heather."

"Of course, sir." The second Jonathan finished his phrase, the call ended. What had just happened? A phone conversation with the Head of the Pentagon? And for whom? For that punk in his custody?

Jonathan returned the phone to Heather. "Follow me." He went past her to the door. Heather caught up with him in the corridor while she was making another phone call. Who was she calling this time? The President himself?

"Are you taking him on your own?" he asked her when they reached Burke's room.

"My men are coming." She closed her phone before she nodded toward the shut door of Burke's room. "I hope you have been keeping him in good condition."

"We don't have lake-view rooms here," Jonathan hissed through clenched teeth as he opened the door.

Heather didn't respond to his *honest* remark as she watched Burke through the open door. Jonathan swore he spotted a faint smile that lasted for a millisecond on her face when Burke called out to her. She ignored the punk and walked away from his sight, her eyes on her peeping phone.

"Satisfied?" Jonathan asked, but again she didn't say a word. All she did was press her lips tightly together.

"My men are standing outside by the door. Would you please let them in?" she coldly asked despite her *gentle* words. Reluctantly, Jonathan motioned his assistant to let Heather's company into the office. In a minute, two jerks joined Heather and Jonathan, who were still standing outside Burke's room. "You know what to do." She nodded with her chin toward the open door.

"These are your men?" Jonathan asked in disapproval as he watched her jerks handcuff Burke and drag him outside. *Who are those punks?* Not the agents he expected the Pentagon would send to escort and protect their valuable asset.

Heather ignored him for the third time and strode ahead of her men toward the office door. Until they took Burke with them outside, the punk didn't stop mumbling about the handcuffs that hurt his wrists.

The moment they all disappeared behind the closed door, Jonathan started to feel something was wrong. *I swear those two idiots are not agents.* "Find out who those two men are. Quickly!" he demanded. His assistant hurried to her computer, her fingers playing smoothly on the keyboard.

"Our connections are temporarily off," his assistant announced.

Jonathan needed a few seconds to digest the news. "What the hell does this mean?"

"Everything is dead now. Internet, intranet, and even landlines."

"No way." Jonathan picked up his cell phone to check the network signal, and indeed it was down. How was that possible? He was sure his device was working fine today. Even Heather managed to make calls with her...

Wait a minute. That connection problem was not a coincidence. It was that bitch; he knew she was up to something.

"Where are you going, Agent Jonathan?" his assistance asked as he hurried to the door.

"Find a way to solve the connection problem," Jonathan urged her, standing at the doorstep. "I will find a damn phone booth."

9. No Way Back

While riding shotgun next to Joshua, who drove like a maniac, Heather kept looking over her shoulder to make sure nobody was following them. Jay and Kenji were doing their best to keep that building offline, she knew, but she had no clue what countermeasures that National Security agent might take. Daniel had warned her of such a reckless move. "We are scientists, Heather," he had told her. "We are not CIA agents to do what you want us to do."

So far her plan was working. Her two IT experts had succeeded in using their magic to convince Agent Jonathan that he was talking to the Secretary of Defense himself. And now she was headed to the naval platform with Burke in the backseat flanked by Kenneth and Daniel. If the coming two hours passed without trouble, they would all be on board the HG-3 departing for the Bermuda Triangle.

"Can you drive fast without drawing too much attention?" Heather nervously asked Joshua who seemed to be enjoying the squealing of the car tires. Some men were just big boys.

"Easy, Josh. Nobody is following us," said Kenneth, a hint of excitement in his tone.

"May I understand what's going on here, Heather?" Burke spoke for the first time since they took him out of that building.

Heather turned to face him. "You said you could take us to that island."

"Of course, I can take you to the island," Burke said hesitantly as he glanced at her colleagues. "But I offered to take *you*, not *all* of you."

"Would that make any difference?"

Burke tilted his head. "No. As long as you will be the one providing the boat. Because they took mine."

"Don't worry about the boat. I have one."

"Excellent." Burke raised his cuffed hands. "Still, I don't understand: am I arrested or what? Because those fellows don't look like agents to me."

"And you don't look like a professor to me." Kenneth elbowed Burke.

"Kenneth." Heather gave him a warning look.

"It's alright," said Burke dryly. "Do you mind taking me home to change my clothes?"

"No need for that," said Heather. "You look just fine."

"What about my handcuffs?"

"I'll remove them at the right time."

"And when does the right time come?"

"When I decide so."

"Don't you trust me?"

"Of course, I trust you." She smirked. "I am just protecting you from any stupid thoughts."

"Is that so? You know me better than I thought, then."

"Can't you shut up for a moment?" Daniel scowled at Burke.

"What's your problem?" Burke peered at Daniel.

"Your presence is a problem, let alone your voice," Daniel countered.

"I was talking to her not to you, and I didn't hear her complain."

Heather ignored Burke and Daniel's boyish rant and called Jay on her cell phone. "We're out. How much time do we have?" she asked Jay.

"Half an hour maximum," replied Jay from the other side.

"No way." Heather was getting nervous. "We won't reach the platform before one hundred minutes. Try to give us more time."

"I will do my best."

The moment she ended her call, Burke asked, "More time for what?"

"Would you do me a favor, Burke? Keep your mouth shut until we arrive."

"Arrive where?"

Heather let out a breath of air, keeping her eyes on the road ahead.

"Are we in trouble?" Burke was determined to bother her, it seemed. "Because I feel we are."

"We will be in trouble if you don't remain silent until we set off for the Triangle," she blustered.

"You were not allowed to take me from that agent, were you?" His tone betrayed his amusement.

"You really need to shut up," Daniel snapped. "We will tell you when you are allowed to talk."

"I will keep my mouth shut as you want," Burke promised. "Just tell me if you're breaking the law to take me with you."

"That's none of your business."

"You're right. But it means a lot to me to know anyway."

Heather exhaled again. He wouldn't stay silent unless she gave him an answer. "Yes, *all* of us are breaking the law to take you with us. You'd better be right about your island, or we are all screwed for good."

A wide smile spread across Burke's face. "Quite a woman you are, Heather."

She wasn't sure if that was a faint attempt of flirtation.

Her secured phone peeped. Only two men had that number, her boss one of them. But this time the caller was the other one. Her new bald, nameless friend.

"I'm impressed, I must say," Mr. Colgate admitted.

Through the window, Heather scanned the clear, blue sky with her eyes. "You can't be watching me right now."

"That's what I do for a living."

"Is my chopper waiting?"

"You'd better hurry before they discover your little trick. I won't be able to help you beyond that level."

I know you will, Heather thought as he hung up and killed the line. She had no doubt he would show up whenever she needed his help, exactly like he did regarding Burke's issue. While Jay and Kenji were tracking the NSA guys' movements to find where they had taken Burke, her secured phone received that call from her bald friend. Somehow, he found out what she was up to. It seemed that her IT experts were tracked as well.

To her surprise, Burke kept his promise and remained silent until they reached the building atop of which the chopper was waiting for Heather and her team. "Your new friend is really powerful, Heather," Daniel remarked the moment he saw the helicopter, Joshua and Kenneth dragging Burke behind them.

"I never thought you might doubt me." In fact, Heather was never sure of the intentions of her *powerful friend* until she saw the chopper for herself.

The one-hour flight saved them around fifteen hours of driving; enough time for the National Security agents to realize they were fooled and track the one who fooled them. While Heather was busying herself with phone calls with the rest of her team to make sure they had already made it to the naval platform in Miami, her colleagues barely talked on board the chopper. It was hard for her to tell if they were nervous because of their one-way mission, or worried about the consequences of their reckless act to free a National Security prisoner.

The helicopter landed outside the naval platform, and at last, Heather and her bounty were getting so close to their escape ark. Wasn't it a bit ironic that her ride to the Devil's Triangle could be her only salvation?

Heather strode ahead of Joshua and Kenneth who held Burke by his arms as they walked him to the platform.

"Easy, tough fellows," she heard Burke protest. "I'm going to fall on my face this way."

"Then move your legs and stop acting like a bitch," Kenneth rebuked him. Irked by the language, Heather couldn't help glancing over her shoulder. "Sorry, Heather."

She might discuss that issue with him later. Or not even at all. Her eyes scanned the place until she found Santino, Linda, and Walter ahead, Susan waving to her. "Move on," she urged the men behind her.

Her cell phone peeped, and this time it wasn't Mr. Colgate. "Yes, Mr. Secretary." She picked up her boss's call.

"Where are you, Heather?" he asked firmly.

"Miami, sir. I'm ten minutes from the HG-3."

She heard a deep sigh from the other side. "Heather, I have just received a call from the office of the Secretary of Defense."

Her heart raced when he stated the news. Silently, she waited in anticipation for more to hear.

"Are you still there, Heather?"

"I am, sir." She exhaled. "I'm just catching my breath after this long walk."

"Heather, they have some urgent questions that need clear answers from your side."

"What questions?" Shouldn't she ask who *they* were?

"Dr. Heather," a stern voice called out to her. Between Linda and her stood six men in black suits. The one addressing her was putting on sunglasses, but from the firm line his lips formed, she didn't expect any good news coming from him.

"You're interrupting an urgent, classified mission." Confidence was her faint hope to get away with this. "You and your friends should better move out of our way."

The man who seemed in charge took off his sunglasses, revealing his narrow gray eyes. "I'm Agent Clark, Dr. Heather. And I'm completely aware of the *urgent*, classified mission you are about to start." He paused for effect, leaning forward. "But who said anything about interrupting it?"

Heather squinted at his face. "What does this mean?"

"Your team can start whatever they are about to start." With his thumb, he referred to her fellows standing behind him. "But I'm afraid I can't let you go before we have a *brief* conversation."

Carefully weighing her next words, Heather evaded her teammates' eyes, especially Daniel's. "Agent Clark, you're making a grave mistake." No turning back now. She had to finish what she had started.

"Not as grave as yours, Dr," Agent Clark coldly said. "You should have thought twice before jeopardizing your *urgent, classified* mission."

* * *

The office was air-conditioned, yet Heather felt those beads of sweat form on her forehead. In a desperate attempt to look confident, she leaned back in her seat, her legs crossed, her arm resting on the desk behind which Clark was sitting. "I hope you tell me soon how I can help you, Agent."

"Jeff Burke." He looked her in the eye. "What is he doing in your team?"

"What do you mean by this question?" Heather stalled, hoping she could come up with something to save her.

Clark folded his arms, his eyes still scanning her. "I thought you were in a hurry, Dr."

"I am indeed. But I wonder why you are concerned about my team members' roles."

"Jeff Burke has been under the custody of the National Security Agency for eight years. Nobody told me he has become a member of your team."

"The decision to take him into my team was made recently. It's not my problem you were not informed." Heather shrugged.

"You can't simply take someone from our custody because you *simply* decided to do so." Clark peered at her.

"I didn't take him by force. Your agent could have just denied my simple request."

"A simple request?" he echoed in disapproval. "There are formal procedures we should follow before we let someone like Jeff Burke go with you." He pointed his finger at her. "You misled our agent to violate those procedures."

"I know shit about misleading your agent or the procedures that hinder an urgent mission like mine," snapped Heather. "If you have a problem with procedures, then you are investigating the wrong person. Ask the one who violated them."

"Would you please show me your phone?"

That request in particular; she couldn't respond to it. Jay had warned against letting the NSA agents come close to her phone. In three minutes, they would be able to unveil their trick. "Excuse me?"

"Your phone, Dr. Heather." Clark extended his arm across the desk. "Would you *please* hand it over?"

"I have personal stuff on that device. You can't violate my privacy."

"Let me decide what is personal and what is not, Dr." Clark glared at her, his arm still extended. "Now give me that phone."

10. Zero Hour

So, Daniel was now in charge.

All eyes were on him. After Jay and Kenji's arrival, everybody was waiting for his decision, he knew, but it wasn't an easy one to make.

Among the rest of the crew, he had been the closest one to Heather for the last three months. He knew that her work at the Pentagon had ruined not only her marriage but also her last fragile love story.

Daniel had met Chris, her second ex (before he became her second ex), a couple of times, and the guy seemed nice. Daniel had hoped that Chris would help Heather move on with her life, but Heather had been totally immersed in the Devil's Triangle.

He remembered that night. They were late at the BUCC, working on the virtual model of the TBM

Avenger. Her phone beeped and she didn't answer. Beeped twice and she swore. At the third time, she did pick up the phone, and God! Daniel wished she hadn't.

"Better be something important." She sounded so irked that Daniel could only pity the guy at the other end of the call. The guy who had barely seen his girlfriend in the last six weeks. Chris must have answered with something like: *You know what, checking on you was a silly mistake.* Because she said, "A *grave* mistake, you mean. I was loud and clear about calling me at this number."

Chris might have said, *Maybe it's better not to call you at all.* Heather's curt answer was, "That would be better indeed." She ended the call, the phone rattling over the table as she shoved it across.

It wasn't the first conversation between Heather and Chris to end like that. However, for some reason, Daniel had a feeling about this one and he hoped he was wrong about it, but he wasn't. It was the last phone call between Heather and Chris.

Speaking of last phone calls, Daniel believed that now was a good moment to hear his wife and daughter's voices.

He picked up his phone and dialed his wife's number. "Hey, Nancy."

"*You don't say! You left early today.*"

Daniel chuckled. "No, hun. Actually, I'm calling to tell you that I might be late tonight. How is my little monkey?"

Nancy sighed. "*Your little monkey will kill you if you do something like that on her performance day. You don't remember when it will be, do you?*"

His daughter's performance day? Had Nancy told him about it in the first place? Anyway, he wouldn't dare to ask his wife now. "Of course, I remember. Now put her on. I want to hear her voice before my break is over."

"*Her break hasn't even started. In case you don't know, she has a ballet lesson today.*"

Daniel could sense the rebuke in Nancy's voice. "Yeah, yeah, you're right." He rubbed his forehead, trying to choose his next words carefully. "Isn't there a way to..." he stammered. "Isn't there a way to pass the phone to her for a second?"

"*What is it, Daniel? Is everything alright?*" Nancy's voice betrayed her worry.

"Everything is fine." Daniel should end this disastrous phone call. That could be his last conversation with his wife, and he ruined it royally. "Gotta go now, hun. Love you."

When Daniel returned the phone to his pocket, he found Santino peering at him.

"Are we aborting mission, Daniel?"

Part of Daniel wished he could do that. But that was quite a big decision to make.

"We have been working hard on this." Daniel heaved a sigh. "We will do ourselves an injustice if we let our efforts go to waste."

"Shame Heather won't be with us," Susan muttered, her head down.

"Shame indeed." Burke had the guts to join the conversation.

"Don't you know when to keep your mouth shut?" Daniel snapped at him. "She won't be with us because of you."

"You blame me?" Burke scoffed. "May I ask you a question: why do you think I'm still here?"

Daniel didn't grasp what Burke was hinting at. "What do you mean?"

"They didn't arrest me, *pal.* I'm not the reason why the agents took her." Burke raised his cuffed hands. "Which reminds me: how long are you going to keep me like this? My wrists are getting itchy."

Jay pulled Daniel gently by the arm. "If we are not aborting this mission, then we must leave now. Once they find Heather's phone, it will only be a matter of a few minutes before they discover how we were all involved."

Jay's words were not helping at all. It wasn't about the mission now. It was about saving their own skins. *Escaping to Bermuda Triangle. Could that be more ironic?* "So, we are simply leaving Heather behind?"

"You think it would help her if we turned ourselves in?" Jay countered. "The only thing we can do for her is succeed in our mission. That might justify everything she did." When Daniel glared at him, he harrumphed. "Everything *we* did."

Running away to save Heather; that wouldn't sound too bad, Daniel must say. He could fool himself for the time being with this lame excuse.

"Santi," Daniel called out. "Gather everybody inside. Kenneth, show our guest his seat next to Major Powell and don't remove his cuffs until we set off." He turned to Burke. "Trust me, you don't want to piss the Major off."

Daniel hopped into the HG3 after everybody was on board. Definitely, it was the hugest hovercraft ever built, yet from the inside it was narrower than it seemed. That protective skeleton probably constituted two-thirds of the vessel size.

Burke was seated beside Powell when Daniel entered the cockpit. "Zero hour has come, Major," Daniel told Powell. "We are good to go."

Looking at Daniel, Powell pointed at Burke's cuffed hands. "What is this?"

Daniel didn't know where he should begin. "Long story. But you can say he is our tour guide to the Triangle."

The marine didn't seem satisfied at all with this answer. "I need to know why a handcuffed man is going to sit by my side on this *mission*."

"See?" Burke gave Daniel a rebuking look. "You could have spared yourself the trouble if you had listened to me from the beginning."

Daniel ignored Burke and took a deep breath. "We will not start with the red and yellow sites," he told Powell. "We shall be headed to an island that no one knows about except him."

Powell looked Burke up and down before he turned to Daniel. "Are you asking me not to adhere to the official protocol of the mission?"

Oh God! Give me patience! "We are the ones who decide the official protocol of the mission, Major." Daniel peered at Powell. "Your job is to make sure we reach the destination we tell you."

"I'm not your damned Uber driver," Powell firmly said. "If this man is not eligible to keep his hands free, then he can't stay on board of my vessel, let alone in *my* cockpit."

"If you insist." Daniel forced a smile before he turned to Kenneth. "The keys."

Kenneth handed Daniel the keys. "For your own good, you had better be serious about your stupid island," Daniel warned Burke. "We have lost Heather because she believed in you and your tale."

"My tale is true, and she was right when she believed in me," Burke hurriedly said. "I will prove you all wrong when you get into the Triangle."

"I hope you will." Daniel unlocked the handcuffs and peered at Powell. "He is eligible now, Major."

Powell chewed on his lip for a moment. "Very well." Reluctantly, he started the HG-3 engines. "The coordinates of our new destination?"

"We don't need them," said Burke. "Just survive the storm and let me worry about the rest."

Powell curled his lip in disdain as he looked from Burke to Daniel.

After heaving another sigh, Daniel leaned toward Burke. "How do you plan to find the island, then, *Dr.* Burke?"

"By following the stars."

"Their constellations, you mean."

Burke nodded.

"Are you both serious?" Powell asked in disapproval.

"We have no other means to guide us in the Triangle," Burke pointed out. "If we survive the electromagnetic storm...I mean *after* we do, the vessel navigation system will be obsolete."

"The HG-3 can stand an electromagnetic storm, I was told." Powell glanced at Daniel.

"Not the one inside the Triangle." Burke smiled at Daniel. "You should have brought some oars, just in case."

Oars? Daniel hoped things would not turn that bad. They were having a bad start already with Heather's absence. The team morale couldn't be worse.

"We must go now, Major." Daniel was not hurried to start the mission as much as he wanted to end the conversation with Burke. "We have ninety-six hours to finish this mission. Let's make every minute count."

Daniel sat next to Kenneth right behind the cockpit. The Major looked back, making a final check that everybody was in place. With the engine already turned on, the HG-3 was ready to move to its...

"Stop, Major! Stop!" Susan waved as she gazed through the window. "I see Heather coming."

11. Into the Vanishing Zone

The sky was clear and the ocean was calm; a perfect day for this expedition despite its rough start.

The HG-3 was twenty minutes away from entering the 'vanishing zone' of the Triangle. Powell had wanted to 'sail' through the ocean to save as much of the engine power as possible for the ugly part of the ride, but Heather insisted on flying to save time. It made sense for the team as they all needed to make good use of their limited time to finish the mission, but to Heather that wasn't her only reason to do so. The farther she got from the Pentagon Headquarters, the more comfortable she felt.

Her heart raced when Powell announced that only fifteen minutes remained before entering the Devil's Triangle. She left her seat and went to Burke at the cockpit. "Are you ready to act as our tour guide?"

"You're the only one who believes in me." He gave her a grateful smile. "I shall not let you down."

I hope so, she thought. "Good." She turned to the marine. "Major Powell, once we are inside the Triangle, we will follow Burke's lead."

Powell nodded without looking at her. "No red or yellow sites, I was told."

"Red and yellow?" Burke gazed at Powell before he asked Heather, "Is our pilot suffering from color blindness?"

Powell frowned at Burke's jest. But probably, Burke wasn't joking in the first place.

"Major Powell is fine." Heather patted Burke on the shoulder. "Those red and yellow points he mentions represent locations of all the disappearance incidents in the Bermuda Triangle." She gestured to Powell. "Would you please show him, Major? Thanks." Powell hadn't responded to her simple request yet, but she thanked him anyway. Reluctantly, he brought the map of events on the dashboard screen, Burke staring at it in obvious concern.

"What are the colors for?" Burke asked.

"Red is for the incidents after the seventies, yellow for before."

"Seventies?" Burke gave her a lopsided smile. "Since 1965, no incident in Bermuda has been recorded except in 2005 and 2007. Why do I see *twelve* red points instead of two?"

That was absurd. "Because there were ten other *classified* incidents, Burke. I guess you know that already."

"I bet the officials responsible for the cover-up of those two incidents were fired."

"We shouldn't reveal everything we know until we understand the reason behind it."

Burke chuckled mockingly. "Now you talk like the Agency guys who used to interrogate me. Come on. You told me you were a scientist."

"I was." What was she saying? "I am."

"Good." Burke's grin was so wide it showed his teeth, which were not perfect like Mr. Colgate's, though. "If I point at a particular point, can you name the incident date?"

"Is that a Bermuda Quiz or what?" Not the right time to test her knowledge. Not when they were that close to the Triangle.

"If you know the dates by heart—as I do—you will notice a pattern."

Heather had to admit he piqued her curiosity—he always knew how to do so. "I don't notice a pattern, but it seems you can show me one." Now she noticed the silence that reigned over the cabin. Her conversation with Burke had grabbed the attention of a curious audience.

"Look. Those happened in the new millennium." He pointed at several scattered circles on the screen. "Those in the eighties and the nineties." He indicated another group. "Those between the forties and the sixties." He gazed at her, as if he was waiting for her answer for this puzzle.

"What? Is it that obvious?"

Burke grinned. "It should be now."

"The range of the Triangle is shrinking." Sitting in his place, Daniel decided to take part in solving the puzzle. From the satisfied look on Burke's face, Heather could tell that Daniel's guess was right.

"Your team is not that bad, though," Burke teased her.

"Maybe you're right—about the Triangle, I mean." Heather ignored his gloating smile. "But where would that lead us?"

"Whatever the force governing Bermuda, it's fading," said Burke. Glancing back, Heather observed the impact of the 'force' on her team.

"We have an island to find, Burke." She managed a smile. "Why don't you focus on how we are going to reach it?"

"You are absolutely right." Burke turned to Powell. "Tell me, Major: can this amazing hovercraft dive?"

"Yes, it can," replied Powell, "Why do you ask?"

"Because you need to get this vessel to a lower altitude and be ready to hit the ocean," said Burke. "Now."

"What is this nonsense?" Powell glanced at Heather. "We don't have to dive, at least for the coming ten minutes. The weather is clear—"

"Do you want to enjoy the experience of free-falling in a hundred-ton hovercraft?" Burke cut him off. "Okay. Be my guest, Major."

"What is it, Burke?" Heather asked

"A storm is coming," replied Burke, "and please don't tell me *it's not on the screen.* In my previous journey, I hadn't received a warning before both the Atlantic Ocean and its sky went mad."

Powell shot Heather an inquisitive look, as if he waited for her say to confirm the order he had just received from Burke.

"We will do what Burke says, Major," Heather decided. "He knows what—"

Her peeping cell cut her off. Wondering why her boss would call her now, she cautiously replied, "Yes?"

"They found your phone, Heather," her boss curtly said.

"What phone, sir?" Heather tried to pretend she didn't understand what he was talking about.

"The one you used to make your fake call." Her boss's voice was getting a bit harsher. "The one you dropped on the road to make us chase a false clue."

Revealing her simple trick wasn't a surprise to her. When she got rid of the phone she had used in tricking that agent Jonathan, she knew she was just buying herself some time until she could get away from the eastern coast. The look on Clark's face was priceless when his technicians told him that Heather's phone—the useless one she had handed him during her brief interrogation—was clean.

What surprised and *irked* her a bit was something else.

"*Us*?" She couldn't help grimacing when she echoed the word. "Were you chasing me as well?"

Her boss sighed. "It's not what it sounds like, Heather. Yes, I was chasing you indeed, but my reasons were different, mind you. You have been improvising for the last few days, and I'm really worried where your reckless moves will take you."

Powell indicated with his fingers that only two minutes remained for entering the Triangle. "I must end this call now, sir. We're about to enter Bermuda."

"You may have managed to get away from *them* this time," said SecNav. "But I assure you, they will be waiting for your *safe* return."

Her safe return? She could only hope. But her faint hope didn't survive more than a couple of seconds. The vessel started to shudder.

"Told ya." Burke gave Powell a gloating smile. "A storm is coming."

12. A List of the Worst Conditions

The vessel was shaking as if it weighed nothing more than a feather in the blowing wind, yet Powell's nervous look gave Burke a sense of satisfaction. *They all doubted me. They all took me for a fool,* Burke thought. Now it was time to see who the real fool here was.

If any of the fools survived in the first place.

The HG-3, or whatever they called it, wobbled so hard that Heather had to clutch Burke's shoulder to maintain her balance—he didn't complain by the way. Burke held her by the arm. "You must go to your seat and buckle up," he urged her. "The storm will only get uglier."

Only a few steps separated the cockpit and the passengers' cabin, yet amid that vigorous wobbling, the distance seemed endless. "Can you make it?" Burke asked her.

She nodded. But the moment she let go of him to head to her seat in the passengers' cabin, she failed to hold her ground, her back slammed against the wall.

"Heather! Are you okay?" Burke left his seat and struggled to reach her, hitting the wall two times before he managed to hold Heather's arm. Daniel unbuckled his seat belt and with one hand he reached out to Heather, the other gripping his seat's armrest. "Hold on to him," Burke urged her, not surprised if Daniel didn't care whether Burke was hurt or not. "Go back to your seats and buckle up," he addressed Daniel and Heather, no one paying him heed, though. Now he had to worry about his return journey to his seat in the cockpit. After falling twice and hitting the floor, he stumbled to his spot next to Powell.

"Damn!" Powell growled. "Where did those clouds come from?"

"I bet you have never seen anything like that." Unlike Burke, who still remembered every moment of his first ride into Bermuda, as if it was yesterday.

Well, not every moment to be honest. He must have lost his consciousness for a few minutes when the waves had slapped him and his boat. He had thought he was drowning, but all of a sudden, he had found himself lying on his back on board his pathetic boat, which had survived the mighty storm by some miracle.

Powell must be doing his best to keep the vessel steady while descending, but Burke wasn't expecting anything more than a desperate attempt. The wind speed went insane without any previous warning, the clouds so heavy that the horizon vanished. "Sit tight, everyone!" A lovely piece of advice from the Major. *What the hell do you think they are doing right now?*

"I thought the HG-3 would be stronger than that," muttered Burke.

"It could be worse." Powell didn't seem sure in his rocking seat.

"It will be worse, Major," Burke managed a smile, his lips pressed together, "if you don't dive with that thing now."

"You survived that storm before, right?" Heather asked from behind him.

"Yes." Burke looked for a gap in the gray curtain ahead of them. "Except that I was on a boat, not hanging in the sky."

"She will make it," said Heather. "I requested that hovercraft to be as such to stand the worst conditions it might encounter."

"Did you provide its makers with a list of those worst conditions?" Burke's head would hit the control panel if it were not for the seatbelt.

"It wasn't a big list." Heather paused for a moment, as if she was trying to recall that list. "But it would do, I think."

"Did it include EMP storms?"

"Fortunately, yes. Would that help?"

"You shall know sooner than you think." Burke's eyes were fixed on the gauges of the dashboard. He knew that moment would come when the...

"The engines are dead!" Powell made the announcement Burke had been anticipating. Screams and shrieks came from the passengers' cabin when the HG-3 started falling. To be honest, Burke wasn't less scared than the men and women behind him. He was never a fan of roller coasters, though he knew that at some point the roller coaster cart would rise again.

Unlike this flipping vessel.

Waiting for the moment of hitting the ocean surface like a bullet, Burke caught a glimpse of Powell, who was sitting tight in his seat as he preached to his passengers. The Major reached down—or up, when the vessel was upside down—for something that Burke didn't know. He was not looking for his phone to make one last tweet, right?

And suddenly, Burke felt himself pulled upward.

He needed a moment to catch his breath, and then he tried to figure out what was happening. Through the windshield, Burke contemplated the ocean surface from a close range. They must be like ten or twenty feet above the water, and they were falling down slowly this time, like a leaf on a warm day.

While the vessel was landing on the water, Burke spotted the handle near Powell's toe. "That's what saved us today, isn't it?" Burke indicated the handle with his chin.

"It activates an emergency parachute brake system." Powell nodded in approval. "And that system works mechanically." That's why it could never be affected by electromagnetic waves.

"I truly admire your composure, Major," Burke addressed Powell. "Even if I knew the place and the function of this handle, I would never remember to use it during such a mad panic."

The team members in the cabin behind Burke were checking on each other. Heather had unbuckled her seatbelt already to see for herself that everybody was okay. *For what?* Burke wondered. They were all sitting tight during the adrenaline-rush ride. *If there is one she must check on, it should be me.*

"The ocean is steady." Powell gazed at the clear horizon ahead. "The storm is over."

"I told you: you have never seen anything like that," said Burke. For a first-timer, it would be hard to believe that this calm ocean had been raging just one minute ago.

Heather came to the cockpit. "Damage report, Major."

"I wish I could be more specific, Dr." Powell gestured at the dead gauges and screens. "But as you see, the HG-3 is turned off."

"You were right, then." Heather nodded toward Burke. For the time being, he would take that as a compliment. "I thought that electromagnetic storms only happen in space."

"Starting from now, forget everything you think you know," Burke said.

Heather stared at him before Daniel interrupted their moment as he said, "Santino, Walter, and I are going to check the engine and turn it on. We need to get some coordinates to know where we are."

"Where do you think we are?" Burke teased him. "We are in Bermuda Triangle, Professor Daniel. By the way, are you Professor yet?"

Daniel countered Burke's jest with a cold look. "We are going, Heather."

"There is a small chance you can revive that engine," Burke pointed out. "But getting coordinates? That's impossible."

Daniel ignored him as he took Santino and Walter to the engine room.

"Even if they manage to revive the engine, we won't be able to communicate with the *outer* world, right?" Heather warily asked Burke.

"The Triangle is designed to keep everything inside and prevent anything outside from entering."

"*Designed*?" Heather arched an eyebrow. "Anyway, it didn't keep you inside."

"Which means you still have a chance to survive Bermuda." He winked.

Heather didn't look amused. "I hope you really mean it, not just trying to be funny." She looked at the orange horizon of dusk. "The sun will go down in less than an hour."

"Which is what we are waiting for," said Burke. "Without satellites and radio, only one way would work. You need darkness to see constellations, remember?"

13. Yellow Lights

Darkness reigned inside and outside the hovercraft.

Two hours had passed, and Heather was still waiting for Daniel, Santino, and Walter to come back from the engine room below the passengers' cabin with good news.

"Haven't you brought fresh fruits with you?" Burke's voice came from behind her as he approached.

"Seriously," she turned to him, "you feel like eating anything in such a situation?"

Burke shrugged carelessly. "What does this situation have to do with my appetite anyway?"

His peace of mind was really impressive yet provocative. As if he had been asleep while the HG-3 was plummeting into the ocean like a rock. As if he wasn't aware that they were stranded on a dead vessel in the heart of the ocean. Should she bring to his attention that they were not having some rest before resuming their lovely cruise in the Devil's Triangle?

"Maybe we find fresh fruits on your island." She smiled crookedly. "Wouldn't that be nice?"

She left Burke in his fruity dreams and bent over the hatch of the engine room. "What if it is not an electromagnetic shock?" Walter's echoing voice came from the room.

"Could it be something else?" Santino asked.

"I don't know," said Walter. "I guess we need to gather the whole team to consider other options."

"Other options? Like what?"

"Lifeboats, Santi."

"And abandon the HG-3?" Heather couldn't help butting into their conversation. Using lifeboats meant losing the HG-3, probably forever. Also, chasing her luck in the middle of the ocean wasn't something she was ready to do.

"The HG-3 is useless if we can't make it move." Daniel came below the hatch, his head up to face her. "We won't stay here until we starve."

She wished she could tell them that help would come soon, but she didn't dare. That wouldn't fool anybody here. *We all knew that from the beginning,* she reminded herself. *We all knew we would be on our own in this mission.*

Next to Nathaniel, the quiet expert of ancient languages, Jay and Kenji were trying every device and gadget they had brought. "Any good news?" she asked them, both of them shaking their heads in denial.

"Heather," Linda called out from the cockpit. Usually, she was that type of person who wouldn't talk to you unless you talked to her first. "You must come and see this." Heather wasn't sure if Linda sounded excited or alarmed.

"What is it?" Heather joined Linda, Susan, Kenneth, and Joshua who crammed Powell's cockpit, their eyes fixed on the windshield. Something ahead of them was grabbing their attention.

"Not sure." Linda shook her head as she made way for Heather to advance. "Can you tell?"

It should be an easy question to answer. Assuming there were no ports nearby, those flashing yellow lights at the horizon must belong to some ship.

A ship that was coming closer to them.

Burke stood on his toes behind Heather. "What's going on?"

"Have you seen that before?" Without looking back, Heather lowered her voice as she gazed at what looked like the shadow of a ship approaching the HG-3.

"I can't see clearly from my spot," Burke protested.

Heather warily peered at him, recalling what Mr. Colgate had told her about the *official* reason why Burke had been fired from the university. *He is not up to any foolish acts, is he?* She nodded to Linda and Susan to step back and let Burke take their spot. "Is the view better now?"

"Much better." He raised his eyebrows as he contemplated the approaching huge vessel.

"You know what it is, don't you?"

Burke shook his head, pressing his lips together. "I never saw anything like that on my first journey."

Disappointed, Heather exhaled.

"It must be another ship," Kenneth nervously said. "I mean: can it be anything other than that?"

Nobody had an answer to his question. Probably, they were too afraid to answer it.

"Why is that ship not dead like our hovercraft?" Powell wondered as he tried every button on the control panel. Again, the answer would be terrifying.

"Because it's not a ship, Major," said Burke, a hint of amusement in his voice. Heather started to doubt whether Burke knew more than he revealed to them, or he was really blessed with this unbelievable quantum of peace of mind.

"What do you know, Burke?" She peered at him.

"I know nothing." Burke shrugged. "I just spit out what I think about. Even just half-baked ideas"

Footsteps crept up from behind her. "What is all this fuss about?" Daniel pointed his torch at the cockpit as he approached, Santino and Walter following him.

"We got company." Heather pointed at the yellow flashing lights coming from that mysterious..."Where did it go?" She squinted at the horizon, which was all black now. The vessel was invisible after the yellow lights were out

"Now what?" Susan wondered.

"This is not promising," Kenneth muttered.

"Why did it stop?" Glancing at Burke, Heather was growing impatient.

"What?" Burke's eyebrows rose. "I am not a fortune teller."

"Dammit!" Heather gnashed her teeth. "Let me through." She gave him a dismissive wave before she strode to the side windows that showed nothing but the silent dark ocean. "Where did it go?" She turned to her IT experts. "You will do us a great favor if you find a way to communicate with that unidentified vessel."

"Unidentified vessel?" Jay exclaimed. "What are we missing?"

Before Heather uttered a word, Powell left the cockpit in a hurry and stopped by every locked side window to look through it. "Something wrong, Major?" she asked him warily.

Powell shushed her as he looked through the second window to the left. His gesture might have irked her on a normal occasion, but right now it made her curious.

And anxious.

"What is it, Major?" Daniel asked, obviously sharing her anxiety.

"Quiet," Powell nervously whispered. "A boat. Get down."

Unable to resist her curiosity, Heather sneaked a peek through the nearest window to her. "Get down, I say," Powell insisted.

"Where is that boat?" Heather asked as she complied with Powell's order.

"Gone," Powell whispered nervously.

For a couple of minutes, no one said a word as they all sat on the floor. Heather wanted to ask Powell how long they would stay like that, but after a second thought she changed her mind. She was not ready for another *shush* from the burly marine.

"Did you hear that?" Susan sounded alarmed, pointing upward...where the light footsteps came from.

Heather's heart pounded as she followed the cautious footsteps with her ears. Whoever he was, he was doing his best to remain unnoticed.

Powell stood below the upper hatch, gesturing with one hand to Heather and her team to stay as they were, the other hand balled into a fist.

"Do you hear that?" Kenneth asked in a low voice when a faint buzzing sound came from behind the very upper hatch Powell stood beneath. In a minute, the buzzing was gone and the hatch was slowly removed. From her angle, Heather could barely see the frame of the intruder's face.

The face that was too long to be human.

14. Humanoid

The darkness made it hard for Heather to see the features of that long face. And obviously, the case was the same for the mysterious intruder, who slowly moved his head right and left, as if he was scanning the vessel from inside. After a minute of absolute silence, Heather doubted if he could see the passengers of the HG-3 in the first place.

And then, the intruder jumped into the vessel. While Heather was petrified like everybody else, Powell made his move.

The marine pulled the intruder by his long, thin arm and slammed his back against the floor. Without giving the unwelcome visitor a reprieve, Powell smashed his jaw with a straight punch in that long face. The intruder screeched like a crow before he collapsed motionless on the floor.

Except for Powell, who was already standing by the fallen creature, nobody dared to move from his spot, as if they wanted to make sure that the intruder was asleep now. A click so close to Heather startled her, but she realized it was only Jay's flashlight. The shell of the HG-3 must have spared it the worst of the electromagnetic storm.

"Oh God!" Susan covered her mouth when Jay approached the fallen intruder, his torchlight showing a long, gray, humanoid face with two narrow eyes that topped a small lipless mouth. The tiny nostrils above that thin mouth were too hard to recognize. Maybe that *thing* did not need to breathe anyway.

"Unbelievable." Heather came closer and bent over the unconscious humanoid, feeling the texture of *his* brown two-piece outfit that covered his body from shoulder to knee. "It feels like leather."

Burke joined her and touched the humanoid's outfit as well. "Because it's leather indeed." He gripped the upper part of the outfit, as if he was going to pull it off. "Well, almost."

"I don't think it's a good idea to touch anything now," Daniel cautiously pointed out.

"Are you so optimistic that you think you can return with *him* as a sample?" Burke scoffed.

"You didn't come with us to be trapped here for life, did you?" Daniel peered at him.

"Gentlemen." Heather wanted to stop a probable pointless argument. Like seriously, how many times would you enter the Bermuda Triangle and encounter an intelligent race other than humans? Unfortunately, she couldn't know the reasons why *he* decided to come to their vessel on his own. "Wasn't there another way to...neutralize *him*?" she asked Powell.

"Did you expect me to offer him a welcome drink?" Powell curled his lip.

Heather sighed. "I said nothing about welcome drinks, Major. I'm just wondering if there is a possible way to communicate with him."

"How would that matter? We would never understand a damn word from this creature."

Only when he harrumphed, Heather remembered that one of her team members was a guy called Nathaniel. "Actually, we can." Probably it was his first time to speak since their departure.

"Did you understand what that creature said?" she asked Nathaniel.

Nathaniel swallowed. "He speaks Latin. *The vessel is not abandoned* was what he said."

Latin? Why wasn't Heather surprised? "The photo you captured." Heather stared at Burke. "He is the one who wrote those words in the sand."

Burke shrugged. "Or one of his people did. We have no idea how many they are."

Of course, that mysterious vessel must be carrying more humanoids. It would be exciting to meet them, but would they be excited as well to meet Heather and her crew?

Another creaky sound coming from the knocked out humanoid startled her, but she realized it wasn't *him*. Powell searched the long-faced intruder and found a spherical gadget from which the voice was coming. "That must be the communicator through which he was reporting that the vessel was not abandoned."

"They are calling him, it seems," said Burke. "Either we reply or leave this vessel immediately."

Heather pondered the two possibilities. "Leave and go where, Burke? To the island?"

"We have no other options," replied Burke. "Shortly, others will come from that mysterious ship to find their missing dude. Don't you have lifeboats on this HG thing?"

Heather shot Powell an inquisitive look. "What do you think?"

"I still don't like the idea of following the lead of this weirdo." Powell shook his head. "But I guess he is right about our options; they are so limited." He peered at Burke as he continued, "I hope you know what you are talking about. We will take the two lifeboats we have into the middle of the dark ocean."

Burke's response was nothing more than his strange smile. A smile that would irritate anybody in such a situation.

And indeed it did.

"Do you really have any idea what damn hole we are stuck in?" Powell held Burke firmly by the shoulders. "Our lives are on the edge."

Burke didn't look bothered that much. "As long as the sky is clear, we still have a chance." He grinned before pushing Powell's arms gently. "Now, if you don't mind. We can talk like civilized people."

Heather heard the worried mumbling of her crew. She was not less anxious than them. From the beginning, she was the one who insisted on bringing Burke on board with her team to Bermuda, but when it was time for a reality check, she did not feel so sure about leaving her destiny, as well as her crew's, in Burke's hands.

The creaking voice started again through the spherical gadget.

"Now what?" Daniel addressed Nathaniel.

"I don't know this time." Nathaniel shrugged. "Maybe they are calling him by his name."

"So be it," said Heather. "We will release the capsules, but first we have to check them to make sure they are not dead." She gestured to the three engineers in her crew to hurry and examine the lifeboats.

"What about that ship?" Santino pointed at the dark figure that could be barely seen through the glass window. "They must be watching us."

"That's why we want to make sure that the diving mode is still working in both boats."

"Diving mode," Burke echoed in excitement. "Interesting. The *capsules* are designed with diving modes." He looked at Heather. "You really did a great job in your preparations for this cruise."

Cruise? "Just pray the EMP didn't kill those capsules."

Burke nodded his chin toward the humanoid. "What are we going to do with *Longface*?"

"We can't leave him here," said Powell. "We can't afford to lose our only means of escape."

"We can't take him with us, either," said Susan.

"Then, what's your suggestion?" Heather asked nervously. "You can't throw him in the ocean."

"Listen, Doctor." Powell wagged a firm finger. "Our plan did not involve humanoid creatures. I'm taking charge from here if you want to survive."

"Mind your tone, Major," Daniel warned.

"Or what? Huh? Or *what?*" Powell glowered at Daniel.

"Major! This is still my expedition!" Heather snarled. "I'm the one in charge here."

"This expedition is over," Powell spat. "Our priority now is to survive this situation until we find a way out."

"They are coming!" Linda announced, alarmed.

"Another boat?" Burke wondered.

"No. It's the ship itself. It's moving!"

Heather looked through the nearest side window to confirm the news. The yellow lights were flashing again from the mysterious ship, which was slowly approaching the HG-3.

"I guess it's time to decide, folks." Burke stood between Heather and Powell. "If we have no problem to be caught by those humanoids, then we can just quarrel until they arrive." He turned to Powell. "We must admit we have lost the HG-3 already, Major. No need to throw anybody anywhere."

"I don't know which is safer." Daniel rubbed his chin. "Following Burke, or getting caught by those humanoids."

"No question, it's getting caught by humanoids." Burke tittered.

"This is ridiculous," Powell muttered. "I can't believe this is the best team the US government has got."

"The capsules are good to go." Santino's voice came out with the first good news in a long time.

"Are you 100% sure?" Heather asked.

"Don't worry, Heather. The shell of HG-3 took the worst of the electromagnetic shock, but the capsules are fine," Santino promised.

"What are you waiting for, guys?" Burke watched through the glass window. "Their ship is getting closer."

Heather had to voice the final say to urge her team to move. "Alright then, everyone. To the capsules. Go! Go!"

The team hurried to the hatch in the floor that led to the life capsules. "After you." Burke ushered Heather with a smile.

"We have no time for this." She grabbed him by the arm, motioning him to follow her colleagues. Only Powell and she remained. The Captain was the last one to leave, she knew. And in this case, Powell should go first.

"Now, Dr." Powell's eyes widened as he gazed at something behind her. Startled one more time, she turned, but all she saw was the humanoid that lay motionless on the floor.

Well, almost motionless. She could have sworn, those slim gray digits made a move.

15. The Island

Through the glass window of the life capsule, Heather could see nothing but the dark water. "What about the other capsule, Santi?" she asked Santino, the *captain* of the encapsulated lifeboat underwater.

"They're just behind us, Heather," Santino replied. "According to the radar, the two capsules are on course."

Heather pondered the situation. She had split the team into two groups, one led by Powell in the capsule behind them, the other included her and Burke. Luckily, radars were still working in both capsules.

"We need to coordinate with Powell when it's time to surface. We're blind in this ocean." She glanced at Burke. "We need him up for the constellations."

"I can hear you, Heather." Through the line already open with the other capsule came Powell's voice over the communicator. "We shall rise after two miles to make sure we're out of sight. Then it's up to your guy."

"You can count on me, Major," said Burke.

"I hope so." Powell's voice was impassive.

Minutes were heavy for Heather, who kept her eyes glued to the window, waiting for stars to show up in her line of sight. *Damn! Can't this capsule go faster?* she thought.

"We are rising," Powell announced from the other end of the line.

As the capsule approached the ocean surface, Heather felt herself lifted up with her seat. Being surrounded by dark water made her so nervous she couldn't wait until she had a view of the sky.

"I guess it's my number now." Burke rose from his seat and stood by the hatch after the capsule had risen to water level.

"We don't need you now, Burke." Santino sounded excited. "I see land on the radar."

"No way." Heather was not less thrilled.

"Confirmed." Powell didn't sound as thrilled as everybody was. "Estimated time to reach land is twenty-four minutes."

"Really?" Burke jerked his head backward. "I guess I can go back home, then."

"Lucky you," Powell's voice came through the communicator. "We will never know whether you are a real scientist or a fraud."

"We risked our careers to get you on board with us." Santino glanced at Heather, a hint of rebuke in his tone.

"Your what?" Burke scoffed. "I'm sorry to ruin your *career,* mi amigo. I must say I admire your optimistic spirit."

"Keep your focus on the radar, Santi," said Heather, who noticed how Santino clenched his teeth.

"We should have left you with Longface, *Dr.* Burke." Powell didn't sound joking about it.

"I'm afraid it's too late, Major. But you may need to have me for lunch when you starve on this island after you finish all your supplies." Burke's suggestion made Heather feel sick.

"I won't hesitate if I have to do so." Powell's answer wasn't less disgusting.

"Enough!" Heather blustered. "I will close that radio if you both don't stop this nonsense."

Silence reigned over the capsule for ten minutes. Heather kept staring at the radar that showed the two capsules as two yellow dots approaching the island. Shortly, two more dots appeared on the radar following their capsules. "What's this?" Heather asked.

"They are after us," replied Santino, alarmed.

"They must have spotted us when we surfaced," said Powell from the other side on the radio. "We must dive again."

The two capsules dove below the surface once more. Again, Heather found herself surrounded by the ocean water.

"Did we lose them?" Heather asked.

"Change the course by thirty degrees to make sure," instructed Powell.

Santino changed the capsule direction as Powell said. The two chasing dots on the radar remained on their course.

"We have lost them," said Burke.

"Good," said Powell. "With their speed, they could have caught us before reaching the shore."

For a minute, Heather, Burke, and Santino kept their eyes on the radar, watching the two capsules escaping the two mysterious followers.

"Thank God." Heather sighed. "Santi, how long until we reach the shore?"

"Thirteen minutes," said Santino. "Unless we return to the original course."

"Negative," Powell answered through the communicator. "We will stick to our current course. We don't want to—"

"Damn!" Santino cut him off. "They are after us again."

"Forward with maximum speed," Powell urged. "Take the shortest route to the shore."

The two capsules adjusted their directions, the two chasers closing in on them.

"Why is Powell a bit faster than us?" Burke asked.

"Funny you ask." Santino glared at Burke. "Because we carry an extra passenger."

Burke looked at Heather. "He doesn't mean me, right?"

"In fact, we wouldn't need to surface if it were not for you," Linda pointed out.

"So much love." Burke smirked.

Heather had enough of that nonsense. "Would you *please* give me a damned break? We have lost our vessel and now we are chased by...whatever they are. So, stop it."

"Is it only me who notices this?" Burke pointed at the radar. "Our chasers have slowed down."

Heather stared at the radar for half a minute. "You're right. They are keeping their distance from us. Their velocity is almost the same as ours. Could this mean anything?"

Nobody replied. Even Burke had no smart remark to add now. Powell broke the silence when he said, "I have no explanation for this, Heather. Anyway, we have to stick to our course until we reach our destination."

The minutes remaining to reach the island passed slowly. As the two capsules approached the coast, they rose to the water surface, the capsule lights revealing the rocky shore.

"The water is getting shallow, Santino," said Powell. "Time to get off."

The two capsules slowed down until they stopped twenty meters away from the shore. The moment Santino opened the hatch, Heather urged her crew, including Santino himself to abandon the capsule. When Heather joined them outside, she found that all passengers of Powell's capsule had exited their vessel already. Holding the few flashlights that had survived the EMP storm, in addition to the gadgets they could carry, her team followed the marine's lead. "Hurry up. We have four minutes to disappear from here."

"What about the capsules?" Santino wondered.

"We don't have enough time for them," said Heather.

The crew trudged in the water with their backpacks until they reached the rocky shore. The flashlights revealed the heavy forested area behind the beach.

"Let's hurry to the woods," Burke urged. "We shall hide there."

"I guess he's right this time," Powell seconded him. "Into the woods."

The options for Heather and her crew were not that many. The ocean was behind them and the forest was upfront, the arrival of their chasers only a matter of a few minutes. And to add a little spice, Heather and her team had to cross that choppy shore with enough caution in this darkness so as not to stumble.

"Freeze," Powell whispered. "Turn off your flashlights."

The Major's warning unnerved Heather. "What's the matter, Powell?" She looked around, but she saw nothing.

"I hear something." Powell was still whispering. "Footsteps."

It was total darkness without the flashlights. Standing in her place, Heather felt somebody next to her.

"It's me," whispered Burke. "Don't be scared. We have to stay close to each other on this moonless night." The calmness in Burke's voice made her doubt if that guy was totally sane. In the last few hours, she had fallen with the HG-3 into the ocean, seen a gray-faced humanoid, and survived a water pursuit. Now she was on an unknown island, cornered by chasers she couldn't see thanks to the darkness that curtained off the world around her. She was a physical geography scientist, not an adventurer who could tolerate such events. How was Burke able to keep his composure so far?

"We must get away from here." Burke held Heather's hand. "Our chasers will appear at any moment from behind. We can win some time in this darkness until we hide in the—"

"Do-not-move."

Heather's heart sank into her boots when she heard that commanding voice. This time it didn't come from Powell or Daniel or even Burke. It didn't come from anybody among her crew.

It didn't come from any human at all.

16. Never Mess with the Humanoids

Heather was sure of what she had just heard. The creaky voice that uttered those three English words resembled that of the gray-faced intruder who encountered her crew in the HG-3.

Obviously, Powell's idea to turn off the flashlights didn't work. Someone had spotted the team anyway. Someone they could not see. Perhaps it was about time she ignored the Major's brilliant plan to lay low.

Heather opened her flashlight despite Powell's protests, and so did Daniel and Susan and Kenneth. Four flashlights were not enough to illuminate the entire woods, but they revealed six figures closing in on them in a semi-circle. Six figures of tall, thin frames that resembled those of the HG-3 intruder. As the humanoids came to the light, Heather could see their gray faces and their brown leather-like outfits which covered their bodies from shoulder to knee.

"Who are you?" Heather tried to make her voice sound commanding. It didn't stop the humanoids from approaching them, though.

"We are outnumbering those fragile creatures," Powell whispered. "We can take them out if we all engage them."

Heather wasn't sure if anybody other than Powell would regard the humanoids as *fragile creatures*. No one among her crew had the Major's mighty fist. And why should they fight those...?

"Wrong."

The creaky cry from the humanoid in the middle startled her. "You-not-defeat-us." The humanoid drew an apple-sized white shiny spheroid strapped to his belt. Heather and, surely, the rest of the crew had never seen that thing before, but from the way the humanoid raised the spheroidal device, she could safely presume it was a weapon.

And he was aiming at them with it.

"I guess it's not wise to attack inhuman creatures that speak English and threaten you with a mango," Burke muttered. "This can be dangerous."

"Only one of them is armed." Santino seemed to be considering Powell's bold suggestion. "And obviously, he is the only one who can understand and speak English."

"With an accent better than yours, Santi," Burke teased.

"Don't call me Santi."

"He is bluffing." Powell tightened his jaw as he peered at the armed humanoid. "The silly ball he holds won't scare us."

"We can't count on that." Heather must bring her crew to their senses before doing something really stupid. "Everybody, stay calm. No surprising moves."

"This is not the time for hesitation, Dr," Powell grunted.

"You are killing us all, Major." Heather forced through clenched teeth, her eyes still on the slim digits gripping the spheroid.

"Heather is right," said Daniel. "There is no need for any hostile actions."

"You fools," Powell growled. "I can't believe you will surrender to these creatures like this."

"Oh my God!" Linda whimpered. "We're going to die!"

"This is insane." Heather felt her nerves shot. The darkness, the creaky voice, Powell's rage, Linda's whimpering; everything was driving her mad.

"Enough."

The gray-faced humanoid demanded as he raised his hand and compressed the spheroid. A beam of light flashed past the entire crew, striking one of the life capsules behind them. In a second, the life capsule turned into a fireball, the explosion shock wave sweeping the other capsule away as if it was a paper boat. With a new source of light behind Heather and her crew, darkness was no longer their main problem.

"Now what, Major? This Longface has made his point." Burke kneeled, putting his hands over his head.

The rest of the crew stared at Burke before they exchanged looks with each other. They were not sure of what should be done now, and neither was Heather. *You are the leader, Heather. You must make a decision.*

"It doesn't hurt, fellows," said Burke. "Trust me; I did this stuff many times before with the agents of the NSA."

Daniel and Santino looked at Heather, as if they were waiting for her to decide. *You must make your move now before Powell does something stupid.* Heather nodded to her colleagues before she knelt next to Burke. The rest did the same except for Powell, who remained standing on his feet.

"Come on, you fool," Burke muttered. "Time to stop this cowboy crap."

"Damn!" Powell gnashed his teeth as he finally acquiesced and went down on his knees. For a moment, she felt that the humanoid was about to destroy the marine with his weapon.

"I hope they won't torture us," said Burke.

Oh thanks! The last thing Heather needed at the moment was such a suggestion of *cheerful* thoughts.

The six humanoids surrounded the whole crew and started to tie every two with a wire-like material. "That's it?" Burke's eyebrows rose in astonishment. "I thought they would contain us in an energy field or something."

One humanoid holding a long wire stood just in front of Heather and Burke. When the humanoid started wrapping Burke's wrist with the wire, Burke winked at Heather. "Look at the bright side. They will tie both of us together. I hope they will pair us face to face." When she glared at him, he cleared his throat. "Or back to back; it will just do."

She really wanted to slap him. Instead, she found herself bursting into laughter.

"So back to back, then?" Burke suggested.

"You are a real jerk, Burke." Heather meant every word. "You must be sent to an asylum after we finish this mission."

Heather felt the humanoid's cold digits grasp her right hand, wrap the wire, and tie it to Burke's left hand. The humanoid pulled them both up from behind to help them get up on their feet.

"Finish this mission?" Burke scoffed. "And you call me a *jerk*?"

With a not-so-gentle push, the humanoid urged them to start walking. All the crew was wired in pairs, except for Powell who was tied from both hands.

"Where are you taking us?" Heather asked the nearest humanoid to her, but again, there was no reply. "Answer me. What are you going to do with us? We are lost here on this island, and we mean no harm. I know you can understand me."

"He-cannot."

Someone else at the front spoke. When Heather looked, she found it was the humanoid pushing Susan and Linda, the only humanoid talking to them from the beginning.

"I-can," the humanoid went on.

"Interesting," Burke muttered. "A well-educated humanoid."

The humanoid kept moving. When the group reached the heavily-forested area near the island shores, Heather bellowed at the leading long-faced creature. "You, alien! You can't ignore me like this! I'm talking to you!"

Though it was Heather who asked him to reply, she was startled when the humanoid turned his gray head toward her. With the narrow eyes he had, it was hard to interpret his facial expressions, if he had any.

"You-wrong." The alien stopped the group and slowly, he returned to Heather and Burke. "We-not-aliens."

Now she found someone whose jokes were worse than Burke's. *Then what else could you be?* she wanted to ask the long-faced dude, who stood just in front of her and Burke, bending forward toward them.

"You-aliens," said the gray-faced creature with his creaky voice before he pointed at Burke. "He-know."

17. Minds Do Not Lie

Heather looked from the alien to Burke and back. The gray-faced creature did refer to him, to the guy who had brought her to this island.

"Excuse me?" Even Burke looked astonished. "Who knows what?"

"Obviously, he is talking about you." Heather glared at the *former* assistant professor.

"No need to give me this look, Heather." Now Burke wasn't able to smile.

"What do you know, Burke?"

"I don't know what he thinks I know."

"You always know something nobody else knows." Heather gripped Burke by the hand. "We were almost drowned in a flipping hovercraft, encountered those humanoids, been chased till we reached this island, and still you look so comfortable."

The rest of her crew herded by the other humanoids stopped to listen to the conversation.

"I knew it from the beginning," said Powell. "There was something fishy about this lunatic."

"I swear I have no idea what this gray freak is talking about," said Burke before he turned to the humanoid. "How do you know what I know, Longface?"

"Mouth-speak-lies," said the alien. "Mind-not-lie."

Burke curled his lip. "What does this crap mean?"

For one rare occasion, Heather found herself ahead of Burke by one step. "Longface reads your mind, it seems." She stared at the tall, gaunt humanoid. "Our minds."

Burke furrowed his brow. "I don't think so. Because in that case, Powell couldn't have been able to stun that humanoid in the HG-3."

"He is right," Susan seconded him.

"Maybe it was too dark there to read," Burke sneered.

Heather looked the talking humanoid in the eye. Did this humanoid really read Burke's thoughts? What did he see?

"No-all-read-minds," said the humanoid. "Few-can. I-can."

"This is stupid." Burke laughed nervously. "So you all decided to just ignore the fact he claims he is not an alien."

"He said you knew they were not," Daniel reminded him. "I guess you are the one who can explain this."

"I can make him explain if they just let me go," Powell offered. It was no secret, Burke lacked popularity among her crew.

"Bullshit," said Burke. "I can't believe how this freak has messed with your minds."

It was Burke who had messed with her mind. It was him who had made her obsessed with this island. His island. But wait. What about the alien who could read their thoughts? Could he implant ideas in their minds as well?

"I not." The humanoid startled her again by answering her unvoiced query. A creepy feeling it was to be close to someone who could read your mind with all its ugly thoughts.

"Whatever you say, I can never tell if you're lying to me." Heather shrugged. "You're the one reading minds here, Mister."

"Shomrunk-can," said the humanoid.

"Shomrunk?" Heather echoed before she shot Burke an inquisitive look.

"Oh yeah, Shomrunk! Unfortunately, I have just deleted him from my phone book," said Burke mockingly.

Heather ignored Burke and turned to the humanoid. "What or who is *Shomrunk*?"

The humanoid jerked his neck toward his fellows, uttering some incomprehensible words before they urged the tied crew members to resume their walk.

"What's going on?" Heather asked the humanoid, who herded her and Burke again, and this time a bit faster. *They are nervous.* Heather noticed that the humanoids didn't stop looking around as they resumed their march, talking in their own language with their creaky voices.

Heather wondered how these humanoids saw their way in the dark while she could hardly see hers. The light coming from the capsule explosion became too faint as they were getting further into the woods, away from the island shore. The humanoid's hand that kept pushing her forward was her only guide until they all reached a vast, plain, grassy area.

"Nathaniel." She looked over her shoulder, trying to spot the ancient languages expert in this darkness.

"Over here," Nathaniel, who was tied to Walter, replied, his voice coming from her left.

"What's going on?"

"We are followed," Nathaniel replied. "They have to move because somebody or something is after us."

"Oh really?" Daniel exclaimed. "Why did they stop here, then?"

Heather contemplated the dark, thin frames of their humanoid captors, who kept checking their surroundings.

"It seems they are waiting for their ride," said Powell. "Look up."

With a noise lower than that of Heather's car, a flying craft five times the size of the HG-3 hovered over them. The darkness made it hard for Heather to know what the craft looked like, but she could tell it had a hemispherical top. "No way. Can it be...?" Her eyes widened as she watched those *familiar* yellow lights. That hovercraft was the same *ship* she saw in the ocean, wasn't it?

She couldn't help glancing at Burke every minute, wishing she had the humanoid's gift in reading minds. Burke had entered that craft before, hadn't he? *What did those humanoids do to you, Burke? What do you know that you don't want us to know?*

The humanoid urged her and her crew onward as the craft landed. "Oh my God! Where are they going to take us?" Linda whimpered. Heather had to admit that the sight of the craft with its open hatch was breathtaking. The notion of entering this ship would unnerve anybody, even if it was a marine like Powell.

"Who or what is following us?" Heather asked Nathaniel.

"I'm not sure what they call it, but it sounded like At—"

An explosion just a few meters away from the craft cut Nathaniel off. "*It's a missile!*" Kenneth's alarmed voice came from somewhere amid this havoc, the humanoids screeching with their creaky voices.

"Oh my God!" Heather was forced to jog as the humanoids shoved her and Burke, her eyes watching the sky in alarm. "What the hell is going on?" she snapped at Burke. "Answer me. I know that you know."

"Why don't you ask your long-faced buddy?" Burke countered.

"*Watch out!*" Powell yelled just a second before another missile hit the ground away from the craft hatch by only a couple of meters.

"Run!" It was the English-speaking humanoid who screamed this time, his voice even scarier when he cried. As the crew was tied in pairs except for Powell, the marine had less trouble in complying with the humanoid's order. Heather almost fell as she tried to match Burke's pace. Behind her, she heard a thud together with Linda's scream and Susan's groan.

"Come on!" Daniel hollered. "We don't know where the next missile is going to hit."

The humanoid responsible for herding Susan and Linda helped them get up and screamed, "To-ship!" Though it sounded ironic, the only haven for Heather and her crew was their captors' vessel.

Heather's heart pounded vigorously when she stepped into the craft with her crew. The yellow lights of the wide hall blinded her for a moment until her eyes accommodated themselves to the illumination inside the vessel. With Linda's entrance, the hatch slowly closed.

"Nicely done," Burke said. "A missile attack to urge us to hurry to their ship."

"Are you serious?" Heather peered at him. "We could have been killed in that attack."

"But we are alive. No one is even hurt. We were not the target, Heather."

"Then what was it? Do you think they were not in need of that attack to take us to their ship?"

"I don't know what they were in need of. I'm just impressed with the way they drove us to our cage. The ship's body didn't even catch the smoke of the explosion."

Well, he wouldn't be Burke if he was less confusing.

Heather started to feel dizzy when the craft rose in the air. *The worst part is yet to come.* Thinking of the possibilities waiting for her and her team at the hands of those humanoids stimulated all the butterflies in her stomach to flutter simultaneously. Would they dissect her body to take a sample? Or lock her in some glass-like cage to observe and study her like a lab rat? *Oh please, be a nightmare!* But it wasn't. That ship was real, and those humanoids were also...

Her forehead collided with Burke's nose when an explosion shook the flying vessel. "Damn!" Burke exclaimed. "It seems we did catch some smoke after all."

Heather was sick of Burke's ridiculous remarks and their even more ridiculous timing. "Nathaniel!" She turned to the language expert. "Who is following us, you said?"

Nathaniel seemed hesitant as he warily watched the humanoids creaking around them.

"They have more urgent matters to worry about as you see." Heather hoped those humanoids were currently too busy to notice Nathaniel's ability to understand them. "Now tell me please that a marine force is following this ship to rescue us."

"I don't think it's the marines." Nathaniel killed her hopes. "If I understand those humanoids right, they are talking about Atlanteans."

18. Akmenios

Heather rubbed her head with both hands, trying to organize all the puzzle pieces she had gathered so far in front of her eyes.

A mysterious island.

Writings in Ancient Egyptian, Latin, and a third unknown language.

Aliens—or humanoids, it didn't matter that much—who spoke Latin and thought of Heather and her team as aliens as well.

Burke; he *knew*.

And now Atlanteans. Where did they come from? Could it be possible they descended from the ancient dwellers of the legendary lost continent of Atlantis? *Legendary?* She inwardly mocked the word. For someone on board an alien vessel with humanoid creatures, meeting real Atlanteans shouldn't be something surprising at all. *Wait, those Atlanteans could be aliens as well.*

The possibilities were endless. But whether they were aliens or humans, Heather had a gut feeling that those Atlanteans were the link between all the loose threads of that expedition. It made much sense to Heather that they were the ones who wrote those lines in Burke's photo in a desperate attempt to seek help against those gray-faced humanoids.

How long had those Atlanteans been trapped with the humanoids?

And what about the disappeared planes and ships and their passengers? Were they abducted by those creatures? What happened to them?

What about Burke? Had he really come here before? Why would he lie about that? What did he hide?

"We're landing," said Powell, whose voice interrupted her thoughts. She could feel the ship losing altitude gradually.

"Here we go," Burke muttered, staring at the slowly opening hatch.

"Oh my God!" Susan exclaimed. "Lots of them."

The whole crew gazed at the dozen gray-faced humanoids waiting outside. Feeling nervous and curious at the same time, Heather knew she was on the verge of the greatest discovery in human history, a discovery that might reveal one of the biggest mysteries that had confounded mankind's scientists for ages.

"Move," said the English-speaking humanoid.

"I'm afraid we don't have many options now." Powell clenched his teeth.

The humanoids in the ship herded the crew outside, where more than thirty humanoids were waiting, all wearing the same leather attire. Yellow spotlights fixed to the gray ceiling lit the "dock" in which the ship had landed. Fifty meters high, Heather estimated. She wondered if they were currently underground.

"True," the humanoid confirmed her doubts.

"It's a whole world down there." Still tied to her, Burke seemed impressed as he looked around.

"Like you don't know." Heather gave him a hard look.

"Please, Heather, not you," said Burke.

"Not me?"

"I know that all of you have suspicions about me," said Burke. "But you have always been the only one to believe me. That's something I don't want to lose."

"I wish I could fully trust you, Burke, but I'm not sure if I can do this now."

"Yes, you can, Heather. Because those suspicions do not make any sense."

"You think? Then what do you have to say to that humanoid's claims?"

"You can't be serious. You trust a *Longface* more than me?"

"He gave me a reason to do that."

"What reason? His broken English?"

"He read your thoughts, Burke." Heather glared at him. "He read mine as well, so I know he doesn't lie. Do you have a stronger reason than that?"

Burke averted his eyes.

"That's what I thought." While she was expecting a clever, sarcastic remark from Burke, he remained silent as they followed the humanoids along a narrow tunnel lit by countless yellow spotlights.

"Where are we going?" Heather asked the English-speaking humanoid ahead of the line. Even if he wasn't looking at her, he must have known whom she was talking to.

"Akmenios-see-you," the humanoid replied.

"What sees me?"

"Akmenios. He-want-see-you."

So, Akmenios was someone. Some humanoid big shot, most probably. *Does Burke know him too?* Heather glanced at the man for whom she had risked everything to include him in the crew of the Bermuda mission.

"You think they might allow us to have some water?" Santino asked from behind her.

"And sleep as well," Linda added.

Sleep? Was that Linda's top concern at the moment? Perhaps Heather needed to remind the newly-wed that she was not on her honeymoon anymore.

Twenty minutes passed, and still, the humanoids herded them in the tunnel. A long march it was after an extremely exhausting day. Heather wondered if those humanoids ever felt tired.

"My legs are killing me," said Kenji.

"You are not alone," said Susan.

The English-speaking humanoid stopped abruptly and stared at both Susan and Kenji.

"What's wrong?" Daniel asked worriedly.

"Apparently, this Longface has misunderstood Kenji," said Burke. "The word 'killing' confused him."

The humanoid turned to Burke, who continued with a cynical smile, "Yeah, yeah. Read my mind, you gray freak. Take your time to understand what I mean."

"No-tricks," said the humanoid. "Akmenios-see-you."

"You are embarrassing me, Longface," said Burke. "Now I can't brag with your English in front of Santino."

Burke should be grateful that the humanoid didn't heed his bad sense of humor. "Move," was all the humanoid said. "Akmenios-wait-there." He pointed his four-digit hand at the visible end of the tunnel.

"Only two more minutes," Heather announced, not less eager than anybody else to get some rest. "Hang on, everybody."

The tunnel led to a vast hall with more humanoids standing in it. A hundred of them, Heather estimated. The hall itself resembled the landing area with its gray walls and yellow lights, except that its ceiling was only around ten meters high.

"What are all these humanoids doing?" Daniel asked warily.

"They look like an army," said Powell.

"They make sure our energy reactors are working."

Heather wasn't the only one startled by this creaky voice. Another English-speaking humanoid, yet more fluent. And a bit taller.

"Damn! That was good," Burke scoffed. "At least if compared to our friendly Longface."

"Not all have the same ability to learn," said the taller humanoid.

"Akmenios?" Heather asked hesitantly.

The tall humanoid turned, contemplating her for a while. "Clever hominum. It is me."

"*Hominum?*" Heather echoed quizzically.

"It's 'human' in Latin," Burke whispered.

So, Burke knew Latin; an interesting fact to know at this very moment. While she was wondering if he hid more things about himself, she was eager to find answers for those questions bugging her. Aside from the invisible island, the humanoids, and those...Atlanteans, there was one urgent question: what were those humanoids going to do with her and her crew?

"So many questions," said Akmenios with his impassive creaky voice.

"You read minds too?" Heather asked.

"Not only yours," Akmenios replied. "All the minds of homines here."

"So perhaps, you know now we are tired and we need some rest," said Santino.

"And thirsty too," said Akmenios.

"What about these?" Heather raised her hand, which was tied to Burke's.

"From what I see in the thoughts of some of you," said Akmenios, "I cannot untie you."

Not a promising start at all. "So, we are prisoners?" Heather wondered.

"Until we find the Shomrunk," said Akmenios. "After that, you will eat and sleep."

Heather turned to the other English-speaking humanoid who had mentioned that Shomrunk once to her.

"I see you heard about it," said Akmenios.

Having a conversation with someone who could read her mind was still an awkward experience. What if she wanted to hide something from him?

"You cannot hide anything from me," said Akmenios. "But the Shomrunk can. That is why we have to make sure he is not one of you."

"I think it is pointless to ask," said Heather. "You already know my next questions."

"Which are so many," said Akmenios. "Anyhow, one particular topic will answer the rest."

From her team members' silence, Heather could tell that she wasn't the only one on her toes here.

"The Shomrunk," said Akmenios. "This is how everything had started. Millions of solar years ago."

"Millions?" Heather didn't mean to utter that out loud, but she was unable to conceal her astonishment. If that humanoid was telling the truth, then he could possibly have records of the ancient history of the universe, way before the existence of mankind.

"We do have records," Akmenios confirmed. "And they are accurate, unlike yours."

"You say I'm going to hear an untold part of history."

Akmenios gazed at her with his narrow eyes. "A different version of history, I would say."

19. History Retold

The humanoids' creaking voice was too annoying to hear. But in Akmenios's case, Heather was ready to make an exception.

"Millions of years ago, we shared the same planet with the Shomrunks, but they had their own lands to live on, separated from ours by one huge ocean," said Akmenios. "They established a great nation, like ours, but the cost was huge. For ages, the Shomrunks haven't learned how to use their resources wisely—unlike us. They consumed their lands until they depleted their resources, and the only salvation for them became our lands.

"A war started, but we were not ready for it. We were a peaceful race, and we used our knowledge only to build, not to destroy."

Heather found some difficulties in believing the last part; she had already seen the spheroidal weapon that turned their life capsule into ashes in seconds.

"Of course, we are not the peaceful community we used to be; we have seen enough from homines—your people." Akmenios peered at her. "I will come to that."

Heather did not want to interrupt Akmenios with her thoughts, but it was nearly impossible for her to control what crossed her mind.

"I know it is too hard for you," said Akmenios.

"Don't mind me, please go on." Heather was growing impatient.

"It is not correct to describe what happened between us and the Shomrunks as a war; it was annihilation," said Akmenios. "Only twenty of us survived. They escaped the Shomrunks' massacre and abandoned the planet that became dominated by Shomrunks. Nobody knows how many years they spent wandering in space until they found Earth."

Heather tried to focus her thoughts on Akmenios's story, but she couldn't help wondering about the technology they used to reach Earth.

"Skip this part, Akmenios," said Heather. "We can discuss it later."

"There were no homines when our ancestors reached Earth," said Akmenios. "The planet was inhabited by those *dinosaurs*, except for that huge island in the ocean; Atlantis. It means 'the new land' in our language."

Struck by what she was listening to, Heather was unable to control her train of thought this time.

Atlantis.

Homines.

Did this mean Latin was..?

"You are a really clever hominum," said Akmenios.

"It was your language from the beginning," Heather concluded, still astounded.

"No way." Daniel shook his head.

"Latin is the fruit of the crossover between our civilization and yours," said Akmenios. "Our original language wasn't much different, though."

"You said dinosaurs?" Susan asked. "Did you witness their extinction?"

"We did. And that was the first time we had to rebuild our civilization, when the Asteroid Interitum hit this planet. We were able to spot that rock ten solar years before its arrival. And we realized that there was no way to survive that collision if we remained on our lands."

"So, you left?" Heather asked.

"Not exactly. We hid in shelters floating in the outer layer of Earth's atmosphere," said Akmenios. "After two years, we returned and re-established Atlantis."

Akmenios leaned forward, addressing Heather, "Now you realize who the real *aliens* here are. We have been living on this Earth *before* you came from nowhere. Though we have no accurate information about when and how you have arrived on Earth, we are quite sure your race has not been there before the Great Collision."

"Is this your way to justify your presence here?" Santino curled his nose. "On *our* planet?"

Akmenios looked at him for a moment. "All this time with homines, and still, I never fully understood their emotions."

"You will never fool us with your mind games." Kenneth was encouraged to challenge the humanoid. "Even your story doesn't make any sense. If your...people came here before us, as you claim, then you would know when we first existed."

"I'm aware of the bloody history of your race...Kenneth," Akmenios replied with his impassive creaky voice. "Your only valid claim for any land here on this planet is always based on power. You don't need me to remind you of what *your* ancestors did to colonize the lands of its original inhabitants."

"Damn!" Burke muttered. "Tell me he is not referring to the Native Americans."

"I'm afraid he is." Heather stared at the humanoid in anticipation. Referring to that example didn't bode well.

"You have no reason to worry," said Akmenios. "Wiping out a whole race by another to replace it and take over its lands is not a notion we totally comprehend. Actually, it is one thing common between you and Shomrunks. You are a really hostile race. And from our experience with you, you prefer war to peace."

Heather couldn't see any positive outcome from the debate about this issue. "Akmenios, can we please get back to your primary story? You said you had to rebuild your civilization in Atlantis twice. What about the second time?" A little trick that had a little chance to work with a mind-reading creature.

"The second time was worse because we did not see it coming," said Akmenios. "It was a great flood that covered the whole planet."

"The Flood of Noah's Day." Santino gaped at the gray humanoid.

"And how did you, I mean your ancestors, survived that?" Daniel asked.

"They did not." Akmenios's answer was shocking. "There was no time to escape."

"Then how did you—?" Heather wondered.

"We are still here thanks to six of our ancestors. They were on a mission at our safe shelters to maintain them," Akmenios replied. "When they returned, they faced a much harder time to rebuild our community than the first one. But eventually, they did it."

Akmenios allowed a moment of silence, as if he was checking Heather and her team's reactions. "Thousands of years later," he continued, "the first homines ship arrived at our shores. They were very primitive compared to us, yet we could see their intelligence from what they constructed in their homelands."

"Now what?" Burke muttered. "Pharaohs maybe?

Akmenios didn't stop at Burke's comment. "We have started to follow your progress since the first encounter with your ancestors. I must say, for a race, whose age does not exceed a few thousand years, your progress is faster than ours. We took millions of years to reach what we have reached by now."

"Thanks for the compliment." Heather smirked. "Then what?"

"More ships came to Atlantis. But they did not seem to be from the same nation of the first ship," said Akmenios. "Those homines settled on Atlantis with us. And we had no problem to establish a shared community with them.

Actually, they learned very fast, became well acquainted with our technology, and became part of the perfect Atlantean society."

"Unbelievable." Daniel was astounded.

"Utopia," Burke muttered. "Plato's Republic. I knew he was right about Atlantis."

"In less than a century," Akmenios went on without any reaction to those comments, "homines became the majority of the Atlantean population—your reproduction rate is much higher than ours—and by the time, our language was affected by theirs, and eventually they became one."

"That's why your language sounds like Latin," Heather said.

"The homines displayed a level of creativity, beyond our expectations," said Akmenios. "The Atlantean nation was much superior to any other known homines nation at that time. And there came the part that we never understood about your race."

Heather tried to expect the next part of Akmenios's tale.

"For ages, we have worked on optimizing the use of power, and we excelled in finding more efficient means to generate energy. But homines always excelled in something else: weaponry," said Akmenios. "First, they told us they were essential to defend our lands from external threats, and we found reason in that. Especially after what we have suffered from the Shomrunks' invasion in the past.

"We helped them construct weapons plants, thinking this would make us safer, but we were wrong. Once you feel superior over others, you seek to control their lands and resources. Your history is full of examples. You never learned how to practice peaceful coexistence with other parties. Even from your own race." Akmenios gave Powell a long gaze. "A soldier like you understands that."

Powell frowned, yet he kept his mouth shut. *Thank God.*

"The Atlantean homines proposed an expansion campaign to us, and we rejected it because there was no need for it. For me, Shomrunks were more logical than your race—at least they had a reason to invade us. As I said, we never found an explanation for your ideology of expansionism."

"And what happened after you rejected their plan?" Heather asked.

Akmenios turned to Heather. "What do you expect? They waged war against us to gain total control on the island of Atlantis and to be able afterward to start their invasion campaign.

"The war was hard on both of us. Both sides were well-equipped. Both sides suffered heavy losses. By the time, we were winning the war, and homines in turn, started to think differently out of despair. Realizing that their defeat was inevitable, they launched a prototype of the Flavi Bomb deep in the heart of Atlantis, aiming to initiate a massive earthquake in our lands. But the results were worse than they expected."

Heather noticed how she forgot her fatigue and thirst. Despite the annoying creaky voice of Akmenios, his talk demanded her full attention. She was sure her team had the same feeling.

"A few survivors passed their memories of that horrifying day to the next generations. It was not a normal earthquake. The land was collapsing under their feet and the Earth's heart was visible to the naked eye. The island sank, and literally, Atlantis was swallowed by the ocean."

"I can't believe I'm hearing this," said Heather. "All you narrate as events are more like myths to us."

"Only seven of us managed to survive the colossal ocean waves," said Akmenios. "And for some reason, four homines accompanied them until they reached the very island we currently reside in, the Domus."

"So, that was the third time to rebuild your society," Heather pointed out.

"Not exactly," said Akmenios. "Our society was never like it was before. We spent a whole century in constructing some primitive reactors to provide us with energy. We forgot our conflicts with homines, and we stood together hand in hand to survive. Everything was fine until we started the isolation."

"The isolation?" Heather echoed.

"When the war between homines started all over the planet in the previous century, we had to take some critical measures to protect our last shelter from this war," said Akmenios.

"I guess he is talking about the World War," Daniel said.

Akmenios continued, "Using all we could gather from the remnants of our ancestors' technology, we built the Shell. It did not only block intruders, it also prevented our lands from being spotted by your radars, and afterward your satellites."

Heather pondered what she had just heard. Was this, at last, the explanation of what became known as the Bermuda Triangle?

So, those humanoid creatures were protecting their lands from intruders...

"Wait a second, Akmenios," said Heather. "If I am getting this right, you didn't *block* intruders. They were swallowed into your *shell*, and they never came back home. What happened to them?"

The hall grew hushed for a few seconds after Heather's question. Akmenios's impassive face did not give any impression of what he was feeling or thinking about.

"We didn't intend to harm anybody," said Akmenios with his creaky voice. "We spared as many souls as we could, but we couldn't rescue all."

Even for an emotionless creature, Akmenios's transparency was shocking. Not even a hollow apology about those who died in the Triangle because of their *Shell*.

"This doesn't make any sense," said Burke, addressing Akmenios. "What satellites and radars are you talking about? We have reported disappearance events from the eighteenth century. What war were you protecting your lands from?"

That was a good point indeed. How did Heather miss that?

"I have no idea about these events," said Akmenios. "Your information might be wrong."

"You're lying, Longface." Burke's sharp tone should have surprised Akmenios if the humanoid had feelings. "The whole thing is about energy. The Shell; you could not maintain it for long, right?"

Akmenios stood still like a statue.

"What are you talking about, Burke?" Heather asked him.

"The map of disappeared ships and planes. The red and yellow dots," said Burke. "There is a pattern, Heather. The range of the Triangle is shrinking. That shell has been consuming their energy, and who knows how long they can keep their island hidden."

Akmenios was still silent.

"Do you have anything to say about this conclusion?" Heather asked.

"Wrong." Akmenios slowly walked toward Burke. "He did not conclude that." He scrutinized Burke's face when he said, "He knew what he said."

Confused, she asked, "What the hell does this mean?"

"Your friend did not think about the issue to reach his conclusion," replied the humanoid. "He was talking as if he was there with us when all those events had occurred." He turned to Burke. "Or as if somebody has told him about our history before." He paused for a couple of seconds, his eyes still on Burke's face. "Somebody implanted these facts in his mind."

While Heather was wondering who would do that, Akmenios continued, "A Shomrunk."

20. Homines and Locusts

Heather wasn't sure she got the last part right. Maybe her mind was confused as it was still processing this new version of mankind's history.

"I see some of you wondering why I am telling you all these events," said Akmenios to Heather and her crew. "Actually, you have finished your primary examination."

"Primary examination?" Heather echoed warily.

"This technique never fails me when I am handling more than one mind at a time," said Akmenios to Heather and her crew. "Telling you something you know reveals most of the information buried in your subconscious mind."

Heather didn't like the idea of being manipulated. A few moments ago, she was excited about the information she had heard from Akmenios. *Damn!* Was he lying to them all this time?

"I was not lying," Akmenios said. "Lying is part of homines ideology, not ours." The humanoid turned again to Burke. "Your friend's mind bears some memories that he seems to have no idea about. Memories that were hidden on purpose. And I know only one creature that can do this."

"Don't you have the same ability?" Heather asked.

"I extract thoughts," replied Akmenios. "I can't implant them."

"Not necessarily you," said Heather. "Anybody else from your race."

Akmenios paused for a moment before he said, "Not all of us can read minds, and nobody else has my ability to handle many minds at the same time."

"What's this?" Burke smirked. "Are you trying to evoke more memories from my mind?"

"Exactly," said Akmenios to Burke. "But it seems that we need further examination to dig deeper into the secret chambers of your mind."

Burke chuckled nervously. "*Secret chambers*? You were reading Harry Potter, not my mind."

Akmenios's face was impassive as usual when he said, "Every mind has its secret chambers. Only the Shomrunk can hide information in it."

"I don't get it, Akmenios." Heather rubbed her forehead. "Aren't those Shomrunks supposed to be on your planet right now?"

Akmenios looked from Heather to Burke more than once in a creepy manner that freaked her out.

"A hundred years ago, we detected a message sent from Earth," said Akmenios. "A message sent from a Shomrunk."

"They are here on Earth?" Heather was stunned. "What was in this message?"

"He is only one," said Akmenios. "It is clear from his message he was sent for one mission: find a new home."

"A new home for whom?" Heather swallowed. "For him?"

"No," Akmenios replied with his creaky voice. "For his entire race. They must have consumed our lands. As they did before with theirs."

From the silence that settled over the place, Heather could tell that Akmenios's bad news had stunned all the crew.

"Oh my God!" Susan muttered. "They are like locusts."

"He must have followed our floating safe hideouts," said Akmenios. "Since he landed on Earth, he has been trying to find our exact location."

"So, the *Shell* was not to protect you from our war, Longface." Burke tilted his head.

"I didn't lie, hominum," said Akmenios. "We built the Shell before the Shomrunk's arrival for the reasons I mentioned earlier. Actually, the Shell became a problem. It might have made the Shomrunk suspicious about the region you call Bermuda Triangle."

Heather gestured with her hand to stop Akmenios. "You said he was looking for a home for his race. What does he want from you?"

"The Shomrunk wants to inform his people of Earth's location," said Akmenios. "The only way to do that is to send a message from here, from the Domus."

"But you said he had already sent a message."

"Yes," said Akmenios. "But his message would never reach its destination. The equipment and power he had at that time were not enough for the task."

Heather wanted to pose another question, but Burke gripped her hand firmly when he said, "Wait a second, Heather." He then addressed Akmenios, "Can you tell us how the hell he knows you have the required equipment? And if you know the answer to this question, can you tell us how you know what he knows?"

Akmenios didn't look bothered by Burke's questions. "It is an assumption," the humanoid replied, "and I tell you something; you should hope it is right."

Heather was trying to gather the fragmented pieces in her mind. "What do you mean by this, Akmenios?"

"Think about it," said Akmenios. "If the Shomrunk finds another way to communicate with his people, he will not need to chase us. At least for now."

Pondering the notion that those Shomrunks might find their way to Earth was horrifying.

"How can we be sure that he hasn't found a way already?" she asked.

"We are sure he has not," Akmenios replied. "We would have detected his message. And most probably, your current technology is not enough for the task."

"So far, you are doing a good job in dodging pitfalls." Burke smirked. "But for some reason, I don't buy all you say. You can read my mind anyway, so no harm if I tell you this."

"It does not matter if you believe it or not," said Akmenios. "Our priority now is to know what is hidden in your mind, hominum." He laid his hand on Burke's shoulders. "I hope your friends now understand what we are going to do with you."

Heather started to feel worried about this part. *What are they going to do with him?* It was true she had some doubts about Burke who seemed to know too much. But leaving him in the hands of those creatures without knowing what was going to happen to him was a scary idea.

"No need to worry." No surprise, Akmenios had read her thoughts. "All I am going to do is connect my mind to his. There is no pain or harm in that."

Burke's sarcastic smile vanished. He must be really anxious when Akmenios called his fellow humanoids to untie him from Heather.

"Where are you taking him?" Heather asked warily.

Akmenios didn't answer her when his fellow humanoids took Burke by the arms and walked him away into a narrow corridor. Still shocked, the former professor didn't utter a word until they were out of sight.

"You need some rest," said Akmenios to the whole crew. "The site here is not prepared to entertain guests, but we have a chamber where you can replenish your energy and use the food you have in your bags."

"A cell you mean." Powell gnashed his teeth.

"It depends on how you see it," said Akmenios. "I will not repeat what I said earlier."

Two humanoids took Heather by the arms toward Powell and tied them together.

"There is something you didn't tell us about, Akmenios," said Heather nervously. "What are you going to do with us after you finish your investigation with Burke?"

As if he didn't hear her, Akmenios headed toward the same corridor the other humanoids dragged Burke into.

"Answer me!" Heather yelled. "You can't ignore this question in particular."

"He will never answer this question, Dr." Powell bit his lower lip. "Whether those creatures find their Shomrunk or not, we are their prisoners."

"Oh God! What are we going to do now?" Alarmed, Linda asked both Heather and Powell.

"There is nothing we can do at the moment, Linda." Heather didn't have more reassuring news to cheer anybody up. "Just pray our fate is better than Burke's."

21. The Secret Chamber

The chair to which Burke was tied had a cold metallic feel to it.

There was not much of a crowd here. Only he, Akmenios, and another humanoid standing by a huge screen that hid one-fourth of the wall of this round room. The walls had the same gray color and yellow lights that were also there in the underground landing area.

The other humanoid was busy with the metal table behind Akmenios. Burke was worried more than curious when the humanoid returned with a silver hairband-like device.

"This is scarier than a dentist's visit," Burke muttered.

"There is nothing to worry about, hominum," said Akmenios. "I am here to help you."

"Oh really?" Burke smiled nervously. "Am I not supposed to be an ally to that *evil* Shomrunk?"

"I assume you are not an ally to the Shomrunk," said Akmenios. "You seem like a victim to me, but I have to assure myself."

The humanoid approached Burke and put the metal hairband-like device on his head. "It's not going to hurt, huh?" Burke watched Akmenios grab another device and put it on his own head.

"No, it is not."

"How could you be so sure? Have you tried this thing before?"

"Yes, hominum. Once."

"Good for you." Burke swallowed. "But what about humans? You can never be sure it is not going to hurt *me*."

"I am quite sure it is not going to hurt you among all other homines."

Burke didn't like the sound of this. "What the hell does this mean?"

"I am not the only one in this room who tried this device." Akmenios assumed another metallic seat opposite Burke. "Welcome back, Burke."

"Welcome back?" Burke repeated Akmenios's words. Those aliens had really worse jokes than his.

"It has been nine years since your last visit," said Akmenios. "We never expected your return."

Burke squeezed his mind, trying to recall all his memories of his first attempt to reach the island. He was sure he had never set foot ashore.

"Don't exhaust your brain," said Akmenios. "I removed all that you saw here from your memory, yet it seems you still have some remaining traces in your subconscious."

That gray-faced Akmenios wasn't messing with him, right?

"You have to relax now," said Akmenios. "This will make things easier for both of us."

"You tie me to a chair, put a stupid device on my head, and tell me I was here before. How the hell can I relax?"

"I know it is confusing, Burke, but don't worry. Your torture will end sooner than you think."

"You brought me here to clear my memory once again, right?" Burke looked him in the eye. "The Shomrunk thing was nothing but bullshit."

"The Shomrunk is real. I am quite sure he is behind sending you back to us."

"Nonsense," said Burke. "I am here on a mission with Heather's team."

"What you say seems somehow true," said Akmenios. "But your return cannot be a coincidence."

"My return?" Burke thought for a while. "Tell me, if you had really captured me before, how did I escape from your island?"

"You didn't escape. We let you go because we were sure the Shomrunk would contact you again to restore all the information you had gathered during your journey."

"You were watching me or what?"

"We were tracing your mind, but somehow he figured out what we were doing. We lost our connection with you soon after you arrived home." Akmenios leaned forward.

"Which confirms our doubts about the Shomrunk; he is currently living in your homeland."

Burke noticed that Akmenios did not move his lipless mouth.

"How did I...?" Burke asked.

"We are now connected, Burke." Akmenios's voice was heard again, despite his closed mouth. "These devices on our heads modulate our brain waves to make us sleep. This makes your mind more vulnerable."

"Damn! I didn't feel myself sleeping. How does this device work on different brains? Do we have the same wave patterns?"

"This is not the time for a scientific discussion, Burke. Focus and tell me; what do you see now?"

Suddenly, Burke found himself in the heart of the sea, the cold water flooding his clothes. *This is not the sea. This is the Atlantic Ocean,* he thought as he spotted his flipping boat, a colossal wave toying with it.

And his turn was coming.

"Your first attempt to reach Domus was a nightmare," Burke heard Akmenios's voice, but he couldn't see the gray-faced humanoid.

"Get me the hell out of here!" Burke gazed at the mountainous wave that was about to swallow him. "I'm drowning!"

"Let's skip this quickly," said the invisible Akmenios.

Burke filled his lungs with air, his eyes fixed on the wave crashing over him.

And then suddenly he was sitting there, without a single drop of water trickling down from him.

This is not real, he reminded himself. But it wasn't a dream, either. That *scene* in the ocean was a memory. A memory he could recall now for the first time.

He wasn't awake yet. Yes, he was sitting down, but he wasn't in that same room he loathed. Through the locked window on his left, he watched the small buildings he was flying above. Looking around, Burke presumed he was in the same craft that escorted him and Heather's team after they had disembarked on the island.

The altitude was not too high. Burke could see the buildings so clearly, but they weren't anything he had ever seen before.

"It's your city." Astounded, Burke realized. "I can't remember to have ever seen this before."

"It seems I have succeeded in deleting this part from your memory," said Akmenios, who appeared to be standing beside Burke in the same craft.

The scene changed again, and this time, Burke was tied to a metal chair, with the by now familiar device on his head.

"So, this is when you erased my memory for the first time." Burke clenched his teeth.

"Not only that," said Akmenios. "I also found some suspicious ideas implanted in your mind."

"Like what?"

"Like your relative who was lost in the ship Proteus."

His relative? An implanted idea? "What do you mean?"

"You never had a relative on that ship," said Akmenios. "That alien idea was introduced to your mind, incubated inside it, until it grew and became a belief that eventually drove you to look for your imaginary relative."

Imaginary? The news petrified Burke for a few seconds. Was it possible that his biggest obsession was based on a lie? He had paid whole years of his life as a price for this delusion.

"No, this is bullshit," Burke spat. "I see the dirty game you're playing, dumbass."

"I play no games, Burke."

"Stop messing with my mind."

"I understand your shock," said Akmenios. "But this is the truth. You have been pushed to do somebody else's bidding."

"I'm not listening to this bullshit."

"There is nothing you can do but listen."

"What do you want from me, scum? Make me doubt everything about my life? Make me doubt who I am? And then what?"

"Calm yourself, Burke. Everything in your life is real. Only a small part of it was faked by the Shomrunk."

"How can you be so sure of that?" Burke growled. "How can you be sure he had not manipulated your mind as well?"

"I thought you would keep your composure better than that," said Akmenios.

"Oh, please! Say that to someone who wasn't forced to spend eight years in solitude."

"Try to focus, Burke. Your thoughts are flowing too fast and into too many directions."

"So what?" Burke shrugged. "You can't see through my mind clearly now?"

"For your own good," said Akmenios. "Let me find any hidden memory with the Shomrunk. It may help us locate him more precisely."

For a second, Burke sensed some honesty in the humanoid's creaky voice. Taking a deep breath, he tried to calm himself down as Akmenios requested. One minute later, the scene in front of Burke changed again. This time he was in his boat, heading back home.

"I remember this," said Burke. "At that moment I thought I had just survived the storm."

He looked right and left, but he couldn't find Akmenios on the boat. "Where are you?" he yelled. "You're driving me nuts with this memory shuffle."

"I'm here, Burke," Akmenios's voice came from nowhere. "I am nearing the truth, and soon we will know where and how you have met the Shomrunk. Just be patient."

"At least you can warn me before you shift places from one to another," Burke mumbled.

"Nothing is going to harm you when you relive your memories."

"You must be kidding me. I was about to drown in the Atlantic."

"Your brain won't let you die in your sleep. It will wake you up just before the moment of death. I beg you to relax now; we are so close to the crucial moment."

Burke was sure he had never had such a vivid dream before. Akmenios's voice was loud and clear, but neither louder nor clearer than the engine of the boat. And there was that smell of brine; strong and slightly *sulfury*. Was he back to reality at last? He wouldn't be happier if that encounter with Heather and the humanoids was just a stupid nightmare.

He realized he was still in his induced 'dream' when everything around him became dark, so dark he was unable to see where he was going or what he was stepping on.

"Where am I now?" Burke asked.

Akmenios was still invisible. "It seems we have found a secret chamber in your mind at last. Everything is well hidden, which confirms my doubts."

What Burke had just heard sounded insane. Anyway, the whole experience was unbelievable so far.

"Do you mean this is the part where I meet the Shomrunk?" asked Burke.

"Most probably," replied Akmenios. "I don't find any other reason to hide a memory in your mind."

"So, will you do something about this darkness?" said Burke. "It scares me."

"Just stay quiet for a moment. I'm trying to focus."

The darkness was gradually fading, and Burke found himself standing in a garden, lit only by soft moonlight. He turned his head to find Akmenios on his right.

"You must be kidding me." Burke was astonished. "My house?"

"We must hurry." Akmenios grabbed Burke by the hand. "My power is going to be depleted soon."

"I will never understand this," Burke muttered as he followed Akmenios to the closed door of the house.

"Now what?" Burke wondered.

"Open the door," said Akmenios. "Find the keys in your pocket."

"What the...?" Burke was at a loss for words when he found the keys in his pocket indeed.

"Just open it now," Akmenios insisted, a bit of tension in his creaky voice.

"I don't get it," said Burke. "Am I supposed to be watching a previous memory that has already occurred? I mean if I didn't open the—"

"There isn't much time for your gibberish," Akmenios interrupted. "Just do as I say."

Burke had a thousand questions to ask, but the humanoid wasn't going to answer them right now. Burke had better listen and obey, and later he might get an explanation. Hopefully.

The keys did unlock the door. *Home sweet home,* Burke thought as he stepped inside after years of exile. Feeling impatient to see his messy place like he had left it, he flicked the nearest light switch. The lights didn't work though.

"Come on." Burke kept flicking the switch again and again.

"Stop and listen." Akmenios gripped Burke's hand.

"What's this?" Burke was a bit scared when he heard a low voice uttering strange words. "The voice is coming from everywhere."

"It's him," Akmenios stated after the voice stopped. "This is when he invaded your mind."

Burke looked around, but the place was too dark to see anything.

"It seems he took more defensive measures than I thought," Akmenios said. "This chamber is well protected."

"What protection?" said Burke. "We are inside my house."

"It's not what you think," said Akmenios slowly. "This is how the chamber is labeled in your mind."

Labeled? Burke wondered how his mind looked like to Akmenios.

"Where did he go?" asked Burke. "Did we fail?"

"I am still trying." Akmenios sounded weaker than before, making Burke wonder what kind of effort would be needed to unveil a *secret chamber* in someone's mind. The humanoid seemed a bit tired and thought he might try later after replenishing his power and...

Wait a second. Had Burke just knew what Akmenios thought of?

"No way." Burke's eyebrows rose. He stared at the gray-faced humanoid who murmured in his Latin language and stepped outside the house.

"You are not going anywhere." Burke hurried after Akmenios. He caught him by the arm, and shoved him against the wall. "It's your turn to answer my questions." Burke pinned Akmenios's arms to the wall with his hands. He had no idea how this happened, but for some reason, he could sense Akmenios's thoughts.

"No, you are not leaving," Burke growled when the humanoid uttered Latin words. "You think your friend on the gadgets will wake you up? This won't happen before you tell me what you want from us. Tell me now."

The much taller humanoid seemed too weak to struggle with Burke. Closing his narrow eyes, Akmenios repeated his Latin words.

"Oh my God!" Burke's head jerked backward. "This can't be your real intention."

Akmenios didn't show any reaction. Without saying a word, the humanoid stared at Burke...and vanished. All of a sudden, Burke found himself standing alone by the wall.

"Son of a bitch! You can't escape now!" Burke punched the wall, frustrated. He could have extracted more information from Akmenios's mind. Having said that, what Burke had gotten so far was scary enough. He must find a way to get out of here and warn the others before the aliens might...

And then it was all black again.

* * *

Akmenios removed the head device and tossed it to the ground. He rose from his chair, staring at Burke who was still asleep.

"How did this hominum breach your mind?" his deputy, Cudelios, asked him in Latin, their native tongue.

"I have no idea." Akmenios felt so weary after this attempt to open the secret chamber of Burke's mind. "It seems we have activated something, a dormant defense system maybe."

"The Shomrunk's defenses are much stronger than we thought. Your mind became vulnerable when you slept."

"I didn't expect anything like that." Akmenios slowly walked to the head device he had thrown to the side. "We need more power for this useless device the next time."

"Next time? With what he has seen? We can't keep this hominum for another or a next time."

"He hasn't seen that much."

"He has seen enough."

Akmenios gazed at Burke for the second time. Whatever this human had seen, he was Akmenios's only hope to find the Shomrunk.

"Erase that session from his memory," said Akmenios. "Make sure he doesn't recall anything at all from it."

22. An Offer You Must Refuse

Those gray-faced idiots! How did they expect Heather to sleep on their cold floor...while her hands were still tied to Powell's?

The whole crew was tied in pairs in the bare quiet round chamber, the walls of which having the same gray color they saw outside. Without windows, the yellow spotlights were the only source of light.

Except for Santino who groaned a couple of times and Susan who wished those humanoids would burn in hell, nobody said a word for five hours. They must be exhausted after this insane ride, but Heather doubted that anybody was able to sleep right now. They could try though, and no one could pretend he was not worried about his fate.

What is Akmenios doing now with you, Burke? The humanoid was going to connect his mind to Burke's, he had told her. Was that process accompanied by much pain? *You had better worry about yourself, Heath.* Well, maybe she was more curious than sympathetic.

"This is ridiculous." She hysterically pulled her tied hand. There must be a way to tear those wires apart to lose that awkward proximity to Powell.

"Whoa! Relax, doc." Powell held his hands still. "You really need to have some rest. Nobody knows how long we will be forced to stay here."

"I can't stay like this. I want to get up," Heather snapped as she rose to her feet, Powell rising with her. The wire that tied them was so short that each tied couple was forced to move together.

Standing in the chamber with Powell, Heather looked at her crew. Though Kenji, Jay, and Walter lay with eyes closed, she doubted they were able to sleep amid this tension. The rest looked gloomy, especially Linda who fidgeted. "All these hours, and still, they didn't bring him back."

She wasn't worried about Burke, Heather guessed. She was worried about herself when and if her turn might come.

"Their suspicions are only about Burke." Though Heather shared Linda's fears, she did her best to reassure the fretting girl. She was not sure if her tone was convincing when she added, "They have no doubts about us."

"So what?" Linda asked. "Will they release us then?"

Heather sighed. "I really don't know."

The chamber door slid open, and the other stuttering humanoid entered accompanied by six more gray-faced fellows. All the crew rose, staring at him in anticipation.

"Akmenios-want-you-all," said the humanoid. "Follow-me."

"Where is Burke?" Heather asked.

The humanoid turned to her. "Akmenios-want-you-now."

"He won't tell us unless their leader wants to," said Powell to Heather.

"We should rather be concerned about why he summons us," Daniel suggested, and Heather couldn't disagree.

"We are about to find out, it seems." Heather pressed her lips tightly together as she motioned for her crew to follow her. "Hopefully, we like the *why*."

The humanoids ushered Heather and her team through the network of twisting corridors that seemed to be endless. *Those bastards never get tired, do they?* she thought as she contemplated their tall, slim figures. Maybe they were tireless because of their light trunks. She still remembered how Powell managed to knock a humanoid out with a single mighty punch.

After about half an hour of marching, Heather realized she had arrived at the same hall Akmenios had received them in. A dozen humanoids or more were spread around the room, Akmenios himself in the center waiting for Heather and her crew. The stuttering humanoid herding the team stopped and so did everybody in the procession. An eerie silence descended over the place for a minute.

"I see you all share the same question," Akmenios spoke at last.

"Then, I hope you will answer it," Heather countered nervously.

"It is an expected concern," said Akmenios. "And that is why I gathered you all here."

A prelude that didn't sound promising. *Bad news is coming.*

"It is logical you want to return home," Akmenios continued in his creaky voice. "But I hope you understand that it is difficult for us to allow this to happen."

"What do you mean by it is *difficult* for you?" Heather asked, a disapproving humming behind her from her crew.

"I told you before; the Shomrunk is after us," said Akmenios. "And we cannot risk exposing our location to him."

"But I think you are quite sure we have nothing to do with that Shomrunk." Heather looked Akmenios in the eye.

"For the time being," said Akmenios. "But we can never allow even a tiny probability to jeopardize our safety, which is your safety as well. He might be waiting for your return to extract the information he has been seeking."

"So, we are your prisoners until we die, or what?" Heather snapped.

"This is your choice, homines," Akmenios replied.

Unable to get where the *choice* lay exactly in this part, Heather glared at the gray-faced humanoid, waiting for more elaboration from him.

"Thousands of years ago, we shared the same lands with homines and established the most civilized nation in Earth's history," he said. "Why don't we do this together once again, where you can be part of this new community with your knowledge and expertise?"

His *offer* took her off guard. To her, staying on this island forever wasn't a better fate than dying on it.

"Don't just discard the idea," said Akmenios, who was surely reading her mind. "Give it a thought, all of you, and you will realize it is for the best of all of us."

He meant for the best of him, Heather reflected.

"Put your emotions aside, Heather," said Akmenios. "Let your mind digest the facts. Take into consideration our suffering with the Shomrunks and with you as well."

"How do I know if your tale about your people's *suffering* is not just bullshit?" Heather asked coldly.

"You will never know because you can't read minds as I can." His blunt reply was a bit shocking. Those humanoids knew nothing about diplomatic answers.

"What options do we have other than accepting your generous invitation?" Heather decided to cut this conversation short.

"I never thought of other options."

Again his bluntness shocked her. *He never thought of other options? What the hell is that?*

"I believe you will not like being tied in your locked chamber for long." Akmenios leaned forward. "You are scientists, and your place is not here." The humanoid glanced at Powell and continued, "I mean most of you."

"What?" Powell growled. "Are you threatening me, you gray freak?"

"Not yet, soldier," Akmenios replied. "It's up to you."

Heather gripped Powell's hand before he might say something foolish. "Easy, Major." She gnashed her teeth, looking Powell in the eye. Despite her expectations, the scowling Major complied and kept his mouth shut.

"A vessel is departing for our city in one hour," Akmenios announced. "Decide if you want to join us. If you don't feel like being part of this, you still have your chamber here." He circled them with slow steps. "One more thing you should know; this is a one-time offer. Make up your minds while I check on your friend."

"Burke?" Heather wondered. "What's wrong with him?"

"Nothing bad," Akmenios replied as he walked away. "He's just in a deep sleep."

* * *

His eyes opened at last.

Burke turned his head right and left, his hands and feet tied to the cold metallic chair, the head device still on his head.

"Welcome back, Burke," said Akmenios, whose assistant removed the device from Burke's head.

"When will we start?" Burke wondered.

"We are already done." Akmenios kept his eyes fixed on Burke's face.

"What about the Shomrunk thing you told me about?"

"We didn't find anything this time, Burke. We may try again later."

"I thought the examination would be painful when you tied me to this chair."

"Tell me, how do you feel now?"

"Nothing. Did you hypnotize me or what?"

"I didn't. We just helped you get some sleep."

"Really? For how long?"

"Five hours."

"What? How can this be possible?"

"What is not possible, Burke?"

"Sleeping all that time without even knowing."

"Is this so different from any time you tried to sleep before? Tell me, do you remember any dreams you had?"

"I don't even know I have slept," Burke sneered. "How can I remember dreams?"

Akmenios leaned forward, looking Burke straight in the eye. "You are lying, Burke. You still remember everything."

Of course, Burke was lying. And yes, he still remembered everything he had seen in the mind-connection session. *Unfortunately*. Only now did he understand why sometimes ignorance was a blessing.

"We underestimated the Shomrunk's power, it seems," said Akmenios to Burke. "The one you met in particular was stronger than anyone we ever encountered."

Burke closed his eyes. He had done it before and read Akmenios's mind. He could do it again.

"What do you think you are doing?" Akmenios asked. "You think you can really see through my mind, hominum?"

"It happened before," Burke said curtly.

"You will never understand how it is done. It was not you who did it in the first place," said Akmenios. "And anyway, it can't work while I'm awake."

"If it wasn't me, then who did it?"

After exchanging a few words with his assistant in their humanoid language, Akmenios turned to Burke. "There is a part of the Shomrunk inside your mind. You may not be aware of it right now, but who knows what else is hidden in your head, hominum."

"So, you will keep me longer until you find out all what you seek, you ugly monsters," Burke spat.

"Monsters?" Akmenios echoed. "You, homines, are so strange. You inflict so much more damage on most of Earth's creatures that any of us, and you dare call us monsters?"

"Stop pretending," Burke grunted. "Who are you trying to fool with your *logical* approach? You are savages, all of you."

"You don't differ much from your race. You bear a bigger brain than ours in your head, but you are still less rational. You don't see the stark truth because you are always blinded by your emotions."

"And just what is that *stark truth*?" Burke scoffed nervously. "Other than you are nothing but monsters."

"It's the food chain, hominum. It all depends on who occupies which rank in that chain or hierarchy. No hard feelings."

A repulsive thought crossed Burke's mind. "Is that why nobody survived the Bermuda Triangle?" The humanoid's silence confirmed his fears. "Oh no!" Burke tried to pull his arms, but the ties held him in his seat. "You are nothing but wild animals."

"Then, I guess this is how your cattle see you too." Akmenios walked away from Burke, heading to the door of the room.

"What about them?" Burke yelled.

Akmenios stopped and slowly looked over his shoulder. "We are not brainless savages as you have just called us, hominum. We know exactly what the best role for each one of your friends is. Some of them are brilliant and can really contribute to our society."

"Some?" Burke was really terrified. "What about the rest?" he asked more than once, but Akmenios simply ignored him and left him in his cold metallic seat alone with the gray-faced assistant. "I know you understand me, gray ass. Tell me: what are you going to do with the rest of us?"

The humanoid assistant resumed his work on his control panel and screen, as if he didn't hear Burke. Whether the humanoid knew English or not, it seemed that nobody would answer Burke's question.

Most probably, he could derive the answer by himself.

23. Atlanteans

Hands were free now. All it took to remove those bloody wires was a 'yes' to Akmenios for his 'generous' offer. The only one who hadn't voiced his approval yet was Powell, but Heather spoke on his behalf whether he liked it or not.

Following Akmenios, she led her team as they headed to the vessel that was supposed to take them to the humanoids' settlement, her wrists still itchy because of those wires. When they reached the vessel, Akmenios stopped by its hatch and so did she.

"I am not coming with you," said Akmenios. "You go."

"So, you will stay to finish those investigations?" Heather doubted he would answer that, but she would lose nothing if she asked, right?

"That is a matter I must oversee myself," Akmenios replied. "He may join you later."

Heather found it hard to believe the gray humanoid. Leaving someone behind was not a suggestion she was even ready to entertain. *Not again.*

Akmenios's narrow eyes were fixed on her face. "You can't blame yourself forever. You need to stop that."

"It's you who needs to stop." Heather glared at him. The mind-reading humanoid must have found that particular dark memory she had been trying to bury. "Don't you ever dare bring that up again."

"I'm just trying to tell you that you must accept that sometimes there are situations that are not under your control," said Akmenios. "Like this one."

Daniel shot Heather an inquisitive look when he passed her, but she motioned him toward the vessel. "I can't help picturing what's happening to Burke," she said to Akmenios.

"This is of no use." His answer was straightforward. "My advice to you, in particular, is to give the coming stage of your life your full focus. You have the potential to contribute so much to this community."

"The coming stage of my life?" Heather echoed faintly, her throat suddenly clogged.

"Yes," he confirmed. "Your life here is going to be different from the one you had before. You should be ready for that."

Except for her, her team was now on board.

"Dubos will escort you." He glanced at the other English-speaking humanoid, who stepped inside the vessel.

"Him?" she asked in disapproval. "Don't you have anybody else with a better fluency?"

"I am sure you can communicate with Dubos," said Akmenios. "Your vessel is leaving."

As usual, he was ending their conversation, leaving her restless with a million questions in her mind. Reluctantly, she dragged her feet and joined her crew inside the vessel. The hatch slid shut behind her, and only a few moments later, the vessel hovered upwards until it reached a huge tunnel at the top of the subterranean dock.

When the sunlight streamed in through the vessel window, she heaved a long sigh, louder than the quiet humming of the craft's engines. After the long day she had spent in the cold humanoids' quarters, the sunlight should soothe her. To her surprise, a shiver ran down her spine. *You have the potential to contribute so much to this community.* The notion of spending the rest of her life here among gray-faced creatures was hard to swallow. All this had better be a nightmare.

"At last." Daniel drew in a deep breath of air, glancing at the silver door isolating the passengers' chamber from the cockpit. "We get a break from their gray faces and creaky voices."

Only now did Heather realize that the humanoids had left them on their own in the passengers' chamber. "Why do these humanoids hate seats?" Heather asked, recalling the first ship that took them to the underground headquarters.

"It looks like a soldiers' transporter," said Powell. "Or perhaps those freaks don't need to sit like us."

The chamber grew hushed. Heather knew that her role as the group leader compelled her to say something to boost the morale of her crew, but the words were stuck in her throat. She wasn't less worried than them about their mysterious fate. *Her* fate.

For the first time, she was able to watch the island in daylight. From above, she could see the dark-green thick forest that covered a vast area of the terrain. At the horizon, a mountainous zone occupied the central part of the island.

"So, their city is constructed between the forest and the mountains." Heather was impressed by the view, she had to admit.

"I can't believe this island has never been detected by our satellites," Daniel muttered.

"Those gray freaks have taken their measures to keep themselves invisible," said Santino. "It's obvious they are so scared of the so-called *Shomrunk*."

"I guess we have to be scared as well." Daniel leaned his weary head on the smooth surface of the vessel wall. If there was something to scare her for the time being, it should be her destiny, not that Shomrunk they were talking about.

Suddenly, an explosion forcefully shook the vessel. For a moment, Heather couldn't feel her pulse.

"Not again!" Susan screamed.

"Those Atlantean scumbags! It must be them!" Santino blustered. "They will get us—"

A second explosion interrupted Santino. This time, the ship swayed sharply.

"Oh my God!" Linda shrieked. "We are falling!"

"We are crash landing!" Powell corrected. "Get down, everybody!" He bent his knees, putting his hands over his head. Since there was nothing to hang on to, everybody followed what Powell did. Waiting for the craft to crash, Heather closed her eyes as she buried her head between her thighs. For the third or fourth time within the last twenty-four hours —she was too confused to count right now—she found herself cornered in a deadly situation.

The ship's hull hit the ground, the shock throwing Heather from her place. After a short while of drifting on the ground, the vessel stopped. Groans replaced screams. Heather bruised her shoulder, and she should be grateful for it being only that. Susan was sobbing as she held her knee. Kenneth seemed to have his shoulder dislocated after being slammed hard against the vessel wall.

Heather struggled as she rose to her feet to go and check Susan's injury. Before she was able to take one step, a third explosion occurred. It was the worst. The vessel hatch was blasted away, the fire swallowing Joshua and Kenji who had been leaning to the very hatch before it was totally blown.

"NOOO!" Heather screamed, staring at the flames that had engulfed her colleagues.

The silver door of the cockpit slid open, Dubos and two other humanoids hurrying out. "Down," the humanoid demanded.

Aiming his spheroidal weapon at the destroyed hatch, Dubos repeated his order as he advanced. Suddenly, two human-sized intruders jumped in through the explosion's smoke and flames. They looked like astronauts with their bright white outfits and helmets that hid their faces. In a blink of an eye, they fired their silver cylindrical weapons, yellow beams cutting through the humanoids' gray heads. No more stuttering for Dubos.

Heather couldn't help but scream. The sight of a dead body was never an easy one to stomach, even if the corpse belonged to a gray-faced humanoid. She heard two creaky screams as the two intruders stormed the cockpit. *What the hell is going on?* Warily, she watched them exit the pilot's room. One of them approached her and said something in a language she couldn't comprehend. Maybe it was also Latin, but she couldn't tell without Nathaniel's help. Anyway, what mattered the most was their voices.

They were humans.

"They want us to follow them," Nathaniel yelled. "There is an exit in the cockpit."

"Who are they?" Roused now, Heather blustered, "Those sons of bitches have just killed two of us!"

The same masked man said something else in Latin. "They say we must leave before more *Griseos* come here."

"Gris...what?" Heather asked nervously.

"Griseos; the Grays in Latin," said Nathaniel, who then exchanged a few words with the masked intruder before he turned back to her. "The Griseos' base is not far from here. We must leave before they catch us."

"As if those are our rescuers." She lunged toward the masked man to slap him on his helmet, but Powell held her by the arm.

"Doctor, wait." Powell's grip was too firm to get rid of. "Look at me. I know you're mad about your friends, but we—"

"You know nothing!" she put in.

"Please, Dr. Heather." Powell's tone was commanding despite his plea. "We have to think rationally at such a critical time. I never liked that Akmenios or his gray people," he gestured to the masked men, "and these two don't seem to be Akmenios's friends. If I am to choose, I would go with them."

"Me too," Kenneth whimpered as he held his injured shoulder. "I don't want to return to those gray humanoids."

"We don't have too many options," Santino pointed out, Linda holding on to him.

"We must act fast, Heather." Daniel gently took her by the hand, Powell letting her go. "It sounds crazy. But I believe you don't want to stay here and wait for those gray creatures."

The intruder she wanted to slap removed his helmet, revealing his human face. While she was contemplating his tanned skin and blue eyes, he yelled in Latin.

"He says he is a human like us." Nathaniel came with the translation. "Can we trust him now?"

Well, after Akmenios had messed with her mind with his version of history, there was nothing she could be sure of. Who knew what exactly those humans were doing on this bloody island? Who knew if they were even real humans in the first place? What if they were *another* race, like the Shomrunks, a race that just looked like humans and resembled them?

"Heather," Daniel snapped. "We must move now." He nodded toward the cockpit. The two strangers were ushering the crew to the exit already. The tan-skinned guy mumbled as he put on his helmet and left Heather and

Daniel in the passengers' chamber. *Maybe it's time to get out of here, Heather.*

Letting Daniel take her by the hand, she skipped through the open sliding door to the cockpit, and from there she exited the craft through another small hatch. Outside the vessel stood a dozen helmeted men, holding what looked like arm cannons. When he hollered in Latin, she was able to recognize the voice of the tan-skinned guy among his fellows. "He is ordering his men to get out of this area immediately," said Nathaniel.

Heather's team complied and followed the arm cannoneers who were retreating from the crash site in studied steps, their heads and weapons up.

Their leader cried out again, but this time, it seemed he was crying at her crew. "He wants us to stay behind his men," Nathaniel said.

She didn't question Nathaniel's translation of their *rescuer's* instructions, her mind busy recalling what she had heard from the gray humanoids about the people called the Atlanteans. It wasn't hard to conclude that those Atlanteans were the descendants of the four humans who had survived the catastrophe that ended the legend of the great continent of Atlantis. Was it a wise decision for Heather and her team to join them? More than once, Akmenios had stressed the hostile history of humans and how they had waged war against his people to take control of Atlantis.

Could it be possible that Akmenios had lied to her? No. She saw for herself how those *humans* had recklessly stormed the craft, killing two of her team members. Upon recalling the dreadful scene and fighting the conjured images her roasted colleagues, she wanted to punch one of those...

"What are they looking at?" she heard Susan asking. Only now did Heather notice that the Atlanteans were concentrating at something in the sky coming from behind her. This time, she didn't need Nathaniel to translate the Atlanteans' firm gestures for her team to duck. And obviously, Powell didn't need to be fluent in Latin to know what was going on. Before Nathaniel performed his usual task of translating, the Major yelled, "Incoming!"

24. Fire Storm

"A missile!" Powell hollered. "Stay down!"

Heather dove, and so did the rest of the crew. But the Atlanteans didn't.

Lying on the ground, she watched one of them aim at that missile with his arm cannon and deter the danger with a counter-missile, an explosion thundering in the sky.

"Oh shit!" Santino cried. "Four more coming in! Run!"

One quick look at the missiles in the sky was enough for Heather to get up and sprint with her team on the grassy fields of this cursed island. Nobody needed to argue if it was a good idea to wait and see whether these cannoneers could block the missiles this time or not. Without looking behind, Heather heard four explosions, yet one of them was so close, much louder than the others.

When she dared to stop and look back, she found three of the cannoneers had fallen, dead.

"Dammit, Heather!" Daniel grabbed Heather by the arm. "You can't stop now!"

His pull forced her to resume her run, the Atlanteans' cries behind her tempting her to look back again. "Ahead, Heather!" Daniel bellowed. "Keep your eyes ahead!"

Running as fast as she could while keeping her eyes forward; it shouldn't be hard to follow that, right? Well, it could be easier if Powell didn't yell, "Duck! Everybody down now!"

So, what the hell should she do? Run or duck? The conflict was resolved in two seconds by another firm pull by Daniel. She was down now. Unable to resist her curiosity this time, she glanced back at the sky as she lay on the grass. Ten more flying objects were coming. "Oh shit!" Heather's jaw fell.

"Your head to the ground, Heather!" Daniel barked.

What would that be good for? Protecting her pretty face from the explosion shock wave? What if those missiles fell *right* on her?

The explosions shook the ground she lay on, every little earthquake startling her, almost causing a cardiac arrest. She buried her head in the grass after the third explosion, the blaze burning her back and the nape of her neck. Or that was what she thought. When she heard the fourth explosion she realized that she wasn't burnt at all. The fifth one was the closest and the worst, the thunderous *BOOM* deafening her for a while. The ground kept wobbling, the air still blazing, and all she heard was a faint clamor of roars and cries. Her lungs yelped for oxygen as the air was laden with choking fumes, making her cough so hard she felt her chest was being torn apart.

And then she was shaken. But this time it wasn't another earthquake, it was Daniel's hand. "Heather?"

"Not dead yet." The cough hurt her parched throat as she let him pull her up. Daniel was haggard, his face darkened by smoke and dirt. Now she had an idea how she looked. "I presume."

The smoke was clearing, but still the field looked like an abandoned tomb, the stench of death saturating the air. "Linda?" Heather called out when she heard her cough. In their situation, a cough was a synonym for 'being alive.' Heather should rather worry about the rest of her *silent* friends. "Jay? Santi? Susan? Walter?" She squinted into the fading smoke, shadows of human beings rising up from the ground, familiar voices coughing, gasping for air and whimpering. *Thank God! They're alive!*

"I see you have forgotten us," Powell's voice came from behind her. With heavy steps, the pilot approached her, Nathaniel following him. "I thought we were part of your team."

Heather was too tired to pretend a smile. *Part of my team?* That reminded her she had already lost two of her colleagues during the Atlanteans' reckless break-in.

"Where is Kenneth?" Only now did she realize he was missing. "Kenneth?" she called out upon spotting a slowly approaching shadow that looked like her teammate. She hurried to him, the smoke so heavy it made her cough again.

But that was not Kenneth. It was the tan-skinned Atlantean. Behind him followed four more shadows of his colleagues, some distance away.

"Dammit!" she cried. "Where is Kenneth?" She turned back where she had found her friends. A scary thought crossed her mind when she saw Santino and Jay kneel at a certain spot. She wished she was wrong, but she wasn't.

"No, Heather." Jay hurried to her, waving with both hands not to get closer. "You don't want to see this."

"No!" Unable to keep her composure any longer, she let her tears fall. "Please, no!" She shoved Jay, who didn't dare to stop her, Daniel and Santino yelling at her to halt. She ignored them both as she stumbled over...Kenneth's head.

"Oh God!" She shrieked, knives cutting through her stomach upon seeing the severed head. Daniel scurried to her, leaving Santino sitting by the headless corpse. While she was unaware of what she was mumbling, Daniel shushed her as he patted her gently on her back.

Despite the repulsive sight, she pushed Daniel away to stare at what remained of Kenneth. "Oh God! What on earth could do that?"

Daniel's voice was low when he held her shoulder. "Maybe it's shrapnel or an explosion fragment." He sighed. "It's useless now, Heather. He is gone."

He was gone indeed. Like Kenji and Joshua. *He is gone;* they had used the same statement in the emergency room to tell her that she had lost her baby. *Gone!*

"Dr. Heather?" Nathaniel called her in a cautious, low voice.

She inhaled deeply, trying to pull herself together. "Yes."

Nathaniel cleared his throat. "According to Tolarus, we have to reach the woods before the humanoids send their troops."

"Tolarus?" Heather turned to Nathaniel, who in turn nodded toward the tan-skinned Atlantean, the man who had caused this entire mess.

"Seems he lost most of his men." She contemplated the four remaining cannoneers of Tolarus's squad.

"Nine of them died in this attack." Nathaniel nodded. "Tolarus told me he understood our sorrow for our friends, but we have to move—"

"Tell him that two of my friends died because of his audacious break-in!" Heather blustered. Nathaniel made one step back and returned to the Atlantean. She wondered if the quiet language expert would convey her fury to the Atlanteans.

Tolarus approached Heather, Nathaniel catching up with him. The Atlantean addressed her in Latin and Nathaniel translated, "He knows his words won't bring your friends back, but he is really sorry. All he wanted was to help, and he lost men from his own squad in the same attack. He wishes you could bear this in mind."

So, what was that Tolarus trying to tell her? His loss was bigger than hers? *Who cares?* She didn't ask for some help that would jeopardize her life as well as her crew's, eventually ending up with three of her colleagues dead.

"All he wanted was to help," Heather echoed, her mind still a bit muddled as she tried to decipher the Atlantean's words. "Help us do what? How did he know we needed his help in the first place?"

For one rare instance, Nathaniel's eyes widened, obviously hesitant to translate that to Tolarus.

"Ask him, exactly as I said it. You hear me?" Heather glared at Nathaniel.

The ancient languages expert pressed his lips together as he turned to Tolarus and spoke with him in Latin. The Atlantean scowled at Heather and replied tensely, his glowing eyes fixed on Heather's face. She didn't need a translator to know he was mad at her.

"He says he has no idea how much we know about the truth of this island," Nathaniel addressed her. "There is too much to tell, yet we have to move as fast as we can now. Your hesitation, *he* says, will end up getting us all killed."

But she had to follow him to have *only* half of her crew killed, right? Actually, she was still wary about those Atlanteans, whose entrance had been nothing but disastrous.

"Heather." Daniel pressed her hand gently. "We have to follow these men."

"How can we make sure they are the right side to join?"

"We can't." Daniel shrugged. "But definitely, I would choose them over those gray-faced creatures."

She scanned her exhausted crew, those who remained, to be precise. They didn't say it, but she knew they were anticipating her approval. They were ready to do anything to get away from every gray face on this damned island.

"Come on," Daniel urged her. "Everything is going to be okay."

"Nothing is okay, Daniel." Heather let out a deep breath of air. "But what other option do we have?"

* * *

When he heard the alarm, Akmenios thought it was the captured hominum. The moment he entered the chamber, his eyes found the sleeping Burke still tied to his seat. *The Shomrunk inside him is under control so far.*

"What is it?" Akmenios asked Cudelios, his second-in-command.

"The Atlanteans attacked our vessel. We lost all our men."

Fury was a human notion Akmenios never grasped, but he knew that, according to human standards, this news was infuriating. "That's unfortunate. What about the homines?"

"The Atlanteans set them all free." Cudelios kept conveying more *unfortunate* news. "I launched the Fire Storm Protocol to make sure those Atlanteans are punished."

While that might mean losing the homines as well, Akmenios didn't protest. *We have lost them already the moment those Atlanteans have found them.* "A good decision," stated Akmenios. "Results?"

"Twelve dead homines, twelve still alive. I'm recharging the missile platform for another wave."

The Atlanteans would have reached their headquarters in the mountains by the time the recharging was complete. And Akmenios had already lost two power reactors last week because of those useless *cannoneers*. "No. We cannot afford to waste our energy like that."

"So, are we letting them go?"

"They know we can raze those mountains to the ground at any moment."

"But we never did."

And we never will, Akmenios thought. It wasn't a secret anyway, even for the Atlanteans themselves. Those homines knew that he must allow them to survive...for his own people's survival.

"They need to be hammered," Akmenios finally said. "We will lay waste to their side, yet we shall leave them room to survive."

"So?" his deputy asked. "Another raid?"

"Not yet. We bombard them first, leaving them in chaos," said Akmenios. "Then, we start hunting."

"Speaking of hunting." Cudelios glanced at Burke. "This hominum has seen too much. Every now and then, his mind retrieves something from the memories he has captured from your head. I had to sedate him when he suddenly raved about the corpses and the tubes. He saw the tubes, Akmenios."

That mind-connection session hadn't gone as expected. "So?" Akmenios asked. "Worried he might tell his friends? His friends must have learned the truth from the Atlanteans anyway." He turned his full attention toward Burke, not sensing any activity from him or *his* Shomrunk. "And he is not going anywhere, is he?"

25. Cattle Farm

For three hours, they had been walking through the woods.

All the trees looked the same, or that was what Heather thought. Somehow those Atlanteans knew how to find their way as they took rights and lefts in this maze of wooden trunks.

"We did nothing more than walk on this damned island," Santino grumbled.

"At least, we are still on our feet," Walter noted, not much joy in his voice. No one could tell if they were more fortunate than their friends who had *gone*.

The Atlanteans stopped at the thickest area of the forest, sunlight barely streaming in through the interlocking green branches of those high trees. "Step back, everyone," Nathaniel translated Tolarus's order. The

Atlantean looked at them as they complied with his order, and then he pressed a button on his belt. A rectangular part of the terrain rose slowly, revealing that it was just a cover for what looked like a secret lift.

"So, it's not only those humanoids who have the good shit." Jay looked impressed.

"Going underground again?" Heather muttered. "I was just starting to enjoy the sun."

The Atlanteans stepped into the secret lift, which was vast enough to accommodate a van, and all members of Heather's crew followed. Nobody uttered a word, neither in Latin nor in English. For a few minutes, Heather felt the lift going down, then moving forward, the air thick with the stink of their sweat. *We have been running and walking like some Olympic athletes since we came to this island.*

The stench and the lack of windows made her edgy. "Will it take forever?" Heather glanced at Nathaniel. "It's hard to breathe in this sardine can."

Nathaniel translated her concern to the Atlantean captain, who only spoke a few words. "We're almost there," the ancient language expert told her.

There where? Another underground camp? She kept her question for herself, hoping she would know the answer soon.

She doubted Nathaniel had translated the word 'almost' right. The smelly metallic box stopped after like twenty minutes. But truth be told, the waiting was worth it.

Heather and her team were stunned when they stepped outside the lift and were greeted with one of the most wonderful landscapes they had ever seen. Mountains surrounded the grassy field from all directions. The ripples of a waterfall whispered from the north, blending with the gentle wind whistling to create majestic background music for the stunning view. Just fifty meters away, a river separated them from a small colony of sprawling two-story buildings.

"At least there is some beauty on this damned island." Susan's eyes widened.

Letting the cool breeze caress her cheeks, Heather watched Nathaniel, who had a brief conversation with Tolarus before the Atlantean walked away. "What is it, Nathaniel?" she asked him.

"He wants us to stay here," answered Nathaniel. "He's going to return to us shortly."

She had no problem allowing herself to enjoy the natural painting carved by the mountains and the waterfall. The tension in the last few hours had been unbearable and so was the pain in her tired legs. The grassy ground was so soft she rested her exhausted body on it. Upon seeing her doing so, most of her crew did the same and lay on the ground, waiting for Tolarus who rode a hovering non-wheeled vehicle that resembled a scooter. Nobody knew where this vehicle came from, but they saw him headed to one of the mountains at the eastern side, the nearest one to them.

"Now what?" Daniel looked around. "They didn't leave anybody to keep an eye on us."

Heather grunted as she raised herself to sit on her haunches. She hoped Daniel wasn't suggesting running away. *Because I'm so tired right now. We all are.*

"They must be watching us somehow," Daniel continued.

Who could tell? "They didn't tie us up so far," she pointed out. "That could be promising."

The place was quieter than it should be. Yes, from her spot, Heather beheld a few Atlanteans wandering on the other side of the river bank. But the way Akmenios referred to the humans' higher reproduction rate made her expect a much bigger and more crowded Atlantean community.

"Here he comes back." Daniel pointed at Tolarus's hovering scooter. When the Atlantean landed, Heather wondered what he was holding. The two identical items he brought looked like two helmets.

Nathaniel rose and exchanged a few words with Tolarus, both of them looking at her. Obviously, she was their topic. Nathaniel took one of those *helmets* and handed it to Heather. "What's this?" She rose to her feet.

"He wants the group leader to put this on," he replied. "He says it makes communication easier."

Heather was hesitant to wear that dreary helmet. But when Tolarus put on his, she warily did the same.

"What is this thing supposed to do?" she addressed Nathaniel.

"It's supposed to help us understand each other."

To her astonishment, the reply came from Tolarus instead of Nathaniel. Somehow, she heard his voice in her head, in English.

"What's this?" she asked. "An instant translator?"

"Not exactly." Tolarus shrugged. "I'm not sure how I can explain this, but it connects our brain waves so we can understand each other."

"A mind reader?"

"No, it doesn't read your thoughts. Not yet, at least with this version." He grinned. "It works on the speech centers of our brains, transferring signals produced in a wavelength that can be comprehended by both of us."

The technology the Atlanteans possessed was impressive, she had to admit. "It seems you have a better understanding of brain functions than we do."

The Atlantean was much more relaxed than he was during their first encounter. "Our scientists, who designed this device, have a better understanding, for sure. But that doesn't apply to me. What I know better is weapons."

Heather nodded toward her crew. "So, they still don't comprehend what you say."

"Neither what you say." He gave her a faint smile. "They can't even hear us. Your words are not coming from your vocal cords while you wear this device."

She was curious about the way this helmet worked. But she had more pressing matters for the time being. "Let's get into the subject." She straightened her back. "What do you want from us?"

"You must be tired like them." He gestured toward her team members. Most of them were still lying or reclining on the ground.

"I'm fine." She ignored his *gentle* offer. "Please, answer my question."

"You never thanked us," said Tolarus, a faint smile still on his face. "Though I lost more men than you did to save you and your crew."

"Which makes me wonder why you and your men would risk your lives so bad," she countered. *Not out of nobility, I bet.*

Tolarus seemed to be weighing his next words. "Alright then. In brief, we are trapped on this island with those humanoids, so actually, we need your help."

"Our help." That reminded her. "You're the ones who wrote 'Help us' on the island shore."

Tolarus's eyes widened. "Did you finally see it?"

"One of us did." Referring to Burke reminded Heather of her guilt. Leaving people behind seems to have become a habit.

"It was a desperate attempt to draw the attention of the outer world. It's amazing how our simplest initiative worked better than the more sophisticated ones."

Heather was about to ask him about the third language they used to write "*Help us*," but the last three words he uttered struck her. "More sophisticated ones?" she echoed doubtfully. "What else have you done to draw the attention of the outer world?"

The Atlantean looked down as he bit his lower lip. *He said too much*, she thought. "What else have you done, Tolarus?"

"Look, Heather." Tolarus sighed. "For centuries, we have been chased by those humanoid beasts. They got us cornered here in this mountainous area so that we wouldn't dare to wander outside unarmed. Otherwise, they will hunt us down and capture us alive. Even here, it's not totally safe. Sometimes, they breach our defenses and we find them here right in the middle of our settlement. Eventually, we have been living *in* those mountains, because defending ourselves there proved to be a bit easier—"

"What else have you done?" Heather cut him off.

Tolarus exhaled. "The Griseos had surrounded the island with an invincible defense system, making the idea of fleeing Domus impossible. The very system that must have swallowed you up and sucked you into this island."

"Are you talking about the storm and the raging ocean?"

"Yes." He nodded. "In the beginning, our ancestors in Atlantis devised that technology to generate energy from stimulated water currents, but those humanoids developed it into something else. Many of us tried to escape, but their attempts were deterred by the Griseos' Storm Shield. And of course, those humanoid cannibals saved the escapees from drowning."

"Cannibals?" The word struck Heather. "Is this a...figure of speech?"

"I thought you knew already." Tolarus raised his eyebrows. "That humanoid race feeds on the energy of our bodies. That's why they will never let us perish here on this island. We are here like a big herd of cattle for them."

Cattle? What about Akmenios's hollow speech about the peaceful coexistence with the primitive hostile humans? *Oh my God! Burke!* "They still have one of our friends. Does that mean he has become...?" *Yes, say it, Heather: Food for those gray-faced monsters. And you left him behind. You always leave someone behind.*

"I'm sorry about your friend." Tolarus pressed his lips together, heaving a deep sigh. "We all lost friends because of those bastards. That's why we changed our stance from defensive to offensive. Our assaults have so far not been massive, yet they are painful for them."

"So, those humanoids have a weak point."

"Yes. They are gluttonous about energy," said Tolarus. "Their technology requires so much power, and currently we are targeting their energy reactors."

Their technology requires so much power? Was there anything about those humanoids Akmenios didn't lie about?

Heather closed her eyes and gestured to Tolarus to stop. *He is evading the question.* "For the third time, what else have you done?"

"A few months ago, we captured an old aircraft of yours during a big raid on one of the Griseos' warehouses. We were looking for their weapons in the first place, but that old aircraft was all that we found."

"An old craft?" A wild thought crossed Heather's mind. "Please, continue."

"It was totally frustrating for us to return home empty-handed, so we took the old aircraft, having no idea what to do with it until an idea came to us. We had many theories about the way the Storm Shield works, and we decided to use your old aircraft to test one of those theories. And it worked. Without a pilot, your aircraft did pass the Shield."

"And where did it go after passing the Shield?" Heather knew the answer already.

"Well, we faced a little problem. After the aircraft had gone past the Shield, we lost control of it."

"And it crashed into a jet carrying more than four hundred passengers," Heather growled. "You killed them all."

"It was an accident..." Tolarus could not find any words to finish his statement.

"It was a disaster."

"You have no idea." Tolarus shook his head. "We went through so much trouble until we managed to learn how to control that aircraft. And after all of that, we were not sure whether we could make it pass through the Storm Shield or not."

His excuses would never be enough to justify his people's recklessness. *It was an accident.* Her mind wasn't able to get over that phrase. That accident caused one of the worst plane crashes of the century.

"Wait a minute, Tolarus." Heather recalled what he had just said. "Why exactly did you send that old plane, I mean the aircraft? To test the Shield? Or to draw the outer world's attention?"

"Both," he replied. "First, it was to test our theory about the Shield, and then we realized it might draw the attention of your world to us. But we really didn't mean to draw attention in that horrible way."

Heather gave his tanned face a studying look. He might be telling the truth, but she had no reason to take what he said for granted.

"Many planes and ships were trapped behind that Shield. What did you do for their passengers?"

"You won't like the answer. But you are the first ones we succeeded in rescuing."

"We lost three friends in your *successful* rescue." Heather would rebuke him for all eternity.

"Heather, please. If you really want to leave this island, then you should stop bothering yourself and me with what we can never change."

"That's what you and I differ about." Heather wondered if the device could transmit her firm voice tone.

"We care about our loved ones, Tolarus. But who can blame you anyway? After all these—"

"Interested in returning to your loved ones back home?" he interrupted. "Because I know a way to get you out of here."

For once, someone interrupted her and she didn't feel offended. "Now you're talking."

Later, she might tell him she had no loved ones waiting for her to come back home.

26. Run or Die

On a paved corridor midway up the northern mountain, Heather and her teammates stepped out of an aircraft that resembled a non-wheeled van. The mix of green and blue colors painted by the grassy terrain and snaky river up there was a view pleasant on their eyes.

During the short aerial ride, Heather had briefed her mates about her conversation with Tolarus. All of them felt a bit conservative about Tolarus's story, except Powell, who seemed much more inclined than the rest of the crew to believe the Atlantean's version.

"It's hard to tell whom we can trust after all we have been through so far," Daniel had said that a few minutes earlier.

Heather could not agree more; however, she had no better suggestions of other allies at the moment. And seriously, she was in bad need of allies on this damned island.

The head device was in her hands, but Heather didn't need Nathaniel's help to understand Tolarus's simple gesture to follow him along the corridor, which seemed to run endlessly deep into the heart of the mountain.

"Too much walking today," Santino complained after ten minutes of their march in the tunnel. "Now what?"

"He told me he needed our help," Heather replied. "I guess he is going to show us what kind of help he needs."

How different that sounded from Akmenios's proposal? Not much, she was afraid. At least, Tolarus and his people would not feed on her and her crew. *Would they?* She shivered at the thought and dismissed it from her mind.

The fenced end of the corridor, where Tolarus stopped, faced a huge man-made pit. Motioning them with his arm, he urged Heather and her remaining team members to hurry. Surprised by the sight, Heather gaped at the aircraft standing on the well-paved ground of that huge pit.

An Avenger TBM from the renowned Flight 19. *Another one,* Heather deduced

When her astonishment faded, Heather put on her head device, and the Atlantean did the same. Now was the time to know what help Tolarus wanted from them.

"You have the whole collection, don't you?" Heather wondered.

Tolarus chuckled. "Not really. The rest of the fleet is still at the Griseos' headquarters. We captured only two aircraft. One of them we have already lost."

Yes, in an accident that resulted in a heavy toll of dead passengers, Heather thought, but she had to postpone that topic for the time being. What was done was done. "I presume you have a proposal." Heather allowed herself a faint smile, her arms folded. "I'm listening."

"The issue is very simple," said Tolarus. "We need to get this plane out of the island to tell the whole world we exist. All humans should send their armies to expel those aliens from the whole planet."

"What are you thinking of? Send a message to all the world nations, asking for an invasion?"

"By humans? We're welcome to such an invasion."

Heather found herself imagining aircraft carriers besieging the island, marines storming the underground headquarters, capturing Akmenios and his people. That would be an ideal scenario to end this situation.

But would they let the Atlanteans rule their island? A worse scenario popped into her head, involving Tolarus and his cannoneers defending their mountainous area against the US marines...

What are you thinking of now, Heather? She was pulled back to reality. How could she be so concerned about such futuristic consequences while she had no idea how to get the hell out of this island in the first place?

"Have you gone somewhere?" Tolarus grinned.

"Not so far, actually." She allowed herself another smile, a wider one this time. "Tell me, how did you manage to get the plane, the old aircraft, past the Storm Shield?"

"As far as I understand, we provided the aircraft with an electromagnetic field that made it 'invisible' to the Shield system," said Tolarus. "It worked just fine, but the problem was about controlling the aircraft outside the Shield."

Heather weighed his words. "You need someone to fly this plane. Am I right?"

"Exactly." Tolarus nodded. "This *plane*, as you call it, is working just fine. But we are not sure we have the right men to steer such a craft in the air manually and reach safe lands. It's the only craft we have left and we can't afford its loss this time."

Heather glanced at Powell before she turned back to Tolarus. "Let's assume we have the right men for this job, what are they supposed to do after they pass the Shield?"

"What was I just saying? Inform your world of our location."

"What if they can't locate this island after they leave? Those aliens have manipulated our satellites, making your island invisible."

"We have taken that into consideration, don't worry. All we need is someone to fly this plane to the right place."

Could this be true? Suddenly, escaping this island became possible.

"When will you be ready?" Heather couldn't wait to see this happen.

"We are indeed. When will you be?"

Heather resisted a strong desire to embrace the Atlantean. "Let me have a little talk with my team."

* * *

For the second time, Heather briefed her team about a conversation she had had with Tolarus. All eyes were on

Powell after Heather had finished. He was the man of the hour, the man who would decide their fate on this island.

"I can do this." Powell straightened his back. "I just need to have a close look to check the engine, fuel, weaponry, and radar."

Heather glanced at Tolarus, who stood aside silently, unable to understand their conversation. "There will be no problem with that."

"So, if I get this right," Linda slowly said. "Powell is going to take the plane out of this island and return home to report everything going on here to the US authorities."

"That's right." Heather nodded to Linda then turned to the rest. "Any more queries?"

"Yes." Linda cleared her throat. "How many of us will accompany Powell on this flight?"

The question struck all of them except Powell, who had no problem with this issue of course. Heather wondered how she didn't think about that. When she shot Powell an inquisitive look, he said, "This bomber can take two passengers in addition to the pilot. It's up to you to decide."

They all looked at each other, each waiting for the other to speak first.

"I'll stay. Anybody else?" Heather looked at the rest of her team. "Except you. You're not allowed to leave without me," she said to Nathaniel who was surely unhappy with that decision.

An awkward silence descended over the place. It was clear everybody was eager to reserve one of the two remaining tickets on the next flight, yet each one of them seemed embarrassed to speak up first.

"Okay, let's all be upfront and transparent," said Daniel. "We are all dying to leave the damned Triangle, right?"

Looking down, Linda, Susan, Santino, Walter, and Jay nodded silently.

"Fine," Daniel said impassively. "We will draw for it, unless we can agree on those two who are going to join Powell."

Heather didn't like the notion of splitting the team. But wasting those two precious chances of salvation wouldn't make any sense.

She knew for sure that Linda and Santino, the newlyweds, wouldn't leave unless they did it together. As for Daniel, she didn't want him to leave her alone in this situation. At moments of panic, he was the only one on her team able to keep his composure and think logically, yet she wouldn't force him to stay if he didn't want to. *He has a wife and a daughter waiting for his return.* Most probably, it would be two of those three: Susan, Walter, and...

Suddenly, an alarming siren rang loudly, startling them all.

"What the hell is going on?" Heather bellowed at Nathaniel, who in turn translated her question to Tolarus. The Atlantean, who wasn't wearing the head device, answered Nathaniel.

"A humanoid breach," Nathaniel told her.

"Oh no! Not again!" While she was harboring a faint hope she might forget those gray faces, they insisted on following her and her team. "What is the extent of this breach? Are they sending their—"

Heather was interrupted by a huge explosion, which literally shook the mountain. The floor of the paved corridor rocked and sand started to trickle down from the ceiling. The Atlantean panicked as he waved to them, crying out in his language.

"We must run away from here!" Nathaniel hollered, and indeed, it was quite a distance to dash through. But what options did they have amidst the falling stones?

All team members sprinted through the corridor. A second louder explosion almost deafened Heather, the earthquake more serious this time, cracking both the corridor floor and ceiling. More sand was falling through the cracked ceiling, forcing the fleeing crew to keep their heads down.

Please! Please! Please! Don't fall down now! Despite the sand flowing through the ceiling fissures, she couldn't help but to peek upwards. That corridor could become a tomb instantly at any moment.

Her pounding heart was almost torn apart, her legs failing her. Possibilities of reaching the end of this corridor before its collapse were diminishing every second.

"Come on, Heather!" Daniel firmly gripped her by the hand, urging her to move forward.

"I can't—" Heather gasped. Talking required an extra effort she couldn't afford at the moment.

"You can't slow down now!" Daniel cried. "We're almost there!"

His pull gave her some momentum to resume her run. However, she was slowing him down. *Oh my God! Linda!* Amid the clamor, Heather recognized her scream and dared to glance back. Because of the floor cracks,

Linda stumbled and fell on the floor, unnoticed by her teammates in this chaos.

"Linda has fallen!" Heather cried as she stopped and turned to her.

"I will get her." Walter, who was one step ahead of Heather and Daniel, returned to aid Linda and help her get up and pushed both Daniel and Heather forward with firm hands. "Go! Go! Go!"

"Come on, Heather!" Daniel hollered, almost dislocating her wrist to force her to start running again.

A third explosion shook the corridor, the worst one so far. The floor was cracking open everywhere beneath their feet. Heather felt she was going to be swallowed into the heart of the mountain at any moment.

"Oh my God!" Heather almost fainted when a massive rock fell just in front of her. Now, the faltering ceiling was not just pouring down sand on their heads. The sight of falling rocks ahead made it obvious they didn't have much time remaining before this corridor collapsed.

A thunderous crackling banged behind her, mixed with horrifying screams that lasted only for a second. She feared to know what happened, but she couldn't help looking back. The terrifying scene froze her legs.

"Noooo!" Heather yelled, staring at the colossal rocks that had buried both Walter and Linda.

"There is nothing we can do for them, Heather!" Daniel dragged her.

"No!" She punched Daniel in the shoulder and yanked her hand from his palm to check the rubble. "We can still get them out. Help me push these rocks!"

"Stop this nonsense, Heather!" Daniel grabbed her by the arm. "You are getting us all killed this way! Can't you see? The damned mountain is collapsing!"

No, she couldn't see. She couldn't stand the idea. Yesterday it was Kenji, Joshua, and Kenneth, today Linda and Walter. Again, she was losing members of her team and *again* she was helpless.

"What the hell are you both doing?" Powell turned to them, falling rocks separating him from Heather and Daniel. "Get out of here!"

"Move your feet!" Daniel urged Heather. Resisting him wasn't her intention, but her cramped legs were not helping.

"Move! Move! Move!"

Having no idea how Powell made his way back through this deadly passage, Heather found him right in front of her and Daniel. The marine grabbed Heather by the hand and threw her over his shoulder. "Don't look back! Run!" He cried at Daniel as he dashed as fast as he could in the cracking corridor.

A few meters separated Powell and Heather from the light. She could hear her colleagues' yelling voices as they hurried Powell up. "Shit!" Powell growled, a shower of rocks falling just before the corridor entrance, almost blocking the only exit. He put Heather down saying, "You can make it through this opening!" He pointed to the only spot of air left by the fallen stones. The only way to pass through was to crawl. "Move it! These stones won't stand for long!"

The idea of creeping below these rocks was terrifying, but the light beaming through this rabbit hole together with Powell's yell urged her to continue going forward. The rocks above scrubbed her head as she crawled, small stone particles landing on her, making her scream as she recalled the sight of rocks piling over her friends.

"Keep moving, Heather!" Powell's voice came from behind her. He pushed her feet to move on.

"Give me your hand, Heather!" It was Daniel's voice from the other side. She reached out with one arm and pushed herself with the other. When Daniel's hand caught her, she stretched the other arm, closed her eyes, and let herself be dragged outside the corridor into the open air.

She was gasping, sweating, and sobbing. "Come on!" Daniel helped her get back up on her feet. "We're almost there!"

Almost? She came back to her senses while Tolarus was pulling Powell out through the hole. The van-like aircraft, which had brought them up the mountain, was luckily still in its place.

"Into the aircraft!" Nathaniel translated Tolarus's loud outcry. There was nothing ahead but the mountain edge. Nobody needed an invitation to survive.

From inside the craft, Heather watched the devastation of the Atlantean colony. The mountains were bombarded by huge missiles falling from the sky. Many similar crafts fled the collapsing mountains, carrying Atlanteans inside.

"Watch out!" Powell hollered.

Barely missing their aircraft, another missile resumed its course until it reached its final destination at the mountain, detonating in a huge explosion that quavered the craft with its shock waves.

A cloud of dust and smoke covered the entire Atlantean valley. Heather kept her eyes fixed on the stunned Tolarus, who was watching his people's last refuge turn into one huge rubble pile. His cry didn't even need a translation from Nathaniel. It was pure grief, pure fury.

"All is over now," Jay muttered as he looked at the collapsed mountains. Heather wished she could lie and disagree, but she couldn't. Their only hope to leave this island was buried beneath the largest pile of rocks she had ever seen.

27. Mind Blown

Five teammates were dead in this damned mission so far.

It was supposed to be a scientific expedition to reveal the secret behind the mysterious disappearance events in the Bermuda Triangle. Many theories had been postulated based on scientific assumptions, and that was why the government had sent a team of scientists and engineers; the best in their specialties she knew. She had taken part in their selection for the Bermuda unit a few years ago.

She had taken part in sending them to their doom.

For the hundredth time in a single hour, Heather rolled on her mattress, trying to sleep in some Atlantean safe house after one of her worst ever days. She had thought of the first day in Bermuda as the worst in her life, but seriously, she should have waited for the second day to judge properly. *Oh God! Two days!* Two unbelievably long days that had devastated her physically, emotionally, and even mentally.

The room had no windows for the sunlight to stream through, as the case was in most of the rooms in the heart of the eastern mountains. She surmised it was close to sunset. The brutal bombardment of the northern and western mountains had lasted for three hours. *Three whole hours.* She had watched those mountains collapse, the green plains covered with debris, rubble and, dust. She and the few remaining of her team had to stay in the aircraft with Tolarus, waiting for the gray cloud to dissipate. But the surrounding air was not clear yet. Landing on such a terrain meant they escaped from being crushed by mountain rocks to die by suffocation.

"Heather," Susan whispered. "Try to sleep."

Heather rolled to the other side to face Susan, who lay on a mattress next to hers. "Am I making so much noise?" Heather whispered, trying not to wake up the rest of the sleeping team. Nobody had slept properly in the last forty-eight hours. Those damned gray humanoids had left them on a plain floor on the first day.

"Your breath is heavy and you roll around too much," Susan said softly. "Let it go, Heather. You're burning yourself out."

Heather allowed a pale smile to escape. Susan continued, "I know you feel responsible for the whole team, but you're burdening yourself beyond your capacity. We all feel grief for those who left us, but there was nothing we could have done for them."

"Thanks, Sue." Heather appreciated Susan's attempt to lift her mood, hoping this would make her sleep at last.

Heather rolled again to her preferred side to sleep on. She took one deep breath, trying to relax. All her trouble was because of those gray-faced aliens. *Those liars.* That Akmenios blabbed too much about his race's peaceful nature, unlike the *homines* who had the lust for power. That rascal had filled her mind with his bullshit.

No, he's not a rascal. He's a killer. A cannibal.

Escaping the island was on the top of her wish list. Now she would add something else: watching Akmenios's head crushed under the same massive rock that had buried Linda and Walter.

"You know what I would do if I could turn the clock back?" said Heather without looking at Susan.

"You would have refused the Bermuda mission, no doubt," Susan replied. Heather could imagine the smile on Susan's face.

"I would have hired marines for this expedition." Heather closed her eyes. "Except for Powell, we are all useless here."

* * *

In his subterranean headquarters, Akmenios monitored the attack aftermath.

"We should postpone the hunters' raid," said Cudelios.

It was not the scenario Akmenios had planned. He wanted to take advantage of the chaotic state of the Atlanteans after the crushing assault, but the attack had consumed too much energy far exceeding their expectations. Razing those mountains to the ground required more missiles than originally estimated, and hence, power reached serious levels at their side. It would be unwise to deplete their scarce energy reserves.

"You're right," Akmenios seconded. "Which gives us some time to have another session with the hominum." He gazed at Burke, who was still tied up in his seat, fidgeting.

"Don't you think we should untie him for a while?" asked Cudelios. "Keeping him tied on this seat for a long time is adding to his restlessness. This may impair his mental focus."

Akmenios knew what his deputy meant by impairing Burke's mental focus. It might produce blurred scenes from Burke's mind.

"His tired mind will decrease his chances of invading mine, like in the previous session," said Akmenios. "This time, I will finally retrieve all I want to know, whatever the defenses implanted by the Shomrunk are."

Akmenios held the two upgraded head devices and walked slowly towards Burke. "Ready for another session, hominum?" he asked his prisoner in English.

"My name is Burke," he taunted. "Burke, you jerk."

"Am I supposed to find that funny or irritating, Burke?"

"You're not supposed to find it anything because you're too stupid to understand that."

"You really don't mean this, unless you don't know what the word 'stupid' really means." Akmenios adjusted the head device on Burke's head. "You know how I define stupidity? Having a brain like yours and not fully utilizing it. Your race is the stupidest I have ever seen, Burke. You barely use one-millionth of your brain powers."

Akmenios put his own gadget on as well and looked at his deputy, who waited for his superior's mark to start connecting the two minds.

"And that's what happens when you possess unexploited resources," Akmenios went on. "Someone else comes and uses them for his own benefit. Don't you think it's fair?"

"Go to hell," Burke snarled.

"You'll never learn," said Akmenios. "Such emotional reactions consume much of your brain power." He turned to Cudelios. "Now."

* * *

Like the previous time, Burke had no idea how it had happened. He just knew it did.

The last thing he recalled was that he had been sitting on this cold metallic chair for long hours. *Damn!* Those humanoids were so cruel. His buttocks were sore.

Now, there was no chair. He was on his feet, untied, standing in a dark familiar office. He stared at the desk stacked with books and papers and grabbed a plastic name tag thrown on the floor.

"Dr. Jeff Burke, College of Earth and Energy, School of Geology and Geophysics," he read out loud.

"Did you miss your office, Dr. Burke?"

Akmenios's voice came from behind him. Burke suddenly found him standing by the window hidden by the curtains.

"So, I'm sleeping once again," Burke scoffed. "And now, we are inside my mind."

"Your body sleeps biologically, but your brain never sleeps."

At last, Burke spotted the light switch beside his desk. He flicked it three times, but nothing changed. Why were his places always dark in his mind?

"So, why did you bring us to my office?" Burke wondered. "What's so particular about this place?"

"It's not about the place, Burke. What matters is the time."

Time? Burke's eyes opened wide. He rushed to his desk, trying to find any indicator of the current date, a newspaper, a paper calendar, or an old cell phone in the drawer. Last time he had been in the university was...

"Nine years ago," Akmenios completed Burke's train of thought. Burke was not that astonished after all he had experienced so far.

"I scanned your memories, Burke," said Akmenios. "Do you remember what I told you before about your 'imaginary' relative? That implanted memory did not exist in your mind nine years ago."

When did Akmenios scan his memories? They had just started their session a few moments earlier.

"This upgraded device is more powerful, it even exceeded my expectations," Akmenios answered Burke's unspoken queries. "Your mind has never been this transparent to me."

"You brought me nine years back when somebody implanted this memory inside my mind. Right?" Burke ignored Akmenios's bragging and tried to focus on understanding what was going on.

"You're not that stupid when you use your mind," said Akmenios.

Again Burke ignored the gray humanoid's comment and said, "So, what do you expect? Someone knocking on the door, greeting me with a smile, *Hi there, I'm the Shomrunk and I want you to go to Bermuda to find your imaginary relative.* Is this really your plan to find him?"

"It will happen more or less like that," said Akmenios. "From what I see in your memories, the Shomrunk is going to contact you at any second now."

At any second? That seemed so close. The notion of meeting that mysterious creature face-to-face unnerved Burke, to be honest.

"Don't worry," said Akmenios. "He won't harm you. You will see his reflection in your memory, not him in person."

"He won't harm me as you will." Burke feigned a smile. "What does he look like? Don't tell me he is as ugly as you."

"Most probably you haven't seen his real form. He can take any shape he wants."

Any shape? That would open a long list of shocking possibilities. "He might have been one of my acquaintances and I had never noticed that."

"He could have been your father, but you would have never known. Even if he showed you his real face, he wouldn't allow you to remember."

His father? That would be interesting indeed. *Wait a minute. Some details don't add up.* "Then what's the point of scanning my memories if the ones we're looking for have been deleted anyway?"

"You are not bad for a hominum," said Akmenios. "Nobody can totally erase any memory from your brain. From our studies on your race, your brains keep everything; every memory, every person, every feeling, every conversation, every word. Recalling those memories depends on where your brain places them. What the Shomrunk does is transfer certain memories to the hidden chambers I told you about before."

"So, we are now in one of those *hidden chambers.*" Burke exhaled heavily. "The one that harbors the moment when the Shomrunk contacts me."

Akmenios nodded. "If my calculations are correct, he is contacting you in—"

A knock on the office door cut the humanoid off.

"Damn!" Burke rubbed his head with both hands. "Are you sure it's him?"

Burke had never noticed any reactions on Akmenios's face during any of their previous conversations, but now he could swear he saw an expression of tension in the humanoid's narrow eyes and mouth.

Another knock on the door.

"Don't you want to open the door yourself?" Burke addressed Akmenios.

"Just ask him to come in." Akmenios lowered his voice, his narrow eyes glued to the door.

"What?" Burke scoffed. "Scared?"

"Do it."

"You're either a coward or a liar. What happened to the crap you've just told me about?"

Akmenios turned to Burke without saying a word. Burke continued, "His reflection won't harm, remember?"

"I'm not quite sure. You feel good now?"

"Not quite sure of what?"

"That it's just his reflection."

"Oh shit! What do you mean?"

Burke almost stopped breathing when all of a sudden, the lights were on. Someone turned the squeaky doorknob, slowly pushing the door open, confident footsteps clicking on the floor.

"You were expecting me, weren't you?"

The familiar voice petrified Burke, a shiver running down his spine. Right now, he was staring at the last face he expected to see.

Heather's face.

28. A Form of Life

"What? As if you both have seen a ghost," Heather taunted.

At a loss for words, Burke gaped at her as she stood by the doorstep. *What the hell does this mean?* He shot Akmenios an inquisitive look, yet the humanoid was standing still.

"You don't remember we knew each other a long time ago, do you?" Heather addressed Burke, a playful smile on her face.

A long time ago? What sort of a silly joke is this? And what happened to the gray freak? Burke contemplated the astounded humanoid, who seemed to have feelings after all. *Why doesn't he say anything?*

"It's not her." Akmenios's creaky voice sounded weaker than any time before.

"Should I feel better now?" Burke looked from Akmenios to Heather. "Because this means it is...*him?*" *Please say no. Please tell me that all Akmenios's folly about the so-called Shomrunk is nothing but a delusion.*

"Himself." Akmenios just squashed Burke's faint hopes.

"Not his reflection?" Burke asked, his eyes still on the *shape* of Heather. "But how?"

Heather laughed. "I can imagine your confusion, Burke. Even this Griseo thinks he understands what's going on, but he really doesn't."

Griseo? Burke peered at Akmenios, part of him hoping that she wasn't referring to the gray humanoid. Because if it was true that Akmenios didn't understand, then Burke could safely presume he was in some really deep shit.

Suddenly, he burst into laughter.

"You're not just a coward and a liar," Burke sneered at Akmenios's helplessness. "You're also a jerk."

The gray-faced humanoid did not seem offended by Burke's mocking words, his eyes fixed on Heather, or what looked like Heather. *He is not in charge. The gray jerk is terrified,* Burke reflected. Quite a pleasant sight for him.

"He's a jerk indeed." Heather nodded with a wicked smile. "Actually, I want to thank him for the power he has provided me with."

Both Burke and Akmenios stared at her in astonishment. "The head device?" the humanoid spoke this time.

Heather chuckled. "The upgraded version is much better. I never felt my connection to Burke's mind that strong."

It's not Heather for sure. Burke was still trying to grasp the situation. But why her? "It seems you're trying to hide your real ugly face."

Heather laughed again. "My real face? Akmenios didn't tell you, did he?"

"Tell me what?" Burke turned to the gray-faced freak.

"A Shomrunk doesn't have a face," Akmenios said, his eyes still glued on Heather's.

Burke was aware he was asleep, aware he was inside his own mind, aware of the heat torching his brain. *A Shomrunk with no real face? Seriously?*

"What the hell are you?" Burke scanned Heather from head to toe. She was flawless, same slender shape, same height, and same pretty face. Everything looked like her, except for the weird smile and the seductive voice.

"You see, Burke." Heather slowly approached him. "This universe harbors many forms of life, and I'm just another form that you'll never understand."

Instinctively, Burke stepped back. "What form?"

He swallowed when she stood right before him. "An unusual form to you. A form that has no body of flesh and blood like yours."

"What are you made of, then?" Burke warily asked.

Heather, or the Shomrunk in Heather's form, lowered her eyes. Obviously, she was giving her answer a thought before she lifted her gaze, looking at him again. "I'm not sure if I can simplify this for you; I'm like a quantum of energy, a wave or a force that is obsolete on its own, but given the proper medium, you'll see and feel it."

A quantum of energy? A wave? A force? What was she talking about?

"I told you; you would never understand." Heather arched one eyebrow. Her mind—the Shomrunk's mind, if *it* had any—was connected to his. That was how she was reading his thoughts. *That's why she's answering me*, Burke realized. This conversation was not *verbally* happening, it was not a real one. Their minds were connected, and somehow, the transmission of thoughts was not one-way.

"Have I told you that you are smarter than the rest I've met so far?" she scoffed. The proximity of such a *creature,* which might tear up Heather's skin to show its true ugly core, made him flinch.

"Your metaphor," Burke tried to collect his thoughts, "is not correct. You're not like a quantum of energy. You're a *form of life* that is only alive in the proper medium."

"Exactly." For a second, Heather's excited reaction was frightening.

"And if I get this right, this *proper* medium is a human body." Burke swallowed again.

"Not necessarily." Heather shook her head, and then glanced at Akmenios with her scary smile. "It could be a Griseo's body." She turned again to Burke. "It could be an animal body as well. The question is: which is better for me? Live as a human or as a dog?"

"It depends on what you're looking for. Do you seek an impervious shell to protect your *life form*? Then, you have many animals on this planet with a physically stronger body to protect you."

"What's the point of spending my life barking or roaring in a jungle? Can you imagine a mind-reading elephant? That would be absurd. I need a brain, and not so many creatures on this planet have an advanced brain like yours." A smile played about her lips when she asked, "Now, do you think you really comprehend what I am?"

"You're more or less like a virus." Burke dared to voice his thoughts.

"A virus?" Heather echoed, a tone of disapproval in her voice. "Speaking of metaphors, this is so irrelevant."

"How so? You need a host to be active."

"I don't flow in the air in a dormant crystalline phase, looking for a host to invade and multiply inside its cells."

"Then, what are you outside a host?"

"Nothing. I don't exist."

That took Burke aback. Her statement was brief and clear, no metaphors in it, but it didn't make any sense. Not existing meant dead. And if dead, how could she find a host in the first place?

"Your knowledge about life forms is limited to the earthly ones you studied before. I'm not a separate species, Burke. I have already been living as a human for more than a hundred years. This is something a virus can't do."

Burke was lost at this point. "This doesn't make any sense." He turned to Akmenios. "What about your war with the Shomrunks who depleted your planet resources? Or was this another one of your lies?"

"I didn't lie." Akmenios stared at Heather. He could say more, Burke knew, but for some reason the humanoid didn't.

"I tell you what he's afraid to say in front of me," Heather addressed Burke, giving Akmenios a scornful look. "We fought the Griseos indeed."

"In their bodies," Burke concluded. "You took over their bodies to be able to fight them."

"What's the meaning of force if there is nothing to impact?" Heather shrugged. "You, humans, devour other animals to survive. Griseos absorb your energy to survive. We have our own way to survive. *C'est la vie.*"

That awkward version of Heather didn't fail to impress.

"I told you," she scoffed. "I have been a human more than you have."

Burke leaned his back against his desk, his head down. It was the worst nightmare he had ever had. From Akmenios's previous conversations, Burke imagined the Shomrunk in many conceptions, but he had never gone that far with his imagination.

"What are you doing here?" Burke lifted his head up. "I'm not your host, am I?"

Her face was closer when she leaned forward, her warm breath brushing his cheeks. "You keep impressing me," she said in a seductive tone before looking over her shoulder at the gray humanoid. "Even he doesn't understand what's going on."

As he was during most of this encounter, Akmenios stood there helpless and clueless like a mindless statue. *Nothing smart to say, huh?*

When Heather turned to him with the alluring smile she wore, Burke wished she had been the real one. "How do you know you're not my host?" she asked playfully.

"If I were so, I wouldn't know it in the first place, right?"

"Absolutely. There will be no you. It will be me."

There will be no me. Burke tried not to overthink it. "Then, what the hell are you doing here?"

"Calm down. You haven't even seen me yet. This is just an extremely tiny part of me inside your mind."

"Can you exist in more than one body simultaneously?" Burke was terrified when he pondered the consequent possibilities.

She chuckled. "I wish I could. Unfortunately, I would be dissipated into nothingness if I tried that. All I did was just embed an almost negligible part of me inside your mind; a very tiny part that wouldn't destroy me, yet sufficient to help me stay connected to your thoughts. I wouldn't be able to control your subconscious to affect your decision," she peered at Akmenios, a gloating smile on her face, "until he brought that upgraded device, which gave more life to this tiny part of me." She slowly approached Akmenios, like a predator toying with its prey "And you know what the best part is? His mind is also connected."

"You can't access my mind," said Akmenios, and Burke knew he was lying. "I added more power to my mind's defenses—"

"To prevent Burke from breaching it," Heather put in. "Like what happened in your last session, right? Do you realize that I'm seeing through your mind now?"

"No way," Akmenios insisted.

"The power you upgraded your device with made your mind immune against this human, but not against me, Akmenios. Not against me. Your stupid assistant has detected you're in trouble. Instead of waking you up, he is providing your device with more power."

"You are just trying to manipulate my thoughts, but I won't let you do that." The humanoid was cornered, and

Burke could only wonder what the Shomrunk might do with him. *What will she do with me after she is done with him?*

"Let's make it more convincing." Heather grinned. Suddenly, she looked like a blurred image before she turned into a gray humanoid, a bit shorter than Akmenios. *His assistant.*

That was no Shomrunk. That must be a demon. Demons did exist.

The "assistant" spoke to Akmenios in his language for a couple of minutes, and Akmenios nodded without saying a word. For the gray humanoid, there was no escape, but that wasn't the case for Burke, who was closer to the door than the Shomrunk. A crazy thought crossed his mind.

"Don't be silly." The assistant turned to Burke, speaking to him in English. "Spring to the door? Seriously? And then what? How far do you think you'll get? We're inside your mind, Burke. You can't run away from me."

How could you lie to somebody who read your thoughts?

"What have you done to him?" Burke cleared his throat, contemplating Akmenios who stood there petrified.

"I was just clearing your way." The Shomrunk's grin grew wide as *it* slowly walked toward Burke. His turn was coming now.

"My way for what?" Burke's heart throbbed.

Again, the assistant's form blurred like a reflection on the water surface and turned into Heather. The same playful look on her face muddled his feelings. He was both charmed and scared to death.

"To save us, Burke," she said softly. "You're our last hope."

"How can I save you? I can't even save myself." *Don't be a fool, Burke. She's manipulating your mind.*

"Send the coordinates of our location to the US Navy. Let them send the troops to sweep those aliens off the island and take us back home," she said warmly. The abrupt transition in her tone made him more confused. And what coordinates was she talking about? How would he send them? He had no clue if...

"The screen, Burke," she interrupted his thoughts. "The one in Akmenios's room. I know you're a genius and you'll figure out how to use it."

Burke took a while to ascertain he correctly understood what she meant by Akmenios's screen. From his metallic chair, he might have had a glance at that screen, but he didn't remember anything meaningful except Akmenios and his assistant tapping on symbols Burke had never seen before.

"Don't worry about the symbols. I told you; you're a genius." She wrapped her arms around his neck, his heart pounding hard in fear and...

It's not her, he reminded himself, unable to stand any more of this farce. "Stop it." He dared to push her hands away.

"Much more resistance than I expected." Heather tilted her head. "Let's make it more convincing, again," she hissed as she stepped back. She looked so creepy when her shape changed for the third time into a taller person.

"No way." Burke gaped at this familiar face.

"I'm sure you don't remember our first encounter," said the Shomrunk in his new form. "You won't remember this one as well."

29. The Signal of Hope

Burke opened his eyes.

Surprisingly, he found himself alone in Akmenios's chamber. The last thing he recalled was Akmenios putting the mind device over his head to start another mind connecting session. He wondered why he hadn't started the session yet.

And by the way, why was Burke alone in the chamber? Those humanoid bastards had left him tied to his damned metallic chair for...

Wait a minute. He now realized that his hands and feet were free. What was going on?

Burke scanned the room as he felt that something was wrong. Akmenios was testing him, or worse, setting a trap for him. Pondering all possibilities behind leaving him on his own in the watch room, Burke couldn't find a rational explanation.

A couple of minutes passed and nothing happened. *They want to see what I'm going to do if I break free*, Burke surmised. A futile idea in his opinion, but why not have some fun? He kept scrutinizing the chamber with his eyes, looking for a weapon, a gadget, or anything that might be useful, but the room was almost bare. All he found was the two metal chairs, the table with the head gadgets on it, and this huge screen with the incomprehensible symbols...

Suddenly, he had a strange feeling. He could see a pattern in those symbols. With cautious steps, he walked toward the screen and gently swiped it. More symbols appeared on the screen in a language he did not understand, and still, Burke's eyes could see the pattern of these symbols. The gray-faced humanoids must have messed with his head in his sleep; there was no other explanation. *They are testing my intellectual capabilities.* Well, he should prove to them how wrong it was to leave him on the loose to use his hacking skills.

"I'm a genius and I know it," he muttered, excited by what he was doing on this screen. His fingers slid gracefully on its surface, more symbols and 3D shapes appearing and vanishing. Regardless of what those humanoids had done to his mind, he wouldn't miss such a chance.

"Stop!" Akmenios's creaky scream came from behind him.

Burke didn't think of even glancing over his shoulder. His message to the US Navy with his location coordinates was almost done. The last thing he needed at this crucial moment was a sort of distraction.

"No!" The gray humanoid shoved Burke, who lost his balance and fell on his back.

"Too late, Grayface." Burke grinned despite his back pain. "It's already sent."

Burke watched Akmenios's assistant hurry into the chamber and join his superior, who was busy swiping and tapping the huge screen rapidly.

"You were right." Burke rose, a smirk on his face. "I'm not that stupid when I use my mind."

"I had enough of you." Akmenios pulled Burke by his shirt. "You must tell me how and why."

"You can't be serious," Burke teased the humanoid. "Do you really need my answer? Come on! Read my mind, Grayface."

Akmenios's eyes were fixed on Burke for a while. "You weren't lying about it."

That confused Burke for real. "I beg your pardon. Lying about what?"

"You really think you were trying to send a message to your headquarters," said Akmenios.

Shit! Think? Trying? What the hell is he talking about?

"You have no idea you were about to bring all the inhabitants of this planet to their doom," Akmenios continued. "Somehow, you managed to deal with our language and composed a message that includes our location, but why? Why were you sending it across the galaxies?"

"Across the galaxies?" Burke's jaw dropped, astounded. He wanted to expose the humanoid's claim, but after a second thought, he didn't find a logical reason for Akmenios to lie this time. All circumstances of this incident didn't make sense. "No way! You don't mean I—"

"You weren't addressing your people, hominum," Akmenios interrupted. "You were exposing our location to the Shomrunks. You were sending a message to their planet."

* * *

Heather stood by the mountain edge, watching the devastated Atlantean fields with sorrow. It would take decades for this terrain to restore its original lush green color. She felt she was looking at her miserable future with those ruins at her sight.

"Heather," she heard Tolarus calling from behind her.

"Tolarus." She turned to him. It was the only word she could say without that Atlantean head gadget.

Grinning, Tolarus handed her a head device before he put his own on his head. "Why are you not staying inside with your friends? The air is still dusty here."

"I just thought of changing the view." She could hear her voice in her mind. It was cold. "I have been locked inside chambers most of the time in the last two days."

"Hopefully, you slept well last night."

"Not so well, but it was better than nothing."

Both paused for a while.

"I'm so sorry for your loss," said Tolarus.

When they first met, she had blamed him for the loss of Kenji, Joshua, and Kenneth. Her grudge had even become worsen when she knew he was behind the tragic jet crash. Now, she sympathized with his loss, which was bigger than hers, she had to admit. However, he was the one trying to calm her.

He seemed to be a nice guy after all.

"Thanks. It's me who should offer condolences to you," she said, afraid to ask about the numbers of dead and injured Atlanteans after yesterday's brutal attack.

Tolarus nodded without saying a word. It seemed he didn't want to discuss the horrible event either.

"I thought of seeing you off before I leave," he said after a momentary silence.

"Seeing me off?" Surprised by his approach, a smile slipped from her face. "Where are you going?"

"It was quite a night yesterday." He sighed. "We decided to finish off those Griseos, once and for all."

"Today?" Heather felt the decision a bit rushed. "I'm not a military expert, but don't you need more time to plan before making such a decision?"

"This is the best chance we may have. We know they are low in energy. We must crush them before they restore their defenses."

"And how are you so sure of their energy status?"

"We have never been more vulnerable to their hunting raids than yesterday. With our devastated defenses, we were easy prey. And yet, they didn't attack us."

"This is not enough. Perhaps they had their reasons not to raid yesterday."

His chest heaved as he took his breath. "Listen, Heather. For centuries, we have been struggling to defend ourselves against those monsters. A few decades ago, we directed our attention to developing offensive weapons, and in the last two years in particular, we succeeded in inflicting some serious damage on them, and that held them off a bit. Currently, their raids aren't as frequent as they used to be because now they need much more time to recharge their weapons.

"We knew it would take some time to gain leverage in our war with the Griseos, but after yesterday's massacre, we couldn't take it anymore. We have been preparing ourselves for this day, the day we annihilate those aliens. But we didn't know it would come so soon."

"Most probably, you're leading your men to another massacre," said Heather, "leaving the rest of your people helpless after losing their only hope for protection."

"Don't you get the message, Heather?" He leaned forward nervously. "They tell us they can destroy our little community whenever they want. And let's not fool ourselves; this valley is their cattle farm. They won't slaughter all their cattle at once, otherwise, they'll starve. But we won't live as cattle anymore. We will die like men."

The Atlantean was shaking, raging with fury. She had been through the same feeling after losing her team members. "Both of us want to see those aliens dead. But if we let our emotions drive us, we won't be able to avenge our friends."

"You think we've made this decision only out of fury, but this is not true," he said. "It's last night's developments that urged us to do so."

"What developments?"

"We detected a signal coming from the woods near the western coast. An incomplete long-range signal that didn't pass the outer atmosphere."

"An incomplete long-range what?"

Tolarus grinned. "It's a message that includes the coordinates of this island. It looks like someone is trying to communicate with outer space."

"Oh my God!" A terrifying thought came to her mind. "The Shomrunk."

"What did you say?" The puzzled look on Tolarus's face surprised her.

"Do you really have no idea about him?"

"I never heard about that Shomrunk. What about him?"

"Ah! Long story." Heather told Tolarus all she had heard from Akmenios about the Shomrunk, starting from the war between its race and the Griseos on their planet until the Griseos' search for the lone Shomrunk lurking on Earth.

"So, this Shomrunk adds more trouble to the Griseos," Tolarus mused. "I'm not quite sure if this is good news for us. Anyway, it won't change our plans. Whoever this message sender and its receiver are; this message has given us a clue about the location of the Griseos' headquarters. We presumed it was underground, but we never knew where. Now, we have a point to start from."

"What about the warehouses you said you raided before? Didn't they get you anywhere closer to the headquarters location?"

"No, they didn't. Those warehouses are usually scattered by the coast, to make it easier for Griseos to take your captured crafts from the ocean and keep them there." Tolarus paused for a while, then he continued, "And speaking of captured crafts, we have some interesting news for you and for us as well."

The way he said it gave her hope.

"Moments after sunrise, we sent our sliders to scout the area around the signal. One of them has visually spotted an abandoned orange vehicle near the shore. I guess it belongs to you." The Atlantean smiled.

"The life capsule." Heather was like a lost wanderer who had just found a well in the desert.

"Leaving that vehicle on the loose confirms our assumption that the Griseos are suffering a serious shortage in their power supplies," said Tolarus. "They rarely leave any abandoned vehicles since they use their metallic skeleton as spare parts."

"What about the HG-3? I mean our main craft?" Heather asked eagerly. "We left it a few miles away from the coast."

Tolarus shook his head. "I have no idea. We didn't inspect the area that far."

She clutched the hope she saw in the horizon. She just needed a little more time to weave a well-crafted plan.

"When will you start your march?" she asked.

Tolarus tilted his head, an inquisitive look on his face. "Tell me: what're you planning to?"

"I don't have a plan yet. I need to consult my teammates to devise a good one."

30. March of the Atlanteans

For some reason, those civilians found it hard not to stare at Tolarus while he was wearing his astronaut suit. Standing ahead of his troops at the mountain foot, the Atlantean seemed to be briefing his officers about their commands.

"It's time for war," Heather muttered.

"War?" Standing by her side, Powell scoffed. *The scientist had no idea,* he thought. "The headcount of these men is barely exceeding a hundred and fifty, and you call this war?"

"This is a decisive battle." Heather nodded her chin toward the Atlanteans. "I believe Tolarus has summoned all who can fight."

"This is going to work, right?" Daniel asked, a pale smile on his face. "Our plan, I mean. It's nearing noon, and we're marching under the clear sunlight."

Failure was not an option. "Our plan depends on our Atlantean friends," said Powell. "The more havoc they'll create, the better our chances to go unnoticed."

Tolarus approached them, holding his helmet in one hand and the head device in the other.

"Let me take it from here." Powell snatched Heather's gadget and adjusted it on his head. The leader of the scientific crew didn't seem to have any problem with that.

"So, you're the fighter of the group." Tolarus grinned at Powell.

Powell nodded. "I need a weapon."

"I can spare a few soldiers to escort you."

"Sending soldiers with us is a good idea, but I still need a weapon."

Tolarus pulled the cylindrical weapon strapped to his belt, handed it to Powell, and pointed at a dotted part near its edge. "Press here to unleash hell on your target."

Powell might have held baby guns in his childhood lighter than this weapon. He aimed at a rock forty feet away and destroyed it with one shot.

Tolarus smiled. "Not bad for starters."

Powell didn't find anything impressive about his shot. "I just wanted to get used to its feeling and weight in my hands. How do you think those aliens will react?"

"Assuming their defenses are not fully charged yet, they will send their guards to defend the eastern warehouse we're headed to. Team beta will be bombing the signal point at the same time."

"Are you sure of your explosives range? We have no idea how deep down their headquarters is."

"We're not going to bomb the surface. We'll use our mine drills to bury our explosives deep down their throats."

"Good." *Provided that the aliens would grant us enough time to dig that hole above their headquarters.* "Such noise will cover our march to the shore."

"Our double attack is intended to cause much more than just *noise.* All those soldiers you see are marching today to cleanse our island from all gray faces on it."

The Atlantean was fearless, Powell would give him that, but his plan of attack was a bit rushed. What if Tolarus's assumptions were wrong? What if those aliens managed to charge their defenses to full power? What if those *Griseos* still had more tricks up their sleeves?

"What about you?" Tolarus interrupted Powell's thoughts. "Do you know what to do when you reach your orange vehicle?"

Powell realized that his concern about his march with Heather's team to the shore should be much more than about the Atlanteans' attack. Nobody could confirm if the HG-3 was still there in the ocean. And if it wasn't found there, nobody could ensure that the life capsule could stand the Storm Shield. *The whole thing is rushed,* Powell thought. But it could be their only chance to escape from this cursed island.

"We'll take our chances," said Powell. "Just hold those gray bastards off as long as you can."

Tolarus's answer was a confident grin. The Atlantean removed the head device and turned to his soldiers, yelling and barking orders at them. Five men split off the Atlantean company and strode to Tolarus, who spoke to them for a while before he put on the head device again and addressed Powell, "These men will escort you to the shore, just in case you face any trouble."

Powell hoped he wouldn't need those Atlanteans, but he was grateful to Tolarus anyway.

"I'll let you keep your head gadget, but after you pass it to Heather," Tolarus said. "There's something I want to tell her."

* * *

Akmenios glanced at the sleeping Burke, who was tied once again to the metallic chair. He had asked Cudelios to make sure the hominum was well tied this time so that nothing would distract them for the time being. Yesterday's incident needed an explanation.

There was something wrong about the last mind-connecting session. All Cudelios had told him was that there was an almost successful attempt to breach his mind. *Almost?* Akmenios was unable to prove it. For some reason, he could not recall anything about that session. He could only *wish* that Cudelios had been right.

What about Burke, the hominum? Akmenios had scanned his mind and found nothing useful. *He is not just useless. The fool was about to summon all the Shomrunks in this universe and bring them to Earth.* Had it not been for Akmenios, the hominum would have finished the Shomrunk's work.

But what about Akmenios himself? The recordings showed him untying Burke from his seat before leaving him in the room on his own. Was the Shomrunk messing with Akmenios too? What about Cudelios? Had the Shomrunk been controlling him as well?

"Are you done yet?" Akmenios asked his subordinate, who was busy with the mind device.

"Not even close. You have to bear in mind this is the first time we do something like this."

"I wonder why we have never tried this before."

"There was no need to visualize thoughts because simply, every time you were supposed to *read* them."

Cudelios had spent the whole night working on the mind device, trying to extract any memories recorded in the form of waves and convert them to a visual format. Akmenios was not sure how much more *visual* Burke's memories could become.

"I have found a peculiar spike in energy levels in the second half of that session," Cudelios stated. "A spike that was concurrent with your mind breach attempt."

Akmenios pondered what he had just heard. A spike in energy level during a mind-connecting session was something he should worry about. "I remember, from our long experience with human brains, they are not able to produce such energy levels," he said.

"You're talking about normal brains, not this one."

Cudelios was right. The link between Burke and the Shomrunk was still unclear, but its existence was undeniable. It was not a coincidence he could see the Shomrunk's actions with Burke's presence.

"We must know what happened in that session." Akmenios held Cudelios's arm. "I see the Shomrunk's tracks and I can tell he's messing with us."

Cudelios gazed at Burke for a while before he said, "Keeping this hominum here is not a good idea anymore."

Akmenios could not agree more. With the confirmed link between the human and the Shomrunk, Burke's presence became threatening.

"Do we still need anything from his mind right now?" Akmenios asked.

"We have extracted all the memories we need," Cudelios replied. "If I understand you right, I can send him now."

It was inevitable. One day, Burke would have the same final destination of all the humans captured in Bermuda: the bio-energy processing room.

For one last time, Akmenios pondered all possible pros and cons of keeping Burke. He tried everything he could to explore this human's mind, but he never found anything decisive about the Shomrunk. On the other hand, he had his concerns that Burke might have become a backdoor for the Shomrunk. And that left him one last way to get any use out of this human.

"So be it," said Akmenios. "Take him out of here."

Cudelios peered at the yellow flashing screen when the notification came. An urgent message from the eastern warehouse.

"What is it?" Akmenios wondered.

"Homines," his subordinate replied. "Around fifty of them."

"Fifty?" A human raid was the last thing Akmenios expected. Yesterday's bombardment should have crushed those Atlanteans. The missile attack was intended to weaken their forces in the first place, but here they were; the Atlanteans were marching with the biggest force he had ever encountered in this island. In all previous raids, he had never faced more than twenty homines.

"How close are they?" Akmenios asked.

"Fifteen minutes."

"They're so close indeed. How didn't we notice them earlier? What happened to our outposts?"

Cudelios looked his boss straight in the eye without saying a word.

"What?" Akmenios asked.

"We're switching our outposts on and off because we're running low on power. Our reactors are still recovering from yesterday's assault."

His subordinate was blaming him. It was Akmenios who had insisted on that attack despite his assistant's warning. But who could have seen that coming? And that soon?

"So, they think they have seen all we got," said Akmenios.

"No, Akmenios. You will not fire the proton cannon."

"Yes, I will. We have no other option. Otherwise, we're simply surrendering our last main warehouse."

"This procedure may shut all our systems down."

"We can make a shunt from the main western reactor."

"This is not an option, Akmenios. You know very well the main reactor is only to keep the Domus Shield working. We won't risk exposing what we have been hiding for more than a hundred years."

Akmenios knew it was a desperate measure. The main western reactor was dedicated to powering their servers, which had been working for many decades to prevent their island's location from being detected by the outer world. Powered by the same reactor was the Storm Shield that captured all intruding flying or floating objects. Akmenios had been the one insisting on constructing that reactor as a standalone unit to prevent any overlap between it and the rest of the power reactors. He never thought he would regret this decision one day.

"So, what are our alternatives? Do we have enough guards to stop such an attack?" Akmenios wondered.

"It won't be easy without the missiles system, but we have to take our chances."

"Our chances? Do you have any idea about the consequences of losing that site? The balance of power will switch to their favor, and soon they will be besieging us."

"We can't risk shutting down our systems, Akmenios. This may mean our doom for good."

"This is correct, provided that those homines know our location."

"And are you sure they don't? Don't forget those scientists who joined the Atlanteans. They may have given them a clue about our headquarters' location."

"No way. They may have been killed in yesterday's attack even."

"And they may be not. We can't—"

Cudelios was interrupted again, but this time by another yellow flash on the screen.

"What's going on?" Akmenios gazed at the screen. This time, the notification came from the headquarters itself.

Cudelios swiped the screen. "One hundred homines are approaching our headquarters."

The number was shocking, and Akmenios was not prepared for this nightmare. The probability of humans attacking their headquarters was never even considered. "Underground?" Akmenios wanted to make sure.

"No. They are marching on the surface, yet their direction doesn't look promising."

Again, Cudelios was right. Those Atlanteans were up to something big with this double attack.

"We're running out of time, Akmenios. We have to act now," Cudelios urged him.

Nine minutes were all that remained for the Atlanteans to reach the warehouse. At this very moment, Akmenios had to make his decision. A crucial one.

"The warehouse guards must hinder the Atlantean march outside the warehouse itself. We have to win as much time as we can to see what the second attack is up to. And that's before using the proton cannons."

"With our current power levels, we have three proton shots at most. Not sure, if they are enough to defeat all these troops."

Three shots would be enough to roast those hundred Atlanteans. But what about the other fifty at the warehouse?

"This is it," Akmenios said. "Crush those fifty with one shot, and let our guards finish the remnants off—if any remained. Keep the two remaining shots for their main attacking force."

"What about this hominum?" Cudelios pointed at Burke.

"Send him to the reactor." With his eyes, Akmenios followed the two moving yellow masses on the screen. Both of them were approaching their destinations. "And bring us weapons. Every one of us must be ready to fight today."

31. Farewell, Burke

Today, the Atlanteans had nothing to lose.

Hidden in the woods, Tolarus led a hundred men marching toward the Griseos' headquarters, followed by the mine drills they brought with them. According to his estimates, his other distracting forces at the warehouse would be engaging the Griseos in a few minutes. Still, twenty minutes remained for him to reach his destination with his men.

As he expected, he didn't encounter any opposition so far. Hope shone from his men's eyes as they approached their target location. Tolarus was not sure whether the Griseos had spotted their march or not, but even if they did, it seemed their defenses were down. He wished he could know what his men at the warehouse were doing at this moment, yet his orders were strict about cutting all communications between the two forces to avoid exposing their plans to the Griseos. *It will be our day today*, Tolarus believed. He would defeat those aliens once and for all, and avenge the relatives and friends he and his people had lost in yesterday's brutal bombardment.

With a hand gesture, he stopped his men when his ears caught a low humming sound. Ahead of him by fifty yards, a huge column was rising slowly from the ground.

This doesn't look promising, he thought when the column glowed. "Spread out," he urged the men lined up behind him.

But he was too late. The glowing column shone like a small sun.

"Duck!" Tolarus hollered. It was difficult for him to tell what happened, but he found himself thrown ahead by a massive explosion before he hit the ground like a stone. The suit he wore was supposed to protect his body, yet his back was singed by unbearable heat. What was that? Tolarus did not see any missiles or rays coming. Only the glowing column was what he saw, and then boom! Hell opened its gates at the very spot on which his men were standing.

Tolarus could hardly raise his head to check on his troops. Half of his men were burnt by the explosion. "Spread out, I say!" he hollered. "Take the drills away from here!"

He gazed at the column that glowed one more time. "No! Not again! Take cover!" Instantaneously, he realized the absurdity of his warning to his soldiers. How could they evade what they couldn't see?

A second explosion blew most of the remaining men apart. The Atlanteans' terrain was turned into a gigantic furnace. With a torn heart and a shocked mind, Tolarus watched what was probably the last shield for his people burn into ashes in just a few seconds. His men did not have a chance to fire even a single shot at their enemies.

That cursed pillar. Lying on the ground, Tolarus pulled himself together, drew the arm cannon strapped to his back, and aimed. With a single missile, the deadly column was destroyed.

"You!" Tolarus yelled at five surviving cannoneers running away from the site of the massacre. "Halt!" Nobody stopped, though. Either they didn't hear his shout, or they just decided to ignore him. Tolarus rose to his feet and sprinted after those escapees. "I didn't give you the order to retreat!"

Only one soldier turned to Tolarus. "It's over! Everything is over!"

"We won't abandon the battlefield like cowards!" Tolarus pulled his cylindrical gun and shot just behind the other four runaways to draw their attention. They froze in place and turned slowly to face Tolarus.

"Have you lost your mind?" the same soldier chided. "What battlefield are you talking about? There is no battle here. We've just been slaughtered."

Tolarus hurried to the soldier and pulled him by his torn suit. "It's not over yet. We won't leave until we dig with the cursed drills and implant the cursed explosives. This is what we came for."

The soldier shoved Tolarus. "You're insane. Look around. Everything is blown up. Even our explosives. Our men were roasted by our own explosives."

Maybe Tolarus should calm down and listen to him. He tried to scan the burnt terrain, but it was not easy at all to look at the charred corpses of his men. Nausea overwhelmed him and he could hardly stop himself from throwing up in front of his remaining cannoneers.

"There!" Tolarus strode to what seemed to be the last hope. One drill machine standing upright. Miraculously, it was still intact.

Tolarus fidgeted when he checked the machine. *Yes*! It was still working. He glanced at his remaining men, who stared at him as if they were watching a lunatic.

"I'll drive this drill onward myself," Tolarus addressed his men.

"This is not going to work." One of the cannoneers shook his head. "What if we encounter another death column?"

"If they had more, then they would have blown us up by now," Tolarus snapped. "We're so close to our target destination."

"What about the explosives? We don't have any."

"We'll use our cannons instead." Tolarus started moving the drill machine. "Come on!"

* * *

"Burke."

Heather's soft voice woke him up. He rose to find himself lying on grassy terrain. Facing him she stood, a lake a few meters behind her.

"It's you," he said coldly.

She arched an eyebrow. "Who do you mean by *you*?"

"I don't know if it's your species name or how your parents called you, but I know you're the Shomrunk."

She laughed, and he knew it wasn't Heather. Burke had no idea how he figured that out, but his awareness of the Shomrunk's presence was growing.

"My parents didn't call me a Shomrunk." She chuckled. "I never knew I had any parents in the first place."

"A different form of life, huh?" Burke scoffed nervously.

"Interesting." Heather gazed at him for a while before she continued, "In your sleep, you can recall our last encounter, although you forget everything when you wake up."

"I recall it as broken scenes, a series of disjointed images." Burke rubbed his forehead. Being aware he was asleep was an awkward feeling. It was a dream that seemed so real. "What's this place?"

"Can't you really recognize it? I have just removed the wires that ruined the view."

Burke looked around. That house looked so familiar.

"Are we in Maine?" His jaw dropped when he recognized the place. Everything was the same; the small villa, the garden, and the lake. The difference was the absence of wires around the perimeter, as well as those brawny agents.

Heather grinned. "This is where we first met. Remember?"

"Stop messing with me. You know that I know you're not Heather," Burke snapped. "Why do you insist on taking her form in my mind?"

Heather laughed. "I searched your memory. She is the person for whom you bear the most positive feelings."

Positive? Burke never thought of his feelings for Heather. He liked her no doubt, but his feelings did not go any further.

"You lie to yourself," Heather scoffed.

"Stop confusing me," Burke warned her. "Tell me, what the hell we are doing here?"

Heather shrugged. "I just love the lake view."

"You love nothing."

"You don't believe me? I love and I hate just like you, Burke."

"Stop pretending to be human. You have no feelings at all."

"How dare you?" Heather blamed him nicely. "My experience with human feelings is much longer than yours."

She turned her back to him, gazing at the lake, and filling her lungs with the cold breeze. "I'm just like you. I love beauty. I enjoy it."

"Impressive for a virus-like form of life."

"Stop it." She looked annoyed when she looked over her shoulder at him. "You know I have nothing to do with viruses." She gazed again at the lake. "Besides, it's not decent of you to see me off like this."

"Really?" He chuckled. "Are you going to leave me at last?"

"I'm not," she slowly said, her tone making him feel anxious. "You are."

"Me? Leaving?" That didn't bode well. "Where?"

"You didn't hear them in your sleep, but I did." She turned, giving him a crooked smile. "As we speak, they are moving you to your final destination as a source of bio-energy."

"What are you talking about?" he blustered. "Who are they?"

She sighed. "Things went mad while you were tied to your stupid chair. Your friends were found by the Atlanteans, and now those Atlanteans are about to launch a double attack on the Griseos."

Surely, Burke would love to know how Heather and her team were doing, but where the hell was the answer to his damned question? "And where am I in all of this?"

"Sometimes I lose my train of thought." She chuckled. "Akmenios is done with you. He failed to benefit from your mind, so he decided to exploit your body."

"No kidding. You're telling me I am going to be fed to the Griseos, yet you're laughing."

"Hey! Chill out." She tried to cup his cheeks, but he pushed her aside harshly, her smile betraying her carelessness about the situation. "As long as you remain asleep, you will never feel any pain. It's like general anesthesia."

The way she lightly talked about his death drove him mad. "What about you? Will you just dissipate?"

"Don't worry about me. That part of me buried in your mind is so negligible I can do without it." She shrugged. "Besides, this may be a whole new experience for me."

"My death is a whole new experience for you." Burke gnashed his teeth. "Even a parasite would show more concern about its host than you do."

"Your death is not what I mean." She waved a careless gesture. "Though I may have liked you a bit, I'm used to this. I witnessed so many dead generations of your race replaced by new ones." Staring at him, she grinned. "I can't wait until they connect those tubes to your body. I'm so curious to see what happens when I flow into the minds of those Griseos."

So, that was the whole matter to her; exciting. She should be keener for his safety though. Alive, he could be more useful to her if she decided to use him inside the Griseos' headquarters as a Trojan horse. But damn! He was too optimistic. She found an alternative that seemed much better.

"You're not sure how this is going to work." Burke desperately tried to discourage her from abandoning him. "This already negligible part inside my mind will be obsolete when it is diluted into many brains."

"You think you know what you are talking about, but you don't." She laughed as she approached him and laid her hand on his shoulder. "Let me worry about this. You have no idea how strong I feel thanks to the energy I acquired from those mind sessions. I guess it is worth trying, and who knows? Instead of having one Trojan horse, I may have ten or even fifty."

"No, you won't." Burke tried to look confident. "You'll be too weak to handle all these minds. Letting me die means losing a golden opportunity to have someone inside their headquarters. You just have been waiting for ages for this moment."

"You're right about the second part." She lifted her hand and slowly ambled in circles in front of him as if she was pondering what he had said. "I have never been that close. I always knew there was something about the region you call the Bermuda Triangle. I was sure the Griseos were behind its mysterious events, but I didn't have any clear idea about their exact location, their headcount, and their equipment. Thanks to you, I was able to get close enough to Akmenios, and I got all the information I needed from his mind."

More bad news to come. According to what he had just heard, his mission was accomplished, and now he was a dead soldier.

"Oh please!" she begged playfully. "Don't take it personally. I'll always remember you, sweetheart." She held his chin. "And to prove that I appreciate all you have done, I'll stay with you in your last hours, unless you want me to leave."

His last hours? He wished this had only been a nightmare. But regarding what she was saying, he understood that his death was an inevitable fact, and it was just a matter of time.

"Is it worth it?" he muttered, his head down. "All those who die on your quest?"

"I don't wish death on anyone." She shrugged. "I just have nothing to do with that."

"You should have just come to the island yourself and finish your task, instead of putting so many lives on the line."

"That was not possible." She shook her head. "I would have drowned if I had done that myself. Why do you think I've sent you here in the first place?"

That bitch. Burke had been so close to death when he had gone nine years ago to Bermuda. Heather's expedition was just another experiment to reach the much-desired island. Now, the Shomrunk knew the way to his salvation.

"Bingo!" She must have read his thoughts. "I wasn't sure of the HG-3 chances to make it through the Storm Shield, but the vessel proved it wasn't that bad after all. With some fine improvements, the next expedition is going to be a success no doubt." She leaned forward and continued, "I may not need another expedition even." She winked.

"Congratulations," he said impassively. Pondering the notion of having a small army of gray-faced humanoids controlled by the Shomrunk was horrifying. The whole Bermuda matter was almost over. Whether the Atlanteans' double attack succeeded or not, the Shomrunk was definitely the only winner in this mess.

Standing by the lake, Burke brooded over his current situation, over the journey that had brought him to this moment, to the view he had been watching for eight years. To be honest, it looked much better without the wires around the lake.

"You know what?" Burke weighed his steps into the lake. "For years in my exile, I never wished anything more than wetting my feet in the water." He looked over his shoulder. "How much time do I have?"

"Twenty hours, more or less."

He swallowed. "Then?"

"Then your body systems will start to collapse. In a week, you'll be nothing but a corpse."

A week. He was terrified. That would be an unbelievably slow death.

"Unfortunately, the energy suction process is a bit slow." Her voice betrayed a hint of sorrow he almost believed.

"A bit?" he echoed, allowing a nervous chuckle. "Are you sure I won't suffer during that week?"

She paused for a moment. "You really don't want to know that."

32. A Mental Duel

The view on the huge screen was split into two, enabling Akmenios and his deputy to follow the scene on both fronts: the warehouse and the headquarters.

"Everything at the warehouse is under control now. Only two Atlanteans survived the proton blast and they are fleeing already."

Akmenios listened to Cudelios while he was watching the unexpected updates near the headquarters. More than ninety Atlanteans were killed by two blasts. But after losing one proton cannon, Akmenios couldn't declare that everything was under control on that battlefield.

"This is not logical," Akmenios pointed at the screen. "These five dots were retreating before this sixth dot joined them and destroyed the cannon. Now they are moving forward, and I wonder what their destination could be."

For two minutes, he watched the slow advance of the six Atlanteans before they stopped completely.

"They are following the incomplete signal, it seems." Akmenios retrieved the source of Burke's signal on the screen. "Now, they're standing just above us."

"We have no underground gates in that area," said Cudelios. "No threat they can pose to us."

His second-in-command was right in his rationale. Gates would be vulnerable access points for the Atlanteans...

What was that? Akmenios gazed at the screen, trying to interpret what he was watching at the moment. Somehow, those homines were approaching their headquarters.

"Drills." Akmenios tapped the screen.

"What?"

"They're digging. If we leave them like this, they will breach this room in three hours." There were no measures for such an attack. All of Akmenios's defense systems were designed to stop aerial and ground raids. The underground area itself was defenseless, and that simply meant that the Atlanteans drill would pursue its journey unopposed.

"Send twenty guards up at once," Akmenios demanded. "The battle must end up there, not here."

* * *

"What if I die here?"

The thought came into Burke's mind as he wetted his knees in the lake. He was sure the Shomrunk had read his mind, even without uttering the idea. But the reaction he saw on Heather's face surprised him. She frowned and tilted her head, an inquisitive look on her face. Was she wondering about his seriousness?

"Excuse me?" she asked.

"You heard me. What if I drown in this lake?" He trudged into the water until it reached his chest.

"You'll never do that," she said flatly.

"Do you notice you don't answer the question?" He felt victorious as she did not look happy with his suggestion.

"Is death what you seek?" She shrugged. "Go ahead then."

"You're lying." Walking backward, he faced her. "I'll wake up because my brain won't let me think I'm dead."

"And why do you want to wake up anyway?" Heather scoffed. "To torture yourself before death?"

"I won't listen to your mind games." He covered his ears with his hands. "For some reason, you insist on making me believe I'm a dead man. Something inside me tells me to take my chances." He pointed at his chest. "I'm a dead man anyway if I stay here."

"You're dead in both cases, so try to make your last moments less painful." She curled her nose. "Trust me, you won't stand the torture of asphyxia."

"We shall see about that." He grinned, giving her one last look before he dipped his head into the water. He hadn't taken a breath before his dive to make his suicide as short as possible. Last time he held his breath underwater had been ten years ago. Seventy seconds was his best record.

But not today.

His lungs began to cry for air. It was time to swallow water, but he didn't dare open his mouth. The more the time he stayed, the more his lips tightened. Suddenly, he couldn't take it anymore, and up he went. He gasped as his head rose to the surface. With the splash he made, he could hear Heather's giggle.

"Why am I not surprised?" She covered her mouth. "Suicide needs balls."

He looked ridiculous, but who would care now? Losing face in front of the Shomrunk wasn't his biggest problem at the moment. It wasn't an issue at all. Actually, her joy confirmed his doubts. *She doesn't want me to leave her in my mind until I die in real life.*

He trudged toward the lakeside with his water-soaked clothes. He ignored her completely, trying to focus his thoughts on accomplishing the task in hand: killing himself. Drowning in the lake seemed to be the best possible option he had in such a simple terrain.

What about those trees in the garden? Perhaps, crushing his skull in one of those trunks would do.

"I'm quite sure it will be fun watching this." She chuckled. "You will really ruin your shirt with your blood."

Again, she read his thoughts and was mocking him, but he insisted on ignoring her. However, he realized how ridiculous his idea was. He would lose his consciousness before committing his suicide.

He wanted something faster.

A glance at the one-story house ahead might have brought the solution he was looking for. A fall from four meters height might not be deadly unless the fall was on his head.

"You won't do that." The way she hissed scared him for a moment before he pulled himself together. He averted his eyes and strode to the house. To his astonishment, he heard her hurrying footsteps behind him. Suddenly, her hand gripped his arm.

"Out of my way." He shoved her, but she did not fall. Instead, she stepped back twice before she lunged forward and punched him in the nose.

Feeling surprised more than hurt, he stared at her while checking his nose, which was fortunately not bleeding. "What was that for?" he mumbled, and she didn't reply with one of her usual snarky comments. The smiling Heather was gone, and a stern one had replaced her.

"You really want me asleep so bad, don't you?" Burke grinned and clenched his fist. He punched, but she simply blocked his blow with her palm.

"I'm in your mind, you idiot," she snapped. "You can't surprise me."

A surprise was all he needed to outrun her to the roof. There was no need to beat her in a hand-to-hand combat.

But how could he possibly trick her? The only way was not to think.

"Just do it." He threw himself on her, squeezed her neck with both hands, and bit her ear until she bled. "Block this, bitch." He stepped on her nose when he rose to his feet, kicking her face with his heel. "I'm surprised myself."

He sprinted upstairs toward the door without looking back, her hurried footsteps cracking on the wooden stairs after him. He pushed the door leading to the roof and slammed it shut behind him. The way to the fence looked clear.

But that was not the case one second later.

From nowhere, a brawny young man appeared in his way. It was one of his former guards; Burke still remembered his face.

"It's you again." Burke stopped, staring at the huge guy who stood still, waiting for his next move.

"Heather is not working with you anymore." The guard's smile looked familiar.

"So, you didn't need to run after me anyway." Burke took a deep breath after this short sprint.

"Some fun won't harm, sissy." The guard smirked.

"Is your ear still hurting you?" Burke grinned cynically, judging the distance to the edge from both sides.

"After all you've seen and you still think of outrunning me?" The Shomrunk in the guard's form raised his eyebrows. "I know you don't have balls, Burke, but at least you still have a brain."

He's trying to confuse me, he reminded himself. Whether the Shomrunk was a she or he, that *thing* was messing with his mind.

He had to surprise the Shomrunk, as he did the previous time. He must act before he even thought.

"Right or left? Right or left?" Burke muttered. One more fast short sprint was all he needed.

"Come on, you—" the guard yelled with a mocking smile, but Burke's unexpected move interrupted him.

He ran directly to the huge guy, arching his back forward, trying to gain momentum to give his larger opponent a powerful head butt in the chest. With his huge palms, the guard received Burke effortlessly and held his shoulders to stop his advance.

But that was not the end of the show. At the same second, Burke punched the guard in his balls. The huge guy stepped back, leaving a room for Burke to reach the edge.

There was no time to think twice. Burke jumped over the fence, letting himself fall with his head down.

33. Awakening

Guarded by the Atlantean cannoneers Tolarus had sent with her, Heather and her crew were still on their march, the cold breeze of the coast kissing their cheeks as they approached it. Along the way, she couldn't help but picture the gray humanoids intercepting their escape with their extremely destructive weapons. Even with those cannoneers on her side, she wasn't sure if they might stand a chance against the Griseos.

"Tolarus gave you this when he saw you off?" Daniel nodded his chin toward the palm-sized blue glass cube in her hand, a pointer hanging in the vacancy inside it.

"Yes." Heather squinted at the pointer. "It's kind of a compass."

"Why would we need a compass?" Daniel asked. "His men are guiding us."

"It's to help us come back." Even Heather couldn't believe she said so. "Tolarus wants us to find him again. Assuming we manage to leave this island."

"Tolarus wants *us* to find him?" Daniel scoffed. "That guy has a crush on you, if you ask me."

"He is not the first," Heather countered.

"You know what?" Santino said, glancing at the compass. "I wish I had half of his optimism."

Heather put the compass in her pocket. "Me too." She still had a long journey ahead that nobody was sure how it would end. Supposing she found the life capsule with her team, she had no idea if they could survive the stormy ocean and get away, far from this damned island.

"Wow! Did you hear that?" Santino's eyes opened wide.

Heather stopped when she heard an explosion. There was no smoke nearby, yet the roaring clamor was loud and menacing. One of the cannoneers gestured to the marching company to stop, the rest looking around with their weapons raised.

"We must continue our march," Powell addressed Heather and the team. "The gray freaks are busy now with the Atlanteans. We must use this in our favor."

Although Heather agreed with him, she was curious to know what was happening to Tolarus and his soldiers. She hoped it was the Griseos who were suffering from those explosions.

"Hey, Nathaniel," Powell called out to the ancient languages expert. "Hurry those folks up. We have a boat to catch."

Nathaniel didn't talk much with the cannoneers before they waved to Heather and her team to resume their march to the shore.

Following the Atlanteans, Heather couldn't help looking toward the direction from which she heard the noise. She was a bit worried about Tolarus, yet she could do nothing. Powell was right. Every moment they wasted might make Tolarus's distracting attack pointless.

* * *

"Tolarus! There is movement behind those woods."

Most of the laser drill body was already underground when Tolarus listened to one of his remaining men without stopping the machine.

"Tolarus! Did you hear me?" the same man asked nervously.

"I heard you." Tolarus gazed at the nearby trees. "Let's hope it's just a wild animal." Because he was currently monitoring the progress of the drill, making sure it was working smoothly.

"This can be serious. Shouldn't we check what's going on?"

"No. Just stand your ground. Whoever approaches us, he mustn't touch this drill."

The spot he was digging in was so exposed. His men would be an easy target if they were attacked from the tree side. Standing on the deck of the descending drill, Tolarus leaned toward the woods in an attempt to ascertain what his man had just heard.

"Now, I hear them." Tolarus's ears caught some movement indeed. He jumped off the drill, drew the cannon strapped to his back, and pointed it at the suspicious spot. "Be ready to fire," he addressed his five surviving cannoneers.

Suddenly, a white ray came out of the woods, striking one of his men dead at once.

"Hunters!" Tolarus warned his fighters. "Spread out!"

Before his men could move, a second beam hit another one of his soldiers. Unable to precisely locate the source of these cursed beams, Tolarus sprinted and shot a missile from his cannon at the woods. He was not sure if he heard a creaky scream coming from the explosion area.

"Fall back!" Tolarus hollered, urging his three remaining men to get away from the firing range of the Griseos, tempting his opponents to abandon their tree cover. He glanced at the drill, which was almost hidden underground, making sure it was out of the Griseos' reach.

Swiftly, Tolarus stepped backward, yet still facing the trees, watching for any deadly white rays coming. A third soldier was nearly struck by another ray that hit the ground instead.

"Come out!" Tolarus hollered at the hidden Griseos. "Come out, you cowards!"

The Atlanteans kept moving backward, their eyes fixed on the trees in anticipation of any alien company. "Those filthy creatures," Tolarus muttered. "What are they waiting for?"

Since he did not wish to be too far away from his drill, Tolarus gestured to his men to stop moving. With the three remaining soldiers, they assumed a line formation.

"Here they are!" one of the soldiers yelled when seven humanoids came out of the trees at last, holding their spheroidal weapons.

Tolarus nodded toward the two cannoneers on his right. Two missiles could wipe those gray creatures out at once if they did not spread out. Tolarus was sure his veteran men knew that, and a gesture from him was supposed to be enough for his cannoneers to execute.

The two soldiers struck the Griseos with their missiles, forcing them to run away. For most of the gray-faced humanoids, it was too late to escape now. Only one humanoid managed to survive and ran back to the woods.

"Don't push forward." Probably, more Griseos were lurking in the woods to stun the Atlanteans whenever they had the chance. Here, in their current position, Tolarus and his men were outside the shooting range of their enemies. "They're testing our patience." He tried to keep the line formation. Speaking of patience, he was losing it himself. He couldn't wait to pursue and finish off that alien for good, but he had to commit to what he preached.

"What about the drill?" the cannoneer on his left asked.

"Don't worry about it. It won't stop until someone turns it off." Tolarus didn't avert his eyes from the woods. "Just keep those trees in your sight."

More aliens came out of the woods while Tolarus was talking. *I knew it.* Fourteen Griseos sprinted from different sides, making themselves harder to be blasted away by one strike. "Stop them!" Tolarus hollered.

While slowly stepping back, the four Atlanteans showered the aliens with their missiles, hitting as many gray faces as possible, but the aliens outnumbered them and were closing in on them. After Tolarus and his men managed to kill seven Griseos, they came into the range of the aliens' weapons. *This is not going to work.* Tolarus stopped his backward march, allowing himself to shoot two aliens in three seconds, before he dove to evade a deadly white beam and struck a third alien while lying on the ground. He swiftly rolled around, and rose to his feet, blasting a fourth gray face.

Tolarus heard a mix of human and alien screams. He couldn't afford a second to glance at his men to check on them, but he noticed there was no more fire coming from his side. It was clear; he was now on his own to finish off one last alien.

But nothing came out of his cannon this time. Tolarus was out of missiles. As the white spheroid glowed in the Griseo's gray palm, the Atlantean knew he had less than a second before he too died.

* * *

He gasped.

As if woken by a nightmare, Burke opened his eyes. The first sight that struck him was the high gray ceiling with its familiar yellow lights. It took him a few seconds to pull himself together. The last view he remembered was the green view from the top of his villa, his *prison.* His pounding heart was still recovering from the free fall feeling that lasted only for one or two seconds.

"It worked, bitch!" He was still gasping. "It worked!"

"You're awake."

When he heard that creaky voice, Burke realized he was lying on his back on a cold metallic bed. His buttocks were still numbed from his long stay in Akmenios's room seated on that damned chair.

What the...? Burke held his head with both hands, but he did not find that mind-connecting device. He was sure he understood what the humanoid had said.

"No! No!" Burke yelled, frustrated. "Not another dream! I'm done with this."

Realizing his legs were free, he rolled over and rose from his bed to stand just in front of the humanoid, who was holding a couple of sharp-ended tubes with both hands.

"Damn!" Burke exclaimed. "You're not Akmenios."

Yet his shock grew even more.

What Burke had just said was not in English.

It was in the aliens' language.

34. Two Minds, One Head

Akmenios was not sure if he could describe what happened atop the underground headquarters as a win. He lost all the guards he had sent in order to stop the Atlantean attack. All the dots on the screen vanished, and there was no sign of life on that battlefield.

"The drill stopped, Akmenios," said Cudelios.

"I guess that was the objective of the whole thing," Akmenios swiped the screen with his finger to scan the whole island, making sure he was done with the Atlantean headache for good. "Yet, the cost was heavy."

Akmenios stopped when he spotted the yellow dots headed to the coast. "Those homines! They're trying to escape. And it seems they have an Atlantean escort. How many guards do we still have here?"

"Twenty."

We've lost twenty already to kill five homines. Akmenios never thought he was losing the battle until this moment. Those remaining twenty guards were all the fighters he had left. He couldn't afford to lose them as well.

"I'll take ten guards with me," said Akmenios. "I must handle this myself."

"You're going out?" his subordinate asked.

"We don't have enough time to discuss this." Akmenios checked the spheroidal weapon strapped to his belt. "Call for ten guards to meet me at the coastal exit. Now."

Akmenios was headed outside when he heard Cudelios saying, "I think you need more guards with you to capture eleven homines."

Akmenios stopped and turned to Cudelios. "More guards means leaving the headquarters without protection." He gave the screen one last look before he continued, "Besides, this is not a hunting raid. Capturing prisoners *alive* is not a priority."

* * *

Burke contemplated the hall he found himself in. It was way much bigger than Akmenios's chamber.

"Damn," Burke muttered. He saw that hall before in Akmenios's mind. It was one of the awful memories he hardly managed to wipe off his head. The room that was full of human bodies connected to the walls with hundreds of tubes.

"This is real, right?" Burke wondered, still stunned by the fact he was speaking Latin at the moment. He had no idea how this happened, but for the time being, he had more pressing problems worth his attention.

Burke stared at the needles at the end of the tubes in the humanoid's hands. *No! These things won't pierce my skin.* He recalled what Powell had said before about those weak, skinny humanoids, and how the burly marine knocked out a *Griseo* with a single punch. Definitely, Powell was much stronger than Burke, yet it was worth trying. That astonished humanoid would not stay petrified for long, and soon he would ask for help.

"You won't be tougher than that guard." Burke clenched his fist and struck the alien in his abdomen. Impressed by the impact of his punch on the two-meter tall humanoid, Burke watched the thin gray creature double over before he clasped his fingers and hammered the humanoid's bald head with both hands.

Easier than I thought. Burke gazed at the fallen humanoid, who was not moving anymore. Looking for a door, Burke scanned the hall with his eyes, and to his surprise, he knew where he would find it. *Bingo.* He hurried to the door before he stopped just in front of it.

Wait, wait, wait, Burke! He tried to understand what had happened to him. It was time to put all the clues he had gathered on the table.

The mind-connecting session with Akmenios.

The Shomrunk inside Burke's mind.

The head device.

The Shomrunk strengthened unintentionally by the energy supplied by the Griseos through the head device.

Akmenios's mind hacked by the Shomrunk during one of the mind-connecting sessions.

Burke pondered the last two points for a while. Putting them together might explain why he knew what he knew at the moment. All the information the Shomrunk gathered from Akmenios's mind came now into Burke's awareness in some way.

All information, including the history of those Griseos...

Oh my God! Burke held his head with both hands, fidgeting. He wasn't dreaming this time. It was real; he got *all* of Akmenios's memories. Some of those memories Burke had learned already from Akmenios himself, but recalling them as if he had witnessed them with his own eyes was quite another experience, a weird one.

And a bit terrifying.

That gray freak is so damn old. That Akmenios had memories of the past three hundred years.

The alien's life cycle with all it included from birth, growth, and decline until death usually took six hundred years. Everything was slower than it was in human life; their metabolism, their need to sleep, their ability to learn even. The Griseos' civilization had been existing for millions of years. However, the gap between them and humans was closing dramatically.

That's why those Griseos are scared, Burke deduced. One day, humans would become a threat to the aliens' existence if they became more advanced than them. For the time being, the Atlanteans were almost head-to-head with the Griseos. Burke remembered how Akmenios referred more than once to the fact that humans were smarter than they thought.

Burke felt a bit dizzy. The surge of information in his mind puzzled him—now he was aware of the two minds inside his head. Gasping, sweating, he leaned against the wall with his head down. *It seems I've downloaded too much*, he reflected self-mockingly, trying to divert his thoughts away from Akmenios's memories, but he couldn't help it. Curiosity killed the cat.

Akmenios didn't lie when he claimed that his people had existed on Earth before humans, before the extinction of dinosaurs. Since the beginning of time, those Griseos had been defending their existence.

For them, humans were aliens.

Most of Akmenios's tale about Atlantis was true except for one small detail: the war that had occurred between the Griseos and the humans was not just a power struggle. Simply, one side refused to be the other's food. That was where everything had started.

Distant creaky voices interrupted Burke's thoughts. He rubbed his forehead and pulled himself together. *Maybe later*. Now was the time to act, to find a way out, to escape.

The door in front of him had no handles. As long as it was not locked from the control panel inside this hall, it would open automatically once he approached it. Burke found himself knowing that, but now he wasn't so astonished. He was still trying to get used to his new condition, though.

Before leaving, he gazed one final time at the dozens of human bodies that lay there on the metallic beds. With those numerous tubes connected to their bodies, there was no way he could save them. They were already dead.

Burke gnashed his teeth and stepped outside. Nobody was there in the corridor that branched at the end into two. One of them would eventually take him to Akmenios's control chamber and the other led directly to the dock. Escaping through the Griseos' dock did not seem like a wise idea though. Probably, it would be guarded by gray faces with spheroidal weapons.

Trying to focus, he hoped he might retrieve any information about emergency exits. It was hard to believe that the humanoids' underground headquarters did not have at least one. He walked cautiously, deliberately making his steps as light as possible. Those corridors were not watched as no threat was expected to come from the inside.

The dock. The chamber. The dock. The chamber. Make your decision, Burke. Think. Think. Think.

Burke did not stop to think. Instead, he let his legs take him to the corridor that would lead him through some right and left turns and then eventually to the dock. *Bad idea. Bad idea.* Burke had no doubt about that, but he hated the other chamber. The metallic chair, the screen, Akmenios, his assistant, the head device; Burke wished he could forget all those memories for good. Trying his luck through the dock was a foolish idea, though.

Is it you again? Burke halted when the thought crossed his mind. Was it possible the Shomrunk was manipulating his mind at the moment? Should Burke go to Akmenios's chamber instead?

No. It doesn't make any sense. The Shomrunk would rather guide him to Akmenios's chamber to try his luck one more time to send a message across the galaxies to all Shomrunks.

Have you forgotten? The Shomrunk doesn't need you now. She or he or it—Burke had no idea—attempted to keep Burke asleep until he would die slowly in the bio-energy reactor.

Burke tried to recall more information about the dock and the usual defense systems. Those defense systems were designed to deter external attacks, but not internal ones. Still, there was the guards' problem. Usually, there were four or five of them securing the dock area. How could Burke handle them?

Weapons. I need one of those mango weapons.

The Griseos had one store for weapon reserves. It was a bit far from the dock, which might increase his chances of encountering more humanoids.

Come on, Burke. You can't just storm the dock and hijack one of their ships unarmed. Burke had no choice but betting on the probability the Griseos would not spot him.

To his astonishment, his way was clear. It was something he wished, yet it piqued his curiosity a little bit. Where were the gray humanoids? The place looked abandoned to him.

Gradually, he was getting more encouraged, and his cautious steps turned into confident strides. Those corridors he went through were supposed to be watched, but obviously, nobody was watching at the moment.

He found the door of the storeroom that he had never seen before except in Akmenios's mind. It was locked by a code Burke didn't have any difficulty in retrieving. In a few seconds, the door slid open, revealing his biggest frustration since he learned that his lost relative was not real.

The chamber was empty. No weapons for Burke today.

Something big is happening. Something that made them arm themselves with all the weapons they have. He hoped the Shomrunk was right about the double Atlantean attack.

The hope that the Griseos might be fighting now with the Atlanteans encouraged him to take his chances at the dock. Maybe it was abandoned at the moment, like all the corridors and chambers so far.

On his way to the dock, Burke strode for fifteen minutes through a network of tunnels. Since he left the bio-energy chamber, he hadn't seen a single gray face, and only occasionally had he heard a few creaky voices.

That tunnel. Now Burke remembered the long corridor he had passed before with Heather and her team, when they were brought in by that stuttering humanoid and his gray mates. Twenty more minutes of walking and Burke would reach the dock.

Heather? Where's she now? He realized, from Akmenios's mind, that the whole team was taken by the Atlanteans to their camp at the mountains before the entire territory was bombarded. Almost half of the mountainous area was razed to the ground. *That son of a bitch.* There was no one Burke wanted to see dead more than Akmenios.

But why bother? Do you think they thought about your fate when they left you here alone? To them, you were always an intruder, a weirdo.

What if Heather was still alive?

And why are you concerned about Heather in particular? You can't be serious, Burke.

She's the person for whom you bear the most positive feelings. The Shomrunk's image taking the form of Heather while saying that crossed Burke's mind.

No, no, no. She was just nice to me. That's all.

I tell you what, you'd better focus on how you're going to escape from this damned island.

Burke stopped at a closed wide gate that led to the dock. *Why don't I remember any closed gates when we came?* The absence of guards, in addition to the closed gates, confirmed his doubts about what was happening outside.

Unlocking the gate was not a problem for Burke. He knew how to handle that small white hemisphere in the middle of the gate. But he had no idea what was waiting for him behind it. *It's all in.* Burke decided to give it a shot. He moved two fingers on the surface of the hemisphere in a circular way. Yellow symbols appeared to him, announcing the gate was now unlocked. Burke watched it open before he warily stepped in, trying not to make any sound that might draw the Griseos' attention to his presence.

Seems I missed a lot while I was sleeping. Whatever happened to those humanoids, it would not matter. Every step forward was getting him closer to his escape. There was no way he would back off now.

The wide yard of the dock was unexpectedly clear, and no one was guarding the two parked ships. The upper portal at the high gray ceiling leading to ground level was open. "The force is with you today, Burke," he muttered when he reached the closed craft hatch. As he did with the locked dock gate, Burke handled it smoothly.

"Stop."

The order coming from behind him was not in English, and the creaky voice was not Akmenios's. As Burke turned slowly, he saw Akmenios's assistant surrounded by ten armed gray guards.

"This is where your journey ends, hominum."

35. Gray Hell

With the greatest detestation, Burke glared at the assistant's face. If this gray humanoid had the ability to read minds like his boss, he would know that Burke wanted to beat him hard.

"You heard me, right?" the humanoid asked in Latin. "I mean you understand what I say."

Burke didn't have a plan in mind, but he decided not to reply.

"What are you thinking?" the Griseo continued. "I watched everything you did, so stop pretending. It's pointless."

He was watching? Then, why did he wait until Burke reached the dock? "Was that yet another investigation of yours?" Burke asked in Latin.

The subordinate seemed to be thinking for a moment before he said, "We all know it's not about you, don't we?"

"Is it the Shomrunk you mean?" Burke noticed that the humanoids made a small step backward when he leaned toward them. The guards tightened their grasp on their weapons. Their narrow eyes and small mouths barely showed any expression, yet Burke could sense from their body language a slight fear. With his back to the craft's hatch, Burke was cornered by the ten guards. They kept their weapons held tight though, as if they were surrounding a band of armed soldiers. *The real threat here is me.*

"We know you're not alone. He's with you. Inside of you," said the humanoid in his annoying creaky voice. "You're not that smart to learn Latin or memorize the structure of our tunnels network that fast."

"So, it's a *he*," Burke scoffed. "Are you sure about that? He almost convinced me of something else."

"You don't know what will happen if you run away, right?" The Griseo ignored Burke's last comment. "Assuming you find a way to pass the Storm Shield, the Shomrunk will guide you through your way back to him, without you knowing anything about it. He'll erase everything about your journey from your mind and will send you back to us. And you know what, this is your best scenario. Because I believe he'll get rid of you and find someone else to do the job you failed in."

Burke wanted to mock what the humanoid said, but it made sense. It had already happened before. "Oh, please! Don't tell me you're trying to persuade me to stay here. I was starting to love the place. Leaving it would tear me up, break my heart."

"Stay?" the humanoid echoed. "I objected to the idea of keeping you in the headquarters, especially after the first mind-connecting session. It was obvious to me that your presence became a threat to us, but Akmenios saw something else. He believed he could use you to lead him to the Shomrunk, and insisted on not listening to me. Look at the mess you've caused so far. Thanks to you, the Atlanteans have almost found our place. Adding to that, I have no idea what information the Shomrunk has extracted from Akmenios's mind about us—I'm sure he has done so; you're a clear piece of evidence to that. With such information, I'm sure the Shomrunk is now much better prepared for his next raid on us. And no one knows what sort of surprises awaits our people."

Was it strange that Burke felt worried in Akmenios's absence? The conversation with his assistant didn't bode well.

"For the first time, our presence on Earth is at risk because of you both, but I can rectify that before it gets worse." The assistant stepped back at the same time the guards advanced.

"You can't do this without Akmenios's permission." Burke swallowed, looking for a way out.

"As I'm the one in charge now, I can do anything I see fit and for the good of our race."

"You are the one in charge?" Burke stalled, trying to buy some time. "What about Akmenios? Where's he? What have you done to him?"

"I did nothing. He left to finish off the remaining of your friends, if that reassures you."

The remaining? Who were those remaining? Was Heather among them? "You should still wait for your leader's return."

"Whether he's back or not," the humanoid said, "he's no longer our leader."

"Are you leading a mutiny?"

"I'm doing what's right for our people. I won't wait to watch more of our men die."

"And what about those humans you killed?" Burke grunted.

"I have wasted enough time with you already." Standing behind his guards, the assistant ordered them, "Kill him."

* * *

Something was flying nearby, Powell could tell.

"Shit! Get down, everybody!" he yelled. "Hide in the bushes!"

The white rays coming from the sky didn't give everybody the chance to abide by Powell's order. Two seconds after his warning, the field was ablaze, two Atlantean cannoneers falling, dead.

"An aerial attack!" Powell rolled on the ground. "Move! Move!" He crawled, trying to shelter himself behind a huge tree trunk from the shower of white rays. He motioned for Heather and Jay to join him behind the colossal trunk. Daniel, Santino, and Susan buried themselves in the bushes opposite the tree. The three remaining cannoneers, who were trying to evade the aliens' shots, were not able to aim at their opponents.

Powell glanced upward and spotted eleven flying scooters, like the one he had seen at the Atlantean camp with Tolarus. The major difference this time was the color of their riders' faces.

But one face in particular made the blood in Powell's veins boil. "Akmenios." He bit his lower lip. "I'm done with this bullshit." Especially after he could smell the tangy salty sea in the air. Failing to escape now, after getting this close to the shore, was not an option.

Powell held the light cylindrical gun, trying to remind his hands of its weight. From his spot, he aimed at the first alien he saw, pressed the dotted part at the edge of his weapon—as Tolarus had taught him—and watched his shot hit the alien, he dropped down dead.

"Not yet, bitches," Powell snarled. "Not yet." The marine sniped one more gray face before he ran from his huge tree to another one. He did not want to direct the aliens' fire to Heather and her colleagues.

The three Atlanteans struck three aliens dead before they lost a cannoneer. "Damn!" Powell gritted his teeth as he watched the scene. The remaining cannoneers took too much time to take cover from the aerial attack, making themselves easy targets for the aliens during their retreat.

Five gray faces were down and now six remained against three humans. Taking into consideration the aliens' aerial superiority, the battle was still skewed. Powell hit one more alien, and immediately he changed his shooting spot. One second later, a white ray shower blasted his previous spot. "Where are you, son of a bitch?" Powell squinted, seeking Akmenios among his fighters.

And at last Powell found him. The gray alien hovered in a curved route, making it hard to shoot him down. For a while, Powell didn't follow the battle and kept his focus on his target. *I swear I'll kill you, even if it's the last thing I do.* Powell remained patient, waiting for a clear shot to finish off the aliens' leader. He didn't want to reveal his spot for nothing.

And his moment was about to come. Akmenios hovered at a lower altitude, slowing down a bit, as if the alien was looking for something.

"Take that." Powell pressed his weapon and watched Akmenios's scooter explode. The gray bastard was history now. *Unless he is immune to fire.*

But the battle wasn't over yet.

Powell realized he had directed the other aliens' fire to himself by revealing his spot. He was only a second late when he dove to dodge the coming white rays that blasted the bushes he was hiding in. He cried out in agony, his legs killing him with an unbearable burning sensation.

"Damn!" Powell growled, lying on his back. Somehow, he was still conscious despite the pain. Seeking the gray aliens, he gazed at the sky, but his supine position didn't allow him to watch the whole scene. All he spotted was the two aliens shooting, most probably, an Atlantean cannoneer. Were there still any survivors from his side? Only one fact he was sure of: there were two damned aliens still alive.

Powell remained unnoticed, and those aliens were busy hunting someone else. Considering his condition at the moment, he had only one shot to kill one gray face. Powell would be a sitting duck the moment the second alien spotted him.

Unless the marine acted fast.

This should work. It had to. *Aim and press, then aim quickly and press,* he reminded himself of what he was about to do. The key was to be faster than his second target. Otherwise, he would be roasted.

Aim and press. Then aim quickly and press. That was what he did. For a second, he forgot his pain when he saw those two fireballs floating in the sky.

"Yes!" Powell was excited, in pain, and infuriated. Now, he could finally have some rest. He allowed his eyelids to close. Everything went black for a while.

"*Powell! Wake up!*" a faint familiar voice called out to him. It sounded as if it was coming from inside a deep well.

"*He's still breathing!*" he heard another louder voice, a hand slapping him on his cheek.

The first face he recognized when he opened his eyes was Daniel's. He was the one slapping Powell, Heather, Santino, Jay, and Susan standing behind him. "He is awake, thank God!" Heather exclaimed.

Having no idea how long he was unconscious, Powell strained his back to raise himself to check on his burned legs. "No need for that, Major." Daniel held him by both arms. "You'll be okay."

The way Daniel said it made Powell worry. Were it not for the pain in his legs, the marine would think he had lost them. "What happened?"

"Could be a third-degree burn." Heather hurried to him, and gently helped him lie down on his back again. "Would you give me a hand here?" She turned to her mates. "We must get rid of those pants first."

"Tell me the truth, Dr," he said tiredly. "How bad is it?"

Heather stared at him, probably thinking of a lie. "You will need a new pair of trousers when we go home."

"Dammit!" Santino snapped. "I can't touch them with my bare hands."

Pressing her lips together, Heather peered at Santino before she turned to Powell, a forced smile on her face. "I told you."

"Guys, guys." Susan's voice was nervous when she gazed at the bushes ahead. "I hear something."

"I hear something, too," Daniel seconded. "We are not done with those Griseos, it seems."

Unfortunately, Daniel was right. From the shrubs rose a gray figure. He was injured, his limp made it obvious. *He should be dead, not injured,* Powell thought, eyeing Akmenios who was holding a spheroidal weapon.

36. The Last Warrior

There was no way out for Burke. In front of him were the aliens, behind him the craft. Death by the lethal white ray was inevitable.

"Get out of here!"

A Latin holler came from behind the humanoids, who turned to face the intruder. Without a second thought, Burke complied, though he wasn't sure how he was supposed to *get out of here* that simple. He dove at the same moment an explosion slammed his back against the outer body of the ship. The pain didn't allow him to check what was happening to the damned Griseos, but their screams made him rest assured that their fate was way worse than his.

Groaning, he forced himself up on his feet. It must be his lucky day to receive such a nasty hit in the back without paralyzing any limbs or fracturing a vertebra.

His rescuer was a bronze-skinned guy wearing a weird astronaut suit. The arm cannon he held was surely the source of the missile that blasted the Griseos. "Thanks," Burke said in Latin, but his rescuer ignored him as he strode toward the aliens' bodies, drew a spheroidal device—similar to those aliens' weapons—from his belt, and started shooting each of the fallen gray-faced creatures.

"Hey! That's enough!" Burke waved both hands, the glare on the shooter's face making him regret interrupting that maniac. "Ok. Never mind."

His intimidating rescuer resumed his bloody work with the aliens' corpses, and when he was done, he returned his weapon to his belt and said, "Never turn your back to those devils until you make sure they're all dead."

Now Burke was relieved. This maniac might be a friend after all. "You're an Atlantean, aren't you?"

The guy stared at Burke before he said, "I'm sure I am. But it seems, you're not, despite your fluency in Latin."

"Burke is my name." He extended his hand to greet his rescuer, but the latter didn't move a muscle.

"You're one of them." A smile spread across the rescuer's face as he extended his hand in return. "Tolarus is my name."

"You've arrived just in time, Tolarus." Burke shook hands with the Atlantean. "How did you find me?"

"I guess there are more important questions to ask right now." Tolarus looked around. "Like: how can we get out of here? Alive?"

* * *

Half an hour earlier ...

Atop the aliens' headquarters, Tolarus stood unarmed, waiting for the Griseo to finish him off with his spheroidal weapon. Dodging a white ray from such a close range was impossible, and his cannon was out of missiles.

But that wasn't the case of another cannon.

Tolarus was startled when he saw the Griseo blown by a missile coming from his right side. Petrified by the shock, Tolarus needed a moment to realize he was still alive, and all credit was due to a seriously injured fellow cannoneer.

Tolarus hurried to his rescuer, who was lying with his back on the ground, his chest blasted open by the Griseos' rays. "You did it." Finding the right words to console a dying comrade was a hard task.

"Only one missile remained." The wounded soldier handed Tolarus his arm cannon. "Make it count. I won't survive this shot."

Tolarus held his soldier's shoulders until he passed away in his arms. *Those monsters,* he thought as he took a moment to look at the brave soldiers he had lost. Tolarus was on his own now, but he still had a mission to complete. *Those soldiers will not have died in vain. No Griseo shall kill an Atlantean after today.*

Tolarus jumped to his feet. From the ground he grabbed the very spheroidal weapon that was about to kill him. Tolarus had never held one before, but he had noticed how the Griseos compressed the spheroid to unleash their deadly white rays. *It's still working.* Wishing the same fate for the drill, he blasted a spot on the field ahead to test his new weapon.

He swiftly walked until he reached the hole the drill had made, but soon he was disappointed. Standing by the edge of the hole, Tolarus eyed the drill stuck on its way down. It was impossible from his spot to figure out what was hindering the machine. *I must jump down to check the drill*, he thought. But the odds of surviving that jump were not high, if they existed at all.

He gave the dead Griseos one last glance. *Those monsters must have come here in some way.* Most probably, the route they had taken to reach him and his cannoneers had a near outlet; he could tell from how soon they showed up after destroying the defense tower.

Tolarus strode toward the woods from which the Griseos had come. Following their fresh tracks could be the way to find their route to reaching this spot. "Here you are," he muttered when he saw a small alien craft standing on the ground. Holding the spheroidal weapon, he cautiously approached the open hatch. Swiftly, he leapt inside, pointing his weapon at different directions, but no more Griseos were waiting for him here. *It seems they were confident of defeating us.* It was strange that the craft was left unguarded.

It wasn't his first time to see a Griseo craft from inside, but he had never flown one before. The control panel design was somehow similar to that of the Atlantean vessels, though. Tolarus had no choice but to use his intuition and touch that circular gray pad at the center. He heard the hatch close, and the Griseo craft started to rise.

It's moving in a preset route. Tolarus wasn't in control of the vessel, which turned slightly to the left and started to land after a couple of minutes without his interference or any input. It didn't slow down. For a moment, Tolarus believed the vessel would hit the ground before a hatch in the ground, hidden by the grass, opened up, and the vessel continued its flight inside. Having no idea whether he managed to break into the Griseos' headquarters or he was captured by this craft, Tolarus didn't try to mess with the control panel until the vessel landed at what looked like an underground dock, one Griseo craft parked beside the one that brought him here.

Tolarus clenched his jaw when the hatch opened. Slowly, he stepped outside with the spheroid in his hand, and surprisingly, the whole place looked abandoned. Not the ambiance he expected in the Griseos' main camp.

Footsteps approached. Realizing he wasn't alone, Tolarus took cover behind one of the parked vessels. *What's going on here?* Tolarus wondered when he saw a dark-haired man walking toward another vessel before a group of Griseos stopped him and surrounded him with their weapons. To Tolarus's astonishment, the cornered man spoke in Latin, though he didn't seem to belong to this island. The guy's outfit resembled those worn by Heather and her people. *They still have one of our friends*, she had told him earlier.

Tolarus could hear bits of the conversation between the man and the Griseos. Surely, the surrounded man was in trouble. But what could Tolarus do against eleven armed Griseos, with only one missile left in his cannon?

Actually, with the Griseos' current formation, it was possible to strike them all with this one missile. The only problem was the man himself who was so close to them. Tolarus wouldn't be able to kill them without taking him out as well. *Think, Tolarus. Think.* The Griseos were already assuming their shooting positions. That anonymous guy was surely dead anyway.

"Get out of here!" Tolarus hollered, shooting at the ground just behind the aliens. If the explosion didn't kill them, he would make sure they were gone for good.

* * *

"This gray freak," Burke pointed at the assistant's corpse, "said something about Akmenios and killing my friends. Do you have any idea where I can find them?"

"Your friends are on their way to the shore," Tolarus replied. "They're escaping."

"Escaping?" Burke was surprised. "How?"

"One of your boats is still there." Tolarus seemed concerned. "They were supposed to reach the shore unnoticed."

"Then we don't have a minute to waste." Burke grabbed Tolarus's hand. "Take us to them before it's too late."

Tolarus didn't move with Burke's pull. "How?"

Burke couldn't understand what the Atlantean's problem was. "Using the same vessel that brought you here?"

"That vessel had a preset route. I'm not sure I can steer it to reach the shore."

"I can. Don't worry." Burke strode toward the vessel, motioning for Tolarus to follow him.

"You speak our language. You steer their vessels. How are you able to do all these things?" The Atlantean furrowed his brow.

"That's a long story, and I'm afraid we're in a hurry. Now, where shall I take us?"

37. Spheroidal Death

Fear was not what Heather felt when she watched Akmenios rise from the bushes holding his spheroidal weapon. It was unadulterated anger and immense fury. No consequences crossed her mind at the moment. All her senses were preoccupied with one thing only: the ugly gray face of Akmenios that reminded her of her late friends.

Kenneth.

Kenji.

Joshua.

Linda.

Walter.

"Enough!" she hollered, stepping forward toward the gray humanoid.

"You're standing in the line of fire," Akmenios said, his creaky voice impassive. "I won't hesitate to kill you if you keep blocking the way."

"No, Heather!" she heard Daniel yell behind her. "Don't do this!"

Heather didn't stop and kept moving toward Akmenios. She had no idea what she was going to do when she would reach him.

"I won't say it again," said Akmenios, his hand still gripping the white spheroid. "Get out of the way."

"What do you want from us?" Heather cried. "Aren't you done killing us?"

"I kill for a purpose." Akmenios didn't lower his hand. "Unlike your blood-thirsty race."

"Your ridiculous lies have become pointless." Heather stopped when she realized that getting closer to the taller humanoid would enable him to aim easily above her head at Powell.

"Stop!" Akmenios was not looking at her when he bellowed and pressed the spheroid with his palm. The white ray went past Heather's left side. Although Heather wasn't touched by the lethal beam, she felt the heat on her body. Terrified, she turned to her team, but the white ray had barely missed them. While Daniel and Jay were dragging Powell behind a tree, Nathaniel, Santino, and Susan ran to the opposite side.

Akmenios shoved Heather out of his way as he chased Daniel and Jay. With his weapon, he struck the tree they were hiding behind, but miraculously, he was a second too late. At the last moment, her two colleagues succeeded in getting Powell out of the blast spot.

Heather couldn't bear watching the *Griseo* hunt down her team. Without too much thinking, she sprinted after Akmenios and jumped, surrounding his trunk with her arms, trying to make him lose his balance. The towering thin humanoid tottered, but he didn't fall. "Your actions don't make any sense." Akmenios forced Heather's arms open and threw her to the ground. "Don't you realize you're getting yourself killed?"

Her back ached, yet she didn't give up. "There are things about humans you can never understand." She pushed to her feet.

"I'm not interested." Akmenios aimed his spheroid at her. "If you still insist on dying, I won't deny you your wish."

He pressed the sides of his weapon. The white spheroid glowed, but only for less than a second. Suddenly, Akmenios fell down after a yellow ray hit the ground behind him. The explosion wave slapped Heather's face, but she managed to keep her feet on the ground. *My chance now.* She hurried toward Akmenios and kicked the spheroid from his hand. Before the gray humanoid protested, she kicked him in the face.

"What do you think you're doing?" Akmenios held Heather's foot, preventing her from hitting him for the third time, and quickly he pulled it. Heather lost her balance and fell down. The humanoid rose and grabbed Heather by the hair, locking her neck with his other arm.

"Hand over your weapons, hominum!" Akmenios yelled at Powell, who hid behind the bushes with Daniel and Jay. The humanoid walked toward the kicked away weapon, dragging Heather with him.

She tried to slow him by pulling herself down. "Let me go!" Heather dug her teeth into Akmenios's thin arm. It was disgusting, but she couldn't think of a better idea at the moment. Akmenios cried out, but didn't loosen the lock on her neck as he kept moving toward the spheroid.

"Let her go!"

They were a few meters away from the weapon when Powell rose, holding the Atlantean cylindrical gun, pointing it at the humanoid. The tenacious marine, who was not able to move his terribly burnt legs a few moments ago, stood on his feet. Heather could feel his pain from his wince and his contorted face.

"I won't say it twice, Gray Face!" Powell yelled.

"Or what?" Akmenios stopped and lifted Heather, shielding his body with hers. "You won't dare to jeopardize her life."

Heather had no idea how Powell managed to stand up all this time with his burnt legs. From the tremble in his limbs, she could tell that the marine had gone far beyond his pain threshold, and she wondered how long he could keep himself on his feet. At any moment they would fail him.

Akmenios seemed to be reading their minds. "Don't fool yourself, soldier," he addressed Powell. "Physically, you're not in your best shape to land a winning shot. Emotionally, you're nervous, as usual, and it's hard for you to take any swift actions at the moment. You might kill her with a foolish attempt from your side, and believe me, you won't be able to live with that—in case you survive this in the first place."

That damned Griseo. Heather could see how Akmenios was messing with Powell's composure, taking advantage of the marine's drained and depleted condition. She desperately tried to wrench herself free of Akmenios's lock, but her attempts failed.

"I forgot to warn you," Akmenios continued. "In case you're thinking of destroying my weapon, then you should know the explosion will be enough to blow me up with your friend. I guess this is your best way out so far."

"Shoot it, Powell!" Heather cried. "Don't listen to him!"

"He won't dare." Akmenios tightened his hold on Heather as he moved toward the spheroid.

"You've forgotten me."

It was Santino's voice. From behind a tree at Akmenios's right, the young widower came and rushed toward the humanoid, falling with him and Heather to the ground.

"This is for Linda." Santino punched the fallen Griseo, but the humanoid held both Santino's arms and kicked him in the belly. Santino growled, and Heather pushed to her feet, hurrying to the spheroid.

"Stop it." She raised the spheroid, facing Akmenios, who slowly stood up, locking Santino's neck with his slim arm.

"You have only two seconds to give me my weapon, or I will break your friend's neck." Akmenios pulled Santino by his hair. "One."

"No."

Heather herself was startled when she realized what she had done. In a fraction of a second, she recalled how Akmenios once had pressed the sides of this spheroid. In another part of the same second, she did what she had just recalled and struck the Griseo's head with the deadly white ray from his own weapon.

"DIEEEEEEEE!" She dropped the spheroid as she rushed toward Akmenios's dead body and kicked it repeatedly. At last, she was able to release all the tension she had been bearing for the last seventy-two hours.

At last, that odious creature was gone forever.

"Everything is okay now, Heather," Daniel's voice came from behind her. She was staring at Akmenios's body, still not believing she had killed the humanoid on her own. She was shaking all over, and she had no idea why.

"It's over at last." Daniel gently patted her on the shoulder.

"That gray bastard killed them all." Heather buried her face in Daniel's shoulder and let her tears pour down and gave in to her sobs.

Daniel softly shushed Heather and brushed her hair, repeating, "Everything is okay now."

Her pounding heart started to slowly calm down. "Come on. Let's get out of this damned island." She parted from Daniel and looked at Powell, who lay on the ground. The marine had exhausted all the stamina he had. "Hurry and help him up." Nodding toward Powell, she addressed Daniel and Santino. The latter stood like a statue for a while, staring at Heather.

"What?" she nervously asked him.

"Nothing." Santino shook his head, an awkward smile on his face. "I still can't believe what you've just had done. You could have killed me, but you did shoot the bastard."

Heather was a bit confused. "Are you blaming me or thanking me?"

"Guys, guys." Daniel pulled Santino by the arm. "Let's get the hell out of here, and later, we shall recall all the *sweet* memories we had on this island."

"Dani is right." It was about time for the leader of this group to regain her composure. "We're less than a hundred meters away from the..."

Heather didn't finish as she spied ten flying scooters in the sky. "No, no, no. Please, no," she muttered, frustrated upon making sure that her eyes were not playing tricks on her. The riders of those flying scooters were more of the damned Griseos.

38. Trust Me, Trust Me Not

Heather felt like falling on her knees upon seeing the aliens' scooters in the sky. It was a nightmare that didn't seem to have an end in sight. "Why more gray faces? Why? Why? Why?"

"We're surrounded." Susan pointed at an aircraft approaching from the left side of the flying scooters.

Both the speed and direction of the aircraft gave Heather a faint hope that Susan was wrong. That vessel wasn't here to surround her and her team.

It had just arrived to hunt the gray-faced humanoids down.

The aircraft was barely harmed when it crashed into nine scooters, missing only one of them. "A miracle," Susan muttered, and this time Heather couldn't agree more. They watched the vessel turn around, pursuing the scooter that tried to escape by maneuvering at a low altitude. Surprisingly, the much larger vessel matched the pace of the scooter and took a vertical downward path until it hit the scooter.

"Oh my God!" Heather screamed. The aircraft was only a few meters away from crashing into the ground before it swiftly raised its front edge horizontally and rose up again to the sky.

Heather wondered who would arrive at such a crucial moment to save her and her team. *Surely, he's one of Tolarus's Atlantean troops, or even Tolarus himself,* she thought, the flying vessel hovering in a circle before it started to slowly land.

"I don't think it's a good idea to wait here." Susan pulled Heather by the arm and waved to the men to hurry up.

"Hey!" Heather gently removed Susan's hand. "Whoever the pilot of this vessel is, he saved us. We shouldn't be running away from him." She looked at Daniel, Santino, Jay, and Nathaniel who were together helping Powell back up on his feet. "Maybe, he can help us get the hell out of here."

"What if he's another gray face?" Susan's eyes were fixed on the aircraft hatch that slowly slid open.

"I don't think so. Why would he shoot down the scooters?" Heather *hoped* she was right. One more gray face at this very moment might cause her a heart attack.

She didn't think twice when she hurried to the Atlantean emerging from the vessel. "I knew it." She threw herself into Tolarus's arms. "I knew it was you."

Tolarus's grin made her realize that they weren't putting on those mind-connecting helmets. She laughed.

"No, it wasn't him."

The familiar voice startled her. *No way,* she thought as she gaped at Burke. It was him in the flesh, standing right before her.

"I guess it's me who deserves a hug," he continued.

"Burke." Heather was still shocked. "You are still...and how do you...Oh my God!" Frozen in her place, she held her face with both hands.

Burke frowned playfully. "I expected a better reception than this."

She chuckled nervously. "I'm really sorry, Burke. I just can't believe it."

"I know, I know." Burke grinned before he shocked her again by addressing Tolarus in Latin. Her shock grew even more when the Atlantean smiled at Burke, replying in the same language.

This is not shocking anymore. This is creepy. And that led Heather to one conclusion she wished it was wrong. "You're not Burke."

"No, Heather. It's me." He laughed. "I know it sounds weird, but for some reason, I know all that Akmenios knew. Let's leave this island for now, and later we may discuss how that happened."

Heather felt hesitant about believing him. She glanced at her team standing behind her, and obviously they were as doubtful as she was.

"Trust me, Heather. It's almost over." Burke's fingers startled her when he touched her arm. He had always been a confusing guy, but never that scary.

"I really wish it were over." She studied him with inquisitive looks, trying to spot anything dubious in his facial expressions, but he seemed honest to her. It was *him* with his cynical smile that seldom left his face, regardless of the darkness of the situation.

"It is over indeed." Burke held her shoulders. "All we need to do is ride the life capsule to leave this island for good."

Heather was still staring at him. "How did you know we were looking for the life capsule?"

"I didn't. Akmenios did, though."

"You just read my mind, didn't you?" She kept her eyes fixed on his.

"Hell no!" Burke's grin faded away. "What's the matter with you? Can't you trust me after all I have been through?"

Again she glanced back at her mates, hoping any of them might provide her with a piece of advice, but all of them looked undecided.

"I'm sorry, Burke." She sighed. "I can't tell what's real from what's not."

"Come on, guessing your next move shouldn't be that hard anyway," he scoffed. "I assume you were not intending to flee the island swimming."

It's him. She felt it in her gut."Of course not. The life capsule was our best and only option we had until you showed up with this aircraft."

"Bad idea." He shook his head. "This vessel won't withstand the Shield storm."

"What about the HG-3? Can't you take us there?"

"It's seized by those Griseos, and now it's kept at one of their warehouses, which is heavily guarded by the way, and we can't break into it with our current numbers. Tolarus has told me about his crushed troops."

Heather was shocked. *Crushed troops.* Upon seeing Tolarus, she assumed the Atlanteans had been victorious in their march. How had Tolarus rescued Burke, then? *It was Burke who rescued the Atlantean, it seems.*

She cleared her throat. "What about his other team? Did he tell you about—?"

"He did. Most probably, they suffered the same destiny of his heavily defeated soldiers." Burke pointed at the coast behind him. "Otherwise, you wouldn't have seen those Griseos with their flying *scooters.*"

"What does this mean?"

"The Griseos' forces have two main rallying points: their underground headquarters—the one we *visited* together—and the northern warehouse. And as I'm quite sure about the current defenseless status of the Griseos' headquarters, I can easily guess where those scooters had come from."

Shocked, Heather's jaw dropped. "Are you saying the Atlanteans have lost their war?"

Burke glanced at Tolarus who was standing completely still. "I'm not sure about Tolarus's future plans, or whether he has reinforcements or not. Because if he doesn't, how will he raise new soldiers? Anyway, it's not our issue to worry about."

The harsh statement left them all hushed.

"Oh, please!" Burke went on, "We have nothing we could do about that. We had better think about something a little bit more important. Like for instance: figuring out a way to leave this island."

It wasn't easy for her to voice her agreement with Burke, especially after all Tolarus and his people had done for them. Yes, what Burke had just said made sense, yet it didn't feel right.

"For once I agree with him," said Powell weakly, still leaning on the other four men of Heather's crew.

"It sounds callous, Heather, I know," said Daniel, "but in fact, the best help we can offer the Atlanteans is to leave this island and go back home to tell everybody about everything that has been going on here. The US government must interfere and aid those humans who have been trapped here for thousands of years."

Heather felt lucky Tolarus knew no English. It would be embarrassing to face the Atlantean with the ugly truth that they were going to leave him alone to face his destiny. How cruel would they seem?

Easy on yourself, Heather. You have no other option.

Or maybe she had.

* * *

Burke didn't understand why Heather was so hesitant. The situation was crystal clear. Even her colleagues shared his opinion.

"Come on, Heather," Burke urged her. "Every minute we waste here increases our chances to be found and caught by the Griseos. Sooner or later, they will realize we're still here, and maybe they will send another force after us."

What was she thinking about? Burke wished he could read her mind like Akmenios, may he rot in Hell, read his. He observed how she glanced a few times at Tolarus. *What the hell is going on? No, it can't be.* He dismissed the thought.

"So, you say taking the aircraft is a bad idea." Heather broke her silence. "What's our better alternative? The life capsule?"

Burke turned to Santino. "How deep can we dive with that thing?"

"Not more than two thousand feet," Santino stated.

"I guess we won't need more than that," Burke said.

"What are you thinking of?" Heather asked.

"Most probably, the Storm Shield will hit us. The only way to minimize the risk of sinking is to sink." Burke knew they would object to his opinion as usual. "I'm sure it sounds strange, but trust me, I know what I'm saying. Can we please postpone our debates for now?"

They all looked at each other. Why was trusting him that difficult?

"What's this all about?" Tolarus spoke at last, only Burke and Nathaniel understanding his Latin.

"They're still not sure how they can leave the island," replied Burke in Latin. "The vessel we brought has become a new option."

"There's no time for this," said Tolarus. "We can never know when the Griseos are going to send more soldiers. You must leave now."

Nathaniel was translating the conversation to Heather and her crew.

"What about you?" asked Burke. "Won't you join us?"

"No, my friend." Tolarus grinned. "This is our land. I won't abandon it that easily and hand it to those aliens on a silver platter."

"You lost so many men, Tolarus."

"So did they. We're even now."

"I'm not sure about that. I think—"

"You're wasting your time, my friend." Tolarus pointed at Heather and her team. "You must take them to your boat and leave the island now. Please, don't forget to tell your people about us when you return home. We will stand our ground, waiting for your reinforcements to come to our aid."

"We won't let you down, my friend." Burke held Tolarus by the shoulder. Truth be told, Burke wasn't sure it was a good idea to let his world know about this island. Most probably, the human invaders would replace the gray ones. The Atlanteans had better defeat those Griseos on their own.

"Tolarus is coming with us," said Heather in English.

"I've asked him already, but he insists on staying with his people." Burke turned to her, trying to put a smile on his face. "Are we leaving yet?"

"We can't leave him here after all he has done for us." Heather frowned. "Tell him what I have just said."

Hell no! I'm not going to do this ridiculous translation thing. "No," was all Burke said.

"Fine." Heather nervously turned to Nathaniel, pointing at Tolarus. "Tell him that leaving him here is pointless. The real help will come from outside the island."

"Come on, Heather," Burke said impatiently.

But Heather didn't listen and insisted on having that futile conversation with her Atlantean crush. Unable to stand watching this farce, he hurried to the aircraft to do something more useful, like checking the radar for incoming Griseos.

Burke couldn't believe Heather really had a crush on Tolarus. *She has lost her mind*, he thought as he stepped into the vessel. Anyway, that was Heather's business, not his. He had better keep his eyes on the damned panel.

Burke moved his fingers over the single gray pad at the center of the control panel. From what he had acquired from Akmenios's mind, he could read the symbols which appeared on the blue screen above the gray pad.

"Shit! Shit! Shit!" Burke stared at the four moving dots on the screen. He sprinted outside and jumped off the vessel. "Four vessels are approaching," Burke announced. "We must run now to the shore."

Heather looked alarmed when she asked, "How much time do we have?"

"Two minutes maximum. Sorry to interrupt your romantic farewell." Burke grunted, nodding toward Tolarus. "I'll explain to him what's going on. Now go."

The Atlantean looked confused when Burke pulled Heather and Nathaniel. "Move, all of you," Burke yelled at the rest of the team before he addressed Tolarus in Latin, "Griseos are coming. Four vessels. You must get out of here."

"Don't you worry." Tolarus patted him on the shoulder, looking him in the eye. "I'll see you again, I hope."

"What are you talking about?"

Tolarus's answer was nothing but a faint smile. The Atlantean left him and hopped onto the aircraft.

"He's not doing this," Burke muttered as he watched Tolarus's vessel fly toward the incoming four crafts. *This guy makes me feel bad about myself,* Burke thought to himself, recalling the moment he had told Heather about not *having anything to do* for the Atlanteans.

Though it was impossible now for the Atlantean to hear him, Burke found himself saying, "I'll see you again, my friend."

39. To Sink Or Not to Sink

Everything had been quiet since Tolarus took off with the vessel. No explosions. No roaring aircraft or buzzing scooters above. Only the murmur of ocean waves. What had happened to the Atlantean would remain a mystery until they met again. *If only we could meet again...*

The water reached Heather's chest when she pulled herself up on board the orange life capsule. Behind her were the rest of her team. Three men were carrying Powell as they trudged through the water. "Almost there, guys." Heather encouraged them as they approached the life capsule. Being the first to hop into their abandoned salvation ark, she went inside to check it out. *Hopefully, it is abandoned indeed.* Encountering a gray face here, at this very moment, would make a horrendous ending for this nightmare.

The life capsule seemed untouched since she had disembarked with her crew. Only some parts of the floor had been splashed by ocean waves through the open hatch during the last three days. No gray faces here. Fortunately.

Three days? It was hard for her to believe it had only been three days. She had seen humanoid aliens who could speak her language; had met descendants of the people who had lived in Atlantis—the continent that, to her, had been nothing more than a myth; had learned new mind-blowing facts about her world and its history. All those massive events in just three days.

And she had lost many friends.

The moment Santino joined her on board, she urged, "Come on, Santino. We want to make sure this capsule is still alive."

She returned to the open hatch of the capsule, urging her mates to hurry up. "Burke!" she called out to him as he was lingering behind her crew for no clear reason. "This is not the time for daydreaming."

No, he is not daydreaming, Heather thought as she squinted at Burke, who had been staring at the sky for a moment. "Burke! You hear something?"

Her team managed to get Powell into the capsule when Burke finally replied, "Nothing. After all these years, I just can't help the feeling that someone is following me."

"We will have time to deal with our issues, Burke, but that happens later, *not* now." She glared at him.

"You're right." Burke nodded and moved at last. When he reached her, he asked, "You are worried about your blue-eyed boyfriend, aren't you?"

The question caught her off guard. "What the hell are you talking about?"

"You heard me. I know you're crazy about those eyes," Burke teased as he went past her into the capsule. "Let's go, folks. What are we waiting for?"

She should rebuke Burke for his ridiculous remark, but instead, she went to Santino. "How are we, Santi?"

Santino was already assuming his position behind the steering panel. "We are good to go." When the hatch slowly closed, he continued, "Sit tight, everybody."

Heather found a seat right behind Santino. "At last," she muttered, gazing through the window at the island she was leaving behind. "Take this horrendous view out of my sight."

"Just one final ride," said Daniel as the life capsule made a turnaround before it moved onward, leaving the cursed island of Domus behind, hopefully for good.

"Burke," Santino called out while steering the capsule away from the island. "You said something about *sinking in order not to sink* or something like that. Can you tell me what the hell this means?"

"It means that we simply need to let the life capsule fall to deactivate the Storm Shield," Burke answered.

"Excuse me?" Santino glanced back at him, unconvinced.

"We have no time for alien hallucinations, Burke," Daniel protested. "This is our only chance."

"You know what, Daniel?" Burke, who sat behind Daniel, leaned forward. "My alien hallucinations are your only hope right now."

Unfortunately, he was right about that, Heather knew. Whether he was hallucinating or not, she and her team had no better options. "You're sure about what you say, right, Burke?" Heather couldn't *dare* to think of any possible destinations for their journey except home.

"This is the only thing I know." Burke shrugged. "I know nothing else."

"Guys, guys, knock it off," Santino interrupted them nervously. "Let me understand what he wants me to do."

"Just wait for the storm to begin," Burke addressed Santino. "And then, you can turn the engines off."

"Turn the engines off?" Santino echoed in disapproval. "For how long?"

"At least before you hit the ocean floor."

"You are so optimistic." Santino gaped at Burke. "There's no way we will hit the ocean floor. The vessel skeleton won't withstand the pressure."

The way Burke was silenced made Heather feel nervous. "Collect your thoughts, Burke," she pleaded. "I don't know what exactly happened to you, but you said you now know all that Akmenios knew. In your mind, there must be a little piece of information that can help us."

"You might be right." Burke leaned back into his seat. "But I have no idea how to find that little piece of information, if it exists in the first place."

"I don't know, either," Heather snapped. "*Nobody* knows. Do you have any suggestions?"

"Sure." Burke's grin didn't make her feel comfortable. "You pray the storm ends before the water pressure crushes us."

Heather didn't know how to answer this. She looked away from Burke and silently watched the ocean from the closed glass window. Waiting for the storm to happen was worse than the storm itself.

"Hey." Jay broke the silence. "How many years do you think they slap us with as a sentence?"

Heather was confused for a while before she realized what Jay was referring to. "Would you trade your seat here for a bed in a cell?" she asked him.

"I never tried either an ocean floor or a bed in a cell," said Jay. "But a cell sounds better to me than a water grave."

"I won't return to a cell." Burke folded his arms. "I'd pick the ocean floor instead."

The vessel started to shake. "Hang on," Santino warned. "It's starting now."

Heather gazed at the rising waves outside. "Oh God," she muttered.

"Now, Santino!" Burke yelled. "Turn it off!"

"This is the stupidest thing I have ever done." Santino seemed hesitant. The capsule swayed in the raging ocean, like a leaf wobbling in the autumn wind. If it were not for the seat belts, the capsule passengers would have been smashed against its walls.

"Now, Santino!" Burke repeated.

Heather could now see nothing through the window but water. She had no idea whether they were swallowed by the ocean, or whether Santino managed to let the vessel sink as Burke suggested. Anyway, it was supposed to be much quieter below the water surface.

"What the hell is that?" Through the front glass, Daniel pointed at the mother of all whirlpools. In Heather's scientific career, she had never seen or heard about a vortex of a diameter that might exceed seven miles. She could estimate the velocity of its vigorous ocean currents to be not less than thirty miles per hour.

"Do something, Santino!" Heather gripped her seat arms tightly. She knew this was useless, but she couldn't help doing so. "Don't let that bitch swallow us! We'll be crunched!"

"What can I possibly do?" Santino's voice betrayed his terror. "With the engines turned off, I can't escape that monstrous vortex!"

"You must turn them on now, Santino!" Daniel urged. "If we get closer, we won't be able to overcome the huge sucking power of that vortex."

"Turning engines on means certain death," Burke reminded them. "The Shield Storm will never stop as long as our engines are still working."

"But we're sinking already, and nothing is happening!" Santino blustered.

"At least we have a probability of surviving in this scenario." Burke glared at Santino, which was unusual. During all of their previous dark situations, Burke had always been calm enough to even find a snarky comment to remark. At this very moment, he looked scared, as anybody in this *death capsule* should be. At this very moment, he acted normally.

Like a human.

"I hope I won't regret this, Burke." Heather looked him in the eye.

"Either way you won't," said Burke impassively. Unfortunately, he was right.

"This is madness," Daniel grunted. "We are already being drawn into the vortex currents. If we wait more than that, we won't stand a chance."

"We'll do what Burke says. We won't discuss this again," she snapped.

Despite its switched-off engines, the life capsule gained more speed as it was nearing the gigantic whirlpool. Could it be possible she had made her worst decision ever?

Her last?

"I can't do this." Santino hit the panel with both hands repeatedly and started to work his fingers on the keys in front of him.

"Not now!" Burke unbuckled his seat belt, rushed toward Santino, and violently pulled him back. "Hold it!"

Santino pushed Burke away from him. "I won't die because of your bullshit!"

Burke's eyes glowed and he threw himself on Santino. "And I said not now!"

"Get off him!" Susan screamed.

Heather knew she must stop this, but her mind was completely blank. The vessel was rocking at a higher pace now. If she unbuckled her seatbelt, she would smash her back against the wall of the vessel. "This is insane," Heather muttered as she could hardly watch Burke and Santino's fight amid this vigorous shaking.

"Look! Look!" Powell spoke at last. "It's retracting!"

Heather stared at the vortex, making sure her eyes weren't fooling her. *Powell is right.* She could swear the whirlpool diameter was shrinking. Even the vessel started to slow down and the shakes slowly subsided. For a while, all sounds in the life capsule grew hushed as all eyes, Burke and Santino's included, were glued to the front glass window.

"Yes!" Daniel hit the seat arm with his palm.

Burke got himself off Santino. "Sorry for this," said Burke as he returned to his seat. "I had to stop you by any means."

Santino's eyes betrayed his fury as he peered at Burke. It seemed it wasn't over yet for the Latino.

"Chill out, man," Jay addressed Santino. "The guy has just apologized to you."

"We shall see about that when we return." Santino frowned.

Heather felt she should say something to Santino. But after a second thought, she chose not to bother herself with this childish squabble.

"What's this?" Heather heard a cracking sound above her head. "Santino! Check the depth!"

"Oh shit!" Santino was awakened by Heather's alarmed voice. "Three thousand feet! We must rise now!"

There was no way to wait for Burke's advice this time, a rift already expanding along the life capsule's roof. The ocean was going to crush them like a car running over a can. "How bad is the damage?"

"Sixty percent and counting! We have a few seconds remaining before the skeleton collapses!"

"We won't make it," Burke muttered. "We're still too deep."

Despite his calmness, Burke's announcement sounded more terrifying than Santino's for some reason. *Because he always means every word he says, even when he jokes,* Heather realized that now.

"Santino?" Daniel asked nervously. "How deep are we now?"

Santino's lips did move, but he didn't answer Daniel. He was muttering with something that only Heather could hear from her seat right behind him.

"*To you, O Lord, I lift up my soul.*"

40. Death Capsule

The capsule wall bulged inward with a terrible rasping, water seeping into the vessel now. At any moment, the ocean would crush that capsule with all its passengers on board.

"Straight up, Santino!" Powell bellowed. "Do you hear me? Straight up!"

Heather grasped what the marine was referring to. "Do it, Santi!" she interrupted Santino's last prayers. "Focus, and you'll do it!"

"I'm already sticking to the protocol—"

"Forget the damned protocol and do what Powell says!" Heather cut him off, cold drops pouring down on her cheeks and forehead. "Do it, Santi!"

"Shell damage is ninety-one percent!" Santino blustered.

"The shell is still holding, for God's sake!" Daniel snapped. "Come on, Santi!"

Santino grunted as he adjusted the course of the life capsule, steering it upward in a sharp angle. Behind Heather Susan shrieked, Jay praying loudly, Powell bellowing out his instructions. On her right, Daniel hollered at Santino, who kept grunting as if he was pushing the capsule upward with his own arms. For once, the only silent man in the room was Burke.

"Only thirty seconds left to surface!" Santino yelled.

Thirty seconds! Thirty long seconds! Heather grasped her seat arms, eyes still closed, waiting for someone to wake her up from this horrendous nightmare. Seeking any happy thoughts in her mind was a total failure. The last three days of her life filled her head with the worst memories ever.

Suddenly the side wall next to Jay collapsed, flooding him with water. "Get out of here! All of you!" Daniel yelled. "The capsule is sinking!"

"Dammit!" Santino was still in his seat. "Only twenty feet! We're almost there!"

"You still have a chance, guys!" Powell shouted. "You can swim that distance."

"He's right." Burke unbuckled his seat belt. "The more we wait here the more we sink. We must abandon this vessel now."

"Take a deep breath, everybody!" Santino commanded. "I'm opening the hatch!"

"Wait!" Heather pointed at Powell. "What about him?"

"I won't make it." Powell motioned for her to go away. "Get out now!"

"Not without you." Burke unbuckled Powell's seat belt and pulled him by the arm. "Daniel and Jay, I need a hand here." He turned to Heather. "What are you still doing here? Get the hell out!"

She knew she must do it. Now. Especially when Santino said, "Hatch open in three, two, one."

Maybe it was the deepest breath Heather had ever taken. Against the heavy influx of water, she could hardly force herself out through the open hatch. She had never been that deep below the water surface, but she *tried* to convince herself it would be like swimming in the pool with only one difference: the direction. *How easy to say that!* Trying not to panic, she reminded herself it was a short distance upward to reach her deliverance. All she had to do was forget how deep it was below. *Dammit!* She brushed that thought aside. *Focus now, Heather. Just keep your legs moving.*

The distance to the surface was longer than it seemed, and her lungs were screaming for air. *Keep moving, Heather. Don't stop fighting now,* she thought inwardly as she tightened her already sealed lips. Her brain should be preoccupied with nothing right now except her legs; one kicking downward, the other moving up. Down and up. That was how it worked.

But she couldn't keep her mouth shut any longer. Cold, salty water filled her mouth now...

And then a steel lock of a grip pulled her by the arm.

Heather coughed and coughed then gasped. Her lungs were yearning for air so badly. After a minute of deep breaths, she turned to her rescuer, who was no one but

Nathaniel. The quiet guy turned out to be competent in stuff other than ancient languages too.

Susan surfaced, and so did Burke and Santino. After a moment, Jay and Daniel arrived together, holding Powell by the arms. Gasps, grunts, hoots, laughs; Heather couldn't tell who did what. But she could safely assume they were all exhilarated.

"Damn!" Burke chuckled. "The water is so cold."

Heather didn't wish to be a party pooper, but she couldn't help reminding him, "We have more serious problems to worry about, I believe." It was right they managed to flee from that cursed island, but they might stay in this abandoned, endless ocean unnoticed until they would die of thirst.

"You can't stay like this for long, guys," Powell addressed Daniel and Jay, who were keeping him from drowning.

"We'll have shifts." Daniel nodded his chin toward Burke and Santino, a tired smile on his face.

"Now what?" Burke wondered. "I hope someone has a working cell phone. It's time to call an Uber."

"How do we know we are *outside* the Triangle in the first place?" Daniel asked.

"I'm sure we are." Burke didn't flinch. "But seriously, we need a ride."

Susan looked around. "Shouldn't we worry about sharks here?"

"You will worry about them if you only live that long," said Santino nervously.

"That won't make any sense," Burke countered. "I didn't survive an electromagnetic storm—twice—and a bunch of aliens trying to suck my energy and life out of me to eventually become some shark's dinner."

"Can anyone hear this?" It was one of Nathaniel's rare talking moments away from translation. Obviously, Heather was the only one who heard him amid this prattle.

"Everybody, quiet!" Heather did hear a faint *chopping* sound coming from the sky.

"Oh my God!" Susan exclaimed upon spying the helicopter. "That was fast."

"They must have tracked the life capsule," Santino guessed. "That's how they knew we were here."

"Hey! Over here!" Jay waved to the helicopter.

How do we know we are outside the Triangle in the first place? Daniel's question kept bugging Heather's mind. Besides, over the last three days, she had developed a habit of doubting any incoming aircraft. But if she remembered right, the Griseos didn't have choppers.

Maybe it was about time to say that her mission was over. Now she had the luxury to worry about the trial waiting for her back home. Strangely enough, she didn't think she might hate her prison cell. *As long as it's on dry land.*

41. Dry Land

Heather thought she would hate any ocean view for good, but from the aircraft carrier deck, it was a different story.

"Nice outfit." Burke joined her, jerking his chin toward the new dry clothes she had received from the rescue team. He himself was wearing the same outfit.

"You didn't go to sleep like the rest. Don't you feel tired?" she asked.

"You didn't go to sleep either."

"The medics insist that I must have some rest, but I can't. I will feel relaxed only when I return home."

"At least you have a home to return to. As for me; I don't know where I'm going. To my villa in Maine, or to a new prison?"

"If you go to jail, then most probably I'll go too." Heather allowed herself a faint smile.

"I have no problem about returning to Maine if you join me. You saw for yourself, my villa had an amazing lake view. Just ignore the wires and you will be fine."

Burke; the last missing part of the puzzle. Heather hoped it was a minor part, though, if compared to the great mystery of the infamous Devil's Triangle.

Suddenly, we find out that he speaks Latin fluently and knows what Akmenios knows. That's not a minor part, Heath.

"So, may I take your silence for a yes?" Burke asked.

Heather peered at him. "Do you need to hear my answer to know it?"

Burke wrinkled his forehead. "Alright, I'm confused now. Is that really a yes?"

What if this Burke is not the same one who came with us?

"You know how to wear a poker face," Burke went on. "I give you that."

The Griseos were suspicious about him for a reason.

"Oh, you're looking for a way to say 'no' in a nice way, aren't you?"

And somehow, he escapes from the Griseos' custody and joins us at the right time.

"Don't sweat it, Heather. Just say it."

He is the Shomrunk. And we are bringing him back with us.

"Heather? Are you okay?"

"You know I'm not." Heather looked him in the eye. "The question is: what are you going to do about it?"

Burke squinted at her, a puzzled look on his face. "About what?"

"I can't help wondering about your next move." Heather didn't mind hiding her thoughts. He would know them anyway. "Will you persuade my boss to send my team again to the Triangle with you? I doubt that would work this time." *Because I will be suspended, if not arrested, for my felony.*

"Send you again? What is this all about, Heather?"

He insisted on playing his role until the end. Very well, then. "I will tell you what this is about. Why don't we start with your Latin fluency for instance?"

"Is that so?" Burke chuckled. "You could ask me directly if you wanted, you know?"

For a second, Heather felt she was talking to the real Burke, the one she had first met in Maine. But she couldn't simply ignore all her doubts about him. She couldn't ignore the fact that it was *him* who had made her obsessed with his island.

"You want to know if Akmenios was right about me." Burke leaned forward, his hands in his pockets. "That's what's troubling your mind, right?"

"I'm quite sure you have an explanation—"

"He was, Heather."

What the hell was that? She was expecting some well-structured story to explain the situation, not this shocking straightforward answer. *He didn't even bother denying my doubts.*

Burke looked around, his voice low. "Listen to me carefully. What I'm going to tell you must remain between us, off the records. Do you understand? Don't tell anybody of your team, not even Daniel—I noticed that you two seem to be like best friends or even more, that's none of my business, I know. Anyway, do not say a word until we find out who the Shomrunk is."

Was he trying to mess with her? "You just admitted that Akmenios was right about you, about the connection between *you* and the Shomrunk. How come you want to convince me now that you are after that very same Shomrunk?"

Burke took her by the hand and walked her to the fenced edge of the deck, away from the soldiers passing by and any listening ears. "I have been pondering all the givens since that chopper took us out of the ocean," he said, keeping his voice low, almost whispering. "All assumptions led me to one conclusion: that Shomrunk works in the Pentagon, Heather."

He was raising more questions instead of answering her previous ones. "What makes you think so?" she asked.

"Remember Paul, my grandfather's brother, who was lost in Proteus? Guess what, my grandfather never had a brother called Paul in the first place."

"What? But you did dedicate years of your life to—"

"To nothing. All those years were in vain, Heather. I'm telling you: that Shomrunk, somehow, implanted that fictional Paul in my head. He made the idea consume my mind until I risked and lost everything to find that damned island and give him its location, or worse, inform his entire race of *our* location. To simply put it: my mission was to send a pin of Earth's location to the Shomrunks across the galaxies."

Everything Burke said confirmed Akmenios's suspicions about him. "But why the Pentagon?" she asked.

"You were always closer to the NSA agents who kept you in their custody."

"If the Shomrunk were in the NSA, he would have never allowed them to transfer me a few days before the Bermuda expedition. If you ask me, the NSA was an obstacle for that Shomrunk."

The NSA was an obstacle indeed. *And I was the pawn he used to overcome that obstacle. I was the pawn he used to bring Burke into the expedition.*

"Oh no!" Heather covered her face with her hands as she realized who the Shomrunk was. "It was him from the beginning."

Burke stared at her. "Do you know who he is?"

Heather shook her head in disbelief, still trying to digest the shock. She wasn't wrong this time. She couldn't be. Actually, she should have realized that earlier, but sometimes, it was difficult to see the most obvious fact.

"Dr. Heather," an officer called out to her from behind.

What did he hear? she wondered as she turned to him.

"We were just informed that a chopper is on its way to escort you and Dr. Burke to Miami," said the officer. "It should be here in eleven minutes."

Only *Dr.* Burke and her? "What about my crew? I can't leave them here."

"I have no orders about them so far, Dr." The officer's voice was firmer now. "Seems they are not that hurried to see them."

"Who are *they*?" Burke peered at the officer.

A smile tugged at the officer's lips as he looked at his watch. "You have ten minutes to get ready."

* * *

All the way to the military airport in Miami, Heather and Burke didn't dare to utter a word. She did not doubt that every single word said on this helicopter was recorded. The question was: recorded by whom? By the NSA? Or the Pentagon?

Who are they?

Sitting side by side, he and Burke were not arrested. *Not yet.* And that made her doubt it was the NSA that sent that chopper. She had fooled them twice; they would never let her get away with that.

It wasn't the NSA. It wasn't the Pentagon, either. It was just one mysterious *creature* that had infiltrated the Pentagon. A creature with a mesmerizing smile and voice.

He was the one orchestrating the whole rescue mission. *He found a way to take me to Burke while he was in NSA custody. Saving me and my team shouldn't be a problem for him.* And that thought made her realize one scary fact: her boss was not aware of anything happening right now. Three hours, and not a phone call from her boss or his office. The chopper that had rescued her and her team, the aircraft carrier, this very flight to Miami; all of that was off the record.

She was on her own against that Shomrunk.

Heather wondered what *he* might want from her. *I'm none of his concern. He is after Burke. After the intel he brought from the island. He just summoned me because it wouldn't make sense to summon Burke alone.*

That should reassure her a bit, right? *Not at all, Heather.* The moment the Shomrunk got the info he was seeking,

Heather would be expendable. Which was not reassuring at all...

"We have arrived," Burke said in an unusual flat voice. He was aware of what was waiting for him down there. "You okay?"

Heather nodded silently.

"Nothing could be worse than what we faced there," he told her. "We are survivors. Don't forget that."

Night fell when the chopper landed at the military airport. While the soldiers were opening the hatch of the helicopter, she thought of asking them where they would be taking her. When the hatch was open, she dropped the idea upon seeing the faces in her reception.

Agent Clark and Agent Jonathan.

"Welcome back, Dr. Heather." Clark feigned a smile. "Glad to see you again, safe and sound."

Jonathan didn't bother smiling at all.

"And Jeff Burke, of course," Clark continued, still wearing his loathsome smile as he beckoned Burke and Heather over. "Please, join us."

Joining them was not something she was looking forward to, but where else would she go?

The moment she and Burke stepped out of the chopper, brawny, dark-suited guys surrounded them as well as the two NSA agents.

"Ah!" Burke smirked. "The well-educated agent."

Jonathan curled his nose. "I see you still keep your sense of humor."

"Agent Jonathan," said Clark firmly. "I suggest we resume our conversation somewhere else." He motioned for Heather and Burke to follow him. "Shall we?"

"You won't take them anywhere."

Heather's heart pounded when she heard that harsh voice. She was wrong. She was not alone.

Her boss was here for her. *SecNav* himself.

"Sir?" Clark looked really surprised. "You came here yourself?"

SecNav stepped ahead of his personal guards. "These two belong to the US Navy," he snarled, wagging a firm finger at Clark's face. "They are not allowed to go with anybody without my orders."

"Mr. Secretary." Clark harrumphed. "I guess you know they are wanted for an investigation."

"They will be investigated by the Navy." SecNav firmly motioned for Heather and Burke to come forward. "If you have any objections, you can call the Secretary of Defense himself." He then glared at Jonathan, saying, "And if you are not satisfied with that, you can go to him and ask him face to face."

Heather enjoyed the show. Now, she could take a breath after her boss left Clark and Jonathan confused.

"You came just in time." Heather glanced at SecNav.

Ignoring her, her boss strode toward a black car. "Get in," he urged Heather. "You too." He motioned Burke to the seat next to the driver before he sat in the back next to Heather.

Immediately, the car took them to another helicopter. Heather and Burke didn't say a word until they followed SecNav into the helicopter that had no one else on board except the pilot.

"Seeing you again is just unbelievable, Heather." Her boss smiled at last. The scowl on his face vanished as the helicopter took off.

"Am I in trouble?" Heather asked.

"Are you talking about those two jerks?" SecNav raised his eyebrows. "They know nothing. I have settled everything with the Secretary of Defense already."

"Great." She sighed. Everything for her was over now.

"Do you remember me, Burke?" her boss asked.

"Not really." Burke squinted at him. "Were you involved in my investigations?"

"Yes, I was." Her boss nodded, his voice cold. "Sorry for not introducing myself; I'm the Secretary of the Navy."

"Really?" Burke's voice betrayed his astonishment. "So, you are the one who ruined my life, right?"

"If you want to say so." SecNav glared. "However, it was you who refused to comply. You must thank me for not sending you to a real prison, where you would experience the real, ugly taste of life behind bars." He turned to Heather, leaving Burke who had nothing to say. "It must have been quite a ride."

Heather didn't know where to start. "Beyond your imagination, sir." She smiled, glancing at Burke.

"You have nothing to hide from him, do you?" SecNav addressed Heather, looking from her to Burke and back. "I assume you two have the same story."

"Not exactly." Burke shrugged. "What I've seen and known is quite different and surely more shocking."

What was Burke doing? *Do not say a word until we find out who the Shomrunk is*, had been his order. Had he forgotten?

"Interesting." SecNav stared at Burke, his fingers crossed. "I'm listening."

Burke leaned forward, looking her boss straight in the eye. "Not before you get me a pardon."

A bargain with SecNav? Was that what Burke was pursuing? *That's a dangerous game, Burke*, she would warn him if she could. Outsmarting her seasoned boss wouldn't be an easy task, even for a clever guy like Burke.

"What about her?" Her boss's question to Burke took her off guard. Burke himself looked dumbfounded.

"What is that supposed to mean?" Heather asked.

"You want to make a deal, right?" SecNav ignored her as he addressed Burke, a peculiar smile of amusement on his face. "I'm telling you that I can offer a pardon to only one person. Would you pick her over yourself?"

"She did nothing wrong," said Burke firmly. "It was all my fault from the beginning."

"Then how did you escape from NSA's custody, may I ask?" SecNav turned to her. "How much was Mr. Colgate involved?"

Mr. what? Nobody could ever know that name. She didn't remember she had ever said that name out loud. It was only...

"...in your mind?" SecNav's grin grew wider.

Heather's heart skipped a beat.

"It's him." Burke's jaw dropped. "I feel it now."

42. Rewind

Heather gaped at SecNav, or whatever the creature sitting before her and Burke was. *It's him indeed. He is inside my mind. Our minds.*

But if that was the Shomrunk, where had her boss gone? Did he still exist?

"Your boss is here, Heather." SecNav leaned forward. "I didn't go anywhere."

"No, you're not," Burke snapped. "You may fool her, but not me."

"Oh, Burke!" Wearing that weird smile, SecNav turned to him. "You can't deny we had some exciting times together."

Heather felt she was having a bad dream. "Somebody tell me what the hell is going on."

"Now, I can tell you the whole story, Heather." Burke glared at SecNav as he went on, "This thing, taking the form of your boss, convinced me somehow that I had a lost relative on the USS Proteus, and based on that I made my first journey to the Domus island, as called by those Griseos. Those gray faces captured me, and Akmenios tried to find anything in my mind that could lead him to the Shomrunk's location, but he didn't find any clue. So, he sent me home again after wiping my memory clean, hoping he could track my return to the Shomrunk. Somehow, the Shomrunk, which is inside this guy sitting with us, lost their tail. Years later, he sent you and your team, and somehow, again, he convinced you to take me with you. That death mission to Bermuda was only for one purpose: sending a message to the rest of his *species* to inform them of the location of Earth. And I almost did that, if it were not for Akmenios who interrupted me before it was too late.

"The plan of this Shomrunk failed. He must be scanning our minds the moment I'm talking to you, trying to find any clue that may lead him to the island's location, so he can send another team to Bermuda in the near future with better preparations to achieve the very same objective. But he'll find nothing."

Heather needed a break to absorb all she had just heard from Burke.

"That was very good indeed, Burke," SecNav raised his eyebrows, "except for some small details."

Burke stared at him quizzically.

"First, I became Heather's boss only yesterday." SecNav gave Heather a wry smile. "Before that, I used to work for a *classified special unit* in the Pentagon."

It was him from the beginning, Heather realized. The charming Mr. Colgate who had persuaded her in their first meeting to take a chopper and visit an NSA prisoner. Now she knew that the devious manipulative bastard wasn't that charming after all.

"Besides." SecNav leaned toward Burke. "Who said I would find nothing? I already did."

"No way." Burke's eyes widened.

"Don't you believe me?" The SecNav shrugged. "You can ask her."

"Me?" Heather was confused. Why her? What did she know? This island had always been hidden from satellites. Nothing changed that fact after the mission.

"The compass, Heather." Her boss looked her straight in the eye.

"No!" Heather blustered. That blue glass cube was supposed to enable her to locate the island one more time and send reinforcements to help the Atlanteans in their war against the aliens. That damned compass was enough to consider the Bermuda mission as a success.

For him.

"I know you still have it," said the SecNav. "You took it out of your wet clothes before you got rid of them, right?"

Heather was too shocked to deny that. This person, *this thing,* knew everything she had done, down to the exact details.

"Didn't you ask yourselves how we found you in the ocean that fast?" SecNav continued, looking at Heather and Burke. "The moment you escaped from the Storm Shield of Bermuda, we detected a small magnetic field that emerged out of the blue. For some reason, I felt it was you."

The compass. Yes, what else? It was the damned compass that had led the Shomrunk to her. What was supposed to be a means of salvation for the Atlanteans would probably accelerate their doom.

"What are you?" Heather asked in a low impassive voice. "What have you done to the man you're inside now? What have you done to the...other guy?"

"As I told Burke before." SecNav shrugged. "I'm just a different form of life. I'm like souls to humans, or energy to engines. I did nothing bad to your boss or anybody I occupied before. On the contrary, I made a better person of each one of them."

"A better person?" Burke echoed in disapproval. "In terms of what? You have *replaced* the guy himself with something else. The man she has known for years does not exist anymore."

"It depends on how you define *existence*, Burke." SecNav tilted his head. "At least, he still exists physically."

"Bullshit!" Burke snapped. "He's gone. The body you're occupying is just a shell for some sort of a virus."

"We discussed this matter before, Burke." SecNav's grin faded. "I'm not a virus."

"Is he aware you're inside his body?" asked Burke. "Like me."

"Your case is different," replied the SecNav. "It's almost a negligible part of me inside your mind; too tiny to overcome your awareness."

"I'm lost." Heather held her head with both hands. Her nightmare was getting worse.

"Your boss is gone," Burke said to Heather, peering at SecNav. "What you see in front of you is just his body, totally dominated by the Shomrunk. It's the Shomrunk who is talking to us right now."

Heather was even more scared. "What about you?" She stared at Burke. "How do I know you're not a damn Shomrunk or some other shit creature? He's inside your mind too, right?"

"Only a very tiny part of him. That part connects him to me only when I sleep or lose consciousness. From what I've encountered so far, this is when our minds are most susceptible to invasion by external ideas."

"Look what you've done with that tiny part." SecNav leaned toward Burke. "After connecting your mind to Akmenios's, you've learned how to speak Latin and how to steer an alien vessel. That was even beyond my expectations, Burke. And that was what also changed my plan."

"Your plan?" Burke wondered. She had the same fears when she heard the word. "For what?"

"I never considered humans as potential hosts." SecNav gestured with his forefinger. "Humans were nothing but a means to reach those Griseos, as you've concluded. But the synergy your mind showed with this tiny part of mine made me reevaluate the potential of the human brain. The Griseos are slightly advanced than you *only* because they have been existing thousands of years more than you have. I should have considered the time factor from the beginning."

SecNav leaned back in his seat with an excited smile. "You know what the funniest part of this whole issue is? It was Akmenios who drew my attention to this point."

Heather recalled the conversation with the gray humanoid when he had addressed that point in particular. The Shomrunk, the *tiny part* of him, must have been listening at that time.

"What do you want?" Heather was eager to know, yet she was scared to receive the answer.

"We're the catalysts of evolution, Heather." SecNav kept his confident smile, as if he was enjoying her sight; frightened and confused. "Imagine a new generation of humans who have one thousand times the learning capacity of the previous generation. Will an intelligent race, like yours, refuse that?"

"Do we look like morons to you?" Burke snapped. "This will be a generation of human spare parts to your race."

"You're using too big words, Burke," SecNav countered. "Do you feel yourself to be a spare part right now?"

"Not for the time being." Burke bit his lower lip. "But who knows what will happen when you send for the rest of your Shomrunk friends."

"I believe you should listen to Heather." SecNav nodded toward her. "She has a different perspective from yours."

Heather was hesitant to express her thoughts, but she recalled the fact that the Shomrunk could read them anyway. "I'm not sure I fully grasp what you both are talking about to get that 'human spare part' thing. Maybe this is why I see the whole notion much simpler than this. Evolution is a natural phenomenon. We can't be sure about the consequences of adding a catalyst to this natural phenomenon. This is not something we may gamble on."

"Damn, Heather! You're talking as if he cares about our approval," Burke scoffed nervously.

"Why not?" Heather shrugged. "Maybe we can reach some sort of agreement. This Shomrunk seems to have some logic after all."

"You don't understand." Burke shook his head. "He's trying to convince you that the Shomrunks' invasion will be something for the good of humanity."

"*Trying* to convince you?" SecNav sneered. "Come on, Burke. You know very well that I *can* convince anyone with all I that want without them even knowing it."

Damn. He's right.

Then why is he bothering to talk to us anyway?

"Sometimes a discussion helps extract some brilliant thoughts, Heather," said SecNav. "But now I'm done with this one."

She felt her blood freeze in her veins when he extended his arm. "The compass, Heather." SecNav stared at her. "Give it to me."

She had no idea why she was complying, but she did. She tucked her hands into her pocket, pulled the blue cube out, and handed it to him.

"Thanks." SecNav's smile widened, then he turned to Burke. "Do you have any problems with that, Burke? I guess you don't."

"No problem, Mr. Secretary." Burke shrugged.

* * *

Heather was startled when she checked her watch. She was pretty sure she had been on the helicopter for only a few minutes.

"I assume we're headed to Virginia, right?" she asked SecNav sitting in front of her.

"You're right." SecNav nodded. "We'll be there in eighteen minutes."

Eighteen minutes? Had she fallen asleep during the flight? The total duration of the journey was supposed to be almost two hours.

"You were so exhausted." SecNav grinned. "You should have seen yourselves when you both fell asleep in your seats."

Burke's eyebrows rose as if he had just realized what had happened. "Damn!" He glanced at her watch. "Did I miss something?"

"Nothing at all." SecNav kept his conservative smile. "It seems I chose the wrong time to discuss the findings of the Bermuda mission. I should have waited until morning."

"We don't have too much to discuss." Heather shrugged. "All we encountered was that huge storm that almost brought the HG-3 down, but we miraculously survived it. We had no other observations."

SecNav shook his head, pressing his lips together. "Unfortunately, your three-day mission to Bermuda didn't provide us with any new clues about the location of the lost AAL 256 plane, but we couldn't go on any longer for safety issues, especially after you've lost five of your crew members because of the horrendous weather conditions. The HG-3 still needs more upgrades to be up to the ocean's unstable condition in the Triangle."

The failure of the mission she had spent years preparing for. What an announcement. What a waste. All her efforts had been in vain. *My baby died in vain.*

"I really appreciate your efforts in this mission, Heather," said SecNav firmly. "With the equipment and expertise you had, no one could have done any better."

Heather inhaled deeply. "Will be there another expedition, sir?"

"We're still not sure about that," SecNav replied. "Anyway, that was your last mission, Heather."

Her what? "But, sir, I—"

"Your work in the Pentagon has ruined your life more than enough. You need a long rest while you still have the chance to mend your life and have a fresh start."

Heather sighed. It was true her position in the Navy had torn her fragile personal life apart, yet it was the same thing that had kept her going and feeling alive so far. Had it not been for immersing her mind in her demanding work, she would have surely committed a suicide.

Was there a way to feel any pleasure in the remaining years of her life as her boss had just suggested? Alone?

No, I'm not alone anymore.

It was really strange. How had she never been aware of her feelings for Burke before this moment?

Epilogue

St. George's Airport, St. David's Island, Bermuda

The governor of Bermuda gazed at the dark-suited Secretary of the Navy stepping out of the plane, burly marines surrounding the American commander. It had been a long time since their last meeting.

A long time, like a century ago or even more.

The governor extended his arm to shake hands when the Secretary of the Navy approached. "Welcome to Bermuda, Mr. Secretary," he said impassively.

"Mr. Governor himself." The Secretary of the Navy smiled decently. "I really appreciate your coming."

"The magnitude of the circumstances imposes so." The Governor was irked by these formal reception rituals. "Come on, let's take a walk."

"You barely waste your time, Stefano." The Secretary of Navy lowered his voice, keeping his smile as he walked next to the governor.

Stefano made sure they were out of earshot before he said, "We don't have much time. This is the best place where we can talk."

"What happened to you?" The Secretary of the Navy furrowed his brow. "Can't you really read my thoughts?"

"Not as clearly as before." The governor sighed. "I see them now only as mere speculations. And my condition is deteriorating."

"This is strange. Do you have any idea why this is happening to you? You're supposed to improve the intellectual capacity of the human you've become."

"I didn't improve anything," snapped Stefano. "It's the human who's overpowering me."

"Haven't you considered occupying another human? Maybe it's time to change."

"Are you kidding me? This is the fifth human I occupy."

"Maybe you picked the wrong humans. So far, it has been working for me."

The governor stopped, staring at the Secretary of Navy. "You use the Shomrunk inside you more than I do."

The Secretary of the Navy slowly looked right and left, as if he was making sure they could not be overheard. "You have a serious problem, Stefano. You're busying your mind with an identity issue. You have to use your Shomrunk abilities without even thinking as one. We're like these waters around this island; we take the shape of our container, yet we're still who we are. Do you get that?"

Stefano, the governor, didn't reply, and he didn't have to anyway. He averted his eyes, his fingers crossed behind his back. "I really don't feel I belong here. I don't even know *what* I am right now."

"Belonging." The Secretary of Navy grinned. "Good. You're talking like a human without even noticing."

"Bullshit." The governor curled his lip. "Does this make me even more human now? Come on."

"Calm down." The Secretary of the Navy kept his face stony as he glanced at his guards. "No need to make a scene here."

"You know what I'm thinking of right now." Stefano lowered his voice.

"You're hinting at your past as a Griseo, right?"

"Exactly." The governor noticed the warning glare on his friend's face. He lowered his voice again as he went on, "Over thousands of years, I never felt any trouble in blending in with those Griseos."

"Because you were not alone at that time. You lived in a whole community of evolved Griseos like you."

"*Evolved?*" Stefano scoffed. "Is that how you see it?"

"Sure thing." The Secretary of the Navy smiled again. "It's all about evolution. And we're the catalysts."

"Catalysts? You can't be serious." Stefano jerked his head backward. "We have been here on this planet for decades and yet we're still unable to transmit our location to the rest of us."

"Because we didn't have the right equipment for such a task." The Secretary of the Navy leaned toward him. "But that's not the case any longer."

That should be interesting, Stefano thought. "Did your inspection team have any success in their last mission?"

The Secretary of Navy paused for a moment, peering at Stefano. "How did you know that? That was a classified mission."

"Officially, Mr. Secretary." The governor tilted his head. "You are not the only one working here."

"This is not the right time to improvise, Stefano. We're so close, and now we know how to reach the transmission device. We will send the message soon."

At last, after decades of waiting, the governor heard good news. "When?"

"In three weeks, the HG-4 will be ready to go with a new team on board. Neither storms nor electromagnetic shocks can stop that mighty machine, so don't worry. Your long wait is about to end, old friend. We are on the verge of a new era."

"The new era of *evolved* humans." The governor inhaled deeply, still unable to swallow the idea. "We shall see about that."

"Fine." The Secretary of Navy gently patted the governor's back. "Now, take us to your office for some formal talks on behalf of the US government regarding the lost plane."

Stefano always hated that part. "How long is this supposed to take?"

"Not more than an hour, I hope. I have a wedding in Miami to attend."

"A wedding? You are really enjoying this," the governor scoffed. "One of your human relatives I presume?"

"One of my best subordinates." The Secretary of Navy grinned. "A former one."

Acknowledgments

I have been obsessed with the Devil's Triangle since I was a kid. It was a story I always wanted to write, but I was never sure how the sci-fi reader in 2019 would receive it. Were it not for the relentless love the story had received on Wattpad, I wouldn't have had the faith to hit "publish." Huge thanks to all who have supported my work for years on the orange cloud.

Thanks to my wizard Stefanie Saw for her brilliant artwork. Again and again, she did it. She always does.

Thanks to my mentor and editor Yasmin Amin. Working with you was a real pleasure, as always.

Special thanks to the sweet Arabella Higgin (aka Bella Higgin). It's no secret, I'm a fan of her writing. Having her as a reader is something I'm very proud of.

My tireless support team and advisors: Katrin Hollister, Gaby Cabezut, Elise Noble, Debbie Joelz, Jessica Fry, Rosa Aimee, Greg Carrico, Rita Kovach, Maria Kristina, and Sandra Grayson. Writing is a long journey that needs friends like you.

Last but not least, a million thanks to my family; my wife and cheerleader May whose faith in our dream keeps me going forward, my sweet angel Soojy for tolerating my occasional mental absence, my baby Groot Mostafa for allowing me to work on my laptop without breaking it, my mother for nurturing my love of books and writing, and my father for providing a five-year-old child with his blank yearly planner to write his first story.

About the Author

Karim Soliman earned his first writing commission through his contribution in the first and last issue of his classroom magazine. Twenty years later, he earned his next commission from Sony Pictures.

Born in Egypt, where he lives with his wonderful wife and two children, Karim works as a brand manager of neuropsychiatric drugs. He holds a Master's degree in Business Administration, just in case he decides to pursue the CEO pathway.

Through Wattpad, Karim has been building his fan base since he started serializing his fantasy and sci-fi novels online. When he is not writing, he struggles with insomnia and continues his search for his next favorite dessert.

Where to find Karim Soliman

Facebook:

https://www.facebook.com/authorKarimSoliman

Twitter:

https://twitter.com/Kariem28

Instagram:

https://www.instagram.com/kariem28/

Made in the USA
Monee, IL
22 April 2021

66511199R00208